CITY
OF
ANGELS

CITY
OF
ANGELS

KRISTI BELCAMINO

Copyright © 2017 by Kristi Belcamino
Cover and jacket design by Georgia Morrissey
Interior designed and formatted by E.M. Tippetts Book Designs

ISBN 978-1-943818-43-3
eISBN 978-1-943818-68-6
Library of Congress Control Number: 2016962840

First hardcover publication May 2017 by Polis Books, LLC
1201 Hudson Street, #211S
Hoboken, NJ 07030
www.PolisBooks.com

POLIS BOOKS

ALSO BY
KRISTI BELCAMINO

Blessed Are the Dead

Blessed Are the Meek

Blessed Are Those Who Weep

Blessed Are Those Who Mourn

Letters From a Serial Killer

To Michael, who makes this crazy writing life possible.

Armed with booze, cigarettes, and guns, my friends paced the hot rooftop of the American Hotel, peering over the waist-high wall, looking for trouble on the streets below.

To the east, wisps of smoke rose as rioters set fire to the palm trees on the 101 Freeway. Helicopters hovered over treetops near Hollywood Bowl. The Rodney King verdict had gone down twenty-four hours ago, triggering a wave of violence and chaos that ricocheted through Los Angeles neighborhoods.

Once again we'd broken the padlocked door to gain access to the roof. This time, not to drink and smoke, but to act as lookouts. Rioters were storming Skid Row, a few blocks away. We were making sure nobody messed with the four-story brick building we called home.

I stood by myself facing the west, thinking of Rain.

Every once in a while one of my friends came to check on me. I was used to being alone, so it felt strange, but good, too. At seventeen, I was the youngest in my group of friends.

"You okay, kiddo?" asked Sadie.

I nodded.

The former cover model was wearing cut-off Levis shorts, platform sandals, and toting some type of big gun like a designer handbag. I took it all in without blinking.

Satisfied, Sadie stalked off, wind whipping her long blond hair as she patrolled the perimeter of the building, leaning precariously over the edge of the wall and occasionally pointing her gun at passerby below.

Danny, who grew up a few blocks away in East L.A., was splayed flat on his back, a black pistol tucked in his waistband, scissoring his arms and legs as if he were making a tar snow angel and periodically shouting, "I wanna burrita!"

His black eyes caught mine for a moment and he cackled loudly, his teeth gleaming in a Cheshire cat grin. I forced a small smile and turned away. Earlier, I'd found him in his room giggling and talking to himself, high on PCP or something. I hoped it wasn't one of those days he thought he could fly.

Although the fires were still blocks away, the reek of burning buildings mingled with the faint diesel smell of the sun-warmed black tar rooftop, which was starting to feel squishy under my combat boots. A tiny shift in the wind brought with it the sweet smell of weed.

Leaning against one wall, the two Iowa farm boys, Taj and John, huddled with Eve. She dipped her head near the flame of a giant purple bong. I worried her mammoth afro would catch fire. Her black-rimmed eyes were smudged. She didn't bother wiping the dark rivulets of makeup-sodden tears trailing down her cheeks.

John held the bong in my direction. "Nikki?"

I shook my head, my dark hair swinging.

Taj took a long sip of his beer without taking his gaze off me. He gave me a slow smile.

We were all there.

All except Rain, of course.

As the sun set on the city, its reddish-orange streaks illuminated our drunk and tear-stained faces. Despite the leaden feeling in my gut, I felt a surge of love looking at my friends. It felt odd calling them that, but that was what they'd become. I also felt a sense of belonging. A new feeling to me. Unfamiliar and a little bit scary, but welcomed all the same.

Shouting and glass breaking on the street below startled me and provoked Sadie's high-pitched shriek. "Get the fuck out of here, motherfuckers!"

Turning back, I searched the horizon to the west, steeling my gaze in the direction where the gleaming white mansion towered over Sunset Boulevard. Smoke mingled with the setting sun, turning the skies blood red. We would strike when it grew dark. Until then, I had to be patient. I pulled up a ripped lawn chair, took a long drag off my cigarette, and settled back to watch L.A. burn.

──CHAPTER──
1

Malibu, Four Months Earlier

Droplets of blood rhythmically splattered in crimson splotches on the Persian carpet at my feet. I swiped at my nose, but couldn't stem the flow.

"Get the kid out of here, she's ruining my goddamn rug," Dean Thomas Kozlak said. He mumbled the words around the cigar clenched between his teeth. His white hair bobbed as he nodded. "That baby put me out thirty grand at auction. I'm talking fifteen hundred bucks a square foot. Was the Shah of Iran's for Christ's sake."

The slight sting on my cheek was fading. I swallowed the blood dripping down the back of my throat, gagging on the metallic taste.

Across the room of sleek leather couches and glass-topped tables, a wall of French doors beckoned. They led to a massive deck. Although the windows had turned into black mirrors as darkness fell, beyond them—and several feet below—was the beach. Freedom. The doors were slightly ajar. A salty ocean breeze drifted in, blowing my hair across my face.

The big-shot movie director with his Andy Warhol hair perched on the arm of a chaise lounge. Unfortunately, he was directly between those French doors and me. Off to one side, way off, was a door to a long hallway. It was the furthest exit from me. The closest door—actually a swinging door—was behind me. The maid, with her plate of fishy finger foods, had come through them earlier

I was still woozy and a little confused from the blow to my head. But a rush of adrenaline jerked me back to life. My body was ready to blow. *Run. Run as fast as you can.*

I lifted my chin to finally look at Chad. The twenty-eight-year-old guy who had been my boyfriend this past month had disappeared. Instead, a stranger shaking with rage stood across the room, downing another shot of the liquid amber in his crystal glass. The stubble on his face hid a weak chin. His lank hair escaping its small ponytail seemed effeminate. He wasn't looking at me, but at Kozlak with a combination of fear, awe, and worship.

"Take her downstairs," the director said. "Now. I'm done being Mr. Nice Guy."

Chad's gaze turned to meet mine. His pupils had morphed into black orbs. I took a step back.

He set his glass down and turned toward me, headed my way. He was going to hit me again. He was mumbling under his breath. "You've embarrassed me, baby. I think it's time to make you a star in a movie you'll never have a chance to see."

"Chad." It was the sternest tone Kozlak had used all night. At his name, Chad froze. But only for a second.

Run! But he was too close. I could almost feel his fingers yanking my long hair if I tried to bolt.

Then I remembered. I slid my eyes over to the big black gun on the table nearby. Kozlak had been showing it off to Chad earlier. Kozlak smirked. He knew. He knew I wouldn't be able to even *pick up* that gun. Pointing it at someone was out of the question.

My nose had finally stopped bleeding. I planted my feet and faced Chad. He grew closer. When he was within reach, I aimed my steel-toed combat boot up into his crotch. He howled and collapsed.

The director leisurely pushed himself up from the arm of the chaise lounge, taking time to carefully arrange his cigar in a crystal ashtray. I didn't wait around to see what he was going to do next.

I raced through the swinging door. It led to a small hallway. Beyond was the kitchen. In the kitchen, I jammed a small wooden chair under the doorknob and looked around for a way out. Less than five feet away, a glass door led outside to a giant garden with high walls. Another door was beside it. I peeked in. A pantry. My hand was on the doorknob to the garden when, out of the corner of my eye, I saw something move.

Across the kitchen, another door cracked open a few inches. Behind it, a girl with pink-streaked blond hair stood silently watching me. I flung the glass back door wide open to the garden. With the girl's eyes on me, I ducked into the pantry instead, pleading with my eyes for her silence. The noises grew louder. The chair I'd propped against the kitchen door slammed to the floor. Right before I pulled the pantry door shut, I held my finger up to my lips. She gave a barely imperceptible nod. Her door closed all but a tiny crack.

My heart thudded in my throat. I froze with one hand on the pantry doorknob. Thirty seconds later, Kozlak's voice boomed—less than a foot away from my hideout.

"Those garden walls are ten feet high. She's not going anywhere. Take this."

"What?" Chad sounded confused.

"Don't worry. Silencer."

"But I—"

"You wanted to play with the big boys?" Kozlak's voice was low and dangerous. "You brought this problem into my house and now you're going to take care of it. She's a goddamn runaway. Nobody's gonna miss her."

"She'll come around," Chad stuttered a little. "I can handle her."

"Like you 'handled' her in there? Get the fuck out."

They were right on the other side of the door. I could practically feel the heat from their bodies.

The doorknob twisted under my palm, triggering a wave of sheer terror. But then I heard a thud—the sound of a door slamming open and hitting a wall.

"Rain." Kozlak's voice was tinged with sudden fury. "Get back in your room."

"No." It was a child's voice, but it was determined. The doorknob untwisted in my hand. "What did you say?"

A door clicked closed.

"How dare—" Kozlak said between what sounded like gritted teeth. After a second of silence, his voice sounded composed again. "You go that way."

Footsteps and then the men's voices grew fainter. All was quiet. I waited a few seconds. I cracked the pantry door. The door across from me opened.

"Take me with you." The girl's voice was frantic. "He's keeping me here. Prisoner."

I looked at her for a long second, remembering the director's proposition to me earlier—starring in a porn flick. When I refused, Chad had slapped me.

I didn't answer, only nodded before I bolted back into the living room, detouring to the couch to grab my bag, which contained my most-prized possession—my Nikon. I looped the bag's strap over my chest. The girl trailed behind me.

I slipped through the large French doors to the deck overlooking the beach and Pacific Ocean. Any minute the men would discover I wasn't in the garden. Out on the sprawling wooden deck, the bracing wind stung my face and tangled my hair. Large clouds drifted over a sliver of moon. Far down the beach, hazy lights cast a big circle on the sand. The waves crashed loudly somewhere in front of me, invisible in the darkness. Below the house, a wooden plank walkway led from the side of the house down to the water. A sound filtered out from the house, triggering a surge of adrenaline. I climbed up onto the rail, one leg hanging over. The girl stood back, hesitating.

I jumped back onto the deck and offered my hand. "It's the only way." Our eyes met for a long second, but she didn't move. I clambered over the side of the rail and hung by my arms, my feet dangling and my bag slamming into my side. The girl stood above me. Voices and footsteps came closer.

The girl looked behind her for a second before scampering over the rail where she hung by my side. "On three," I said in a whisper.

I counted, closed my eyes, and let go, landing on my butt on the sand below. There was a small thud as the girl fell nearby. Within seconds I had scrambled to my feet and raced over to the walkway.

My combat boots pounded noisily on the wooden planks leading to the surf. The girl's footsteps echoed behind me. The walkway ended several yards from the water. As soon as my feet left the wood, they sunk into deep sand and everything slowed. I trudged along the beach in seemingly slow motion, slogging through the deep sand like in a bad dream.

When my feet hit packed, wet sand, I paused to catch my breath, panting as the white froth of the ocean slapped against my boots. The girl caught up. She was quiet beside me.

"Are you hurt?" My own body ached from the fall.

She shook her head. The fear and adrenaline shooting through me made me anxious to keep running, and yet some small part of me balked. By running down that beach, I was leaving everything behind. I would have no boyfriend, no home, nothing but the clothes on my back. I would be alone in L.A. But I also knew that even if I didn't run, that life was over.

High on the deck of the brightly lit home, the director's bulky, dark silhouette stood at the rail overlooking the beach. A tiny orange glow, a cigarette, moved from his waist to his head. An icy chill rippled across my scalp. Through the darkness, with the surf crashing behind me, I could feel the menace drifting toward me across the beach. The figure, a mass of black without clear shape or form, seemed to stand preternaturally still. Watching.

—CHAPTER—
2

The lights were further down the beach than I had thought. I ran along the wet, packed sand with the girl close on my heels like a shadow. My ribs hurt from landing on the sand funny and my side was getting a cramp from running.

And yet, sprinting like this, fueled by adrenaline, helped tamp down something inside me—an anxiety that was always just below the surface. I wanted to run until I collapsed, right past that circle of light and into the darkness. I thought for a brief second that maybe if I did, it would dispel that bubble of anguish inside me—that pressure that had settled in my core after my mom died.

When I had met Chad as an extra on the set of a commercial he was filming in Chicago, I had thought running away to California with him would smother the recklessness surging through me.

But deep down inside I had known it wouldn't go away that easily.

A small sound behind me brought me to a stop. The girl had tripped and fallen a few feet back. Behind her, headlights on the beach headed our way. I hesitated. Stopping to help her could give them the time they need to catch up. I trudged back through the sand as fast as I could, pulling her up and holding her hand. We ran until we reached the edge of the orangish circle of light surrounding a beach parking lot.

Two surfers loading their boards onto the top of a beat-up VW van looked up when we scrambled over the three-foot sea wall. I stooped over, my hands on my knees, panting. The girl stood beside me, her small chest heaving.

"Dude," said one surfer, a boy about my age with a buzzed head and unzipped wetsuit hanging down around his waist.

I squeaked out, "Help," gesturing behind me.

The surfer's eyebrows pulled together. "Did you say help?"

I gasped out the words. "Yes. Hit me. Wants to kill me. Locked her up. Please. Take me—" I glanced at the girl "—us—with you."

His nose scrunched up. His buddy, who wore baggy swim trunks and had long wet hair, elbowed him. "Whoa, look. She's right. Somebody's coming. Let's bail."

He jerked open the van's side door and hopped in, waving frantically for us to join him.

Without bothering to look behind me, I pushed the girl inside before tumbling in myself.

As the boy turned the ignition, a Suicidal Tendencies song blared through the speakers. He peeled out with the van door still open, sending us flying against the other wall. The van tore through the parking lot, fishtailing on the sand-strewn pavement. Behind us, a large Jeep with piercing fog lights on its roll bar stopped on the other side of the sea wall, shining its lights into our back window as one of the boys closed the side door. But we were already gone, squealing onto the Pacific Coast Highway.

The surfers whooped with excitement.

"That was killer," said the boy in the wetsuit. He offered me his seat.

The driver threw his fist in the air and cranked up a Violent Femmes song that came on the radio. He sang along, looking over at me and winking. The van reeked of coconut suntan oil and incense.

I rolled my eyes at him, but cracked a slight smile. The girl sat against one wall in the back. She was digging in a small backpack she'd been wearing. It wasn't until the song ended and we were miles away from that beach that the driver turned down the music and glanced over at me. "What was that crazy shit back there about?"

"It's complicated." I looked away. "Hanging with the wrong crowd."

The driver shrugged, but the wetsuit boy stared at me intensely, making me squirm.

"You look familiar." He snapped his fingers. "I know! You look like that girl in the *Blue Lagoon.*" He sat back, nodding his head. "Yeah, a lot like her except your hair is darker. Dude, she was total nectar. What's her name again?"

"Brooke Shields," I said, fishing in my bag for my cigarettes. "It's the eyebrows."

The driver glanced at me and nodded. "Totally, dude."

"Hey," wetsuit boy said. "You got blood or something on your face."

I pulled the visor mirror down, sucking on the long sleeve of my worn t-shirt and dabbing at the dried blood. My hand was shaking but I managed to get most of it off.

"What's your name, anyway?" the driver asked.

"I'm Alex," I lied. My real name was Veronica Black. I took a drag off my cigarette. It was a bad habit of mine. Both of them were. Lying and smoking.

The wetsuit guy turned to the girl. "You got a name?"

"Rain," she mumbled.

"You sisters?"

"No." I said it louder than I meant to and the two boys exchanged a glance.

"I'm Jonathan," said the driver, who kept tossing his long wet hair over his shoulder, sending small drops of water flying. "And this is Charlie. We go to USC. You like to party? We've got some Super Skunk back at our pad."

"I don't get high." It sounded snottier than I'd intended. "And besides, look at her, she's just a kid."

The driver nodded and turned the music back up, bobbing his head along to the beat.

I rummaged in my bag and took my camera out of its leather case. I snapped off a few shots. The other surfer, Charlie, had climbed into the back and was strumming a beat up guitar. The driver kept glancing over at me and winking. I snapped a few shots then tucked my camera back in my bag. It seemed to work fine despite my rough landing from the deck.

Taking a long drag from my cigarette, I closed my eyes, relaxing back into the passenger seat as the adrenaline that had kept me going the past half hour started to fade. My anger at Chad and the director had fueled me, helped me escape, but now it was turning into fear and worry.

I had no idea how I was going to survive in L.A. on my own. I didn't even know where I was going to sleep that night. The only thing I knew was that I couldn't go back to Chad's place.

Earlier today, I'd read in the *L.A. Weekly* that a band I knew from Chicago was playing at a downtown bar tonight. I'd wanted to go, but then Chad had told me about dinner at the Malibu house. He'd been so stoked. The director was giving him his big break—a shot as the director of photography in a new action film. One word from Dean Thomas Kozlak could make or break someone's entire Hollywood career, Chad said. Kozlak was a Big Shot Director.

It was only after dinner that I found out there was a price for the director's largesse.

Me.

Because I looked much younger than my seventeen years, Chad had lured me from Chicago to offer me up for Kozlak's side business— child porn. Apparently, I wasn't the only one. I peeked back at the girl. She was just a little kid. A sour taste filled my mouth.

I sort of knew the drummer of that band from Chicago. Maybe he could loan me some money or help me find a place to crash tonight. I didn't remember mentioning the band to Chad so he wouldn't know to look for me there.

The L.A. night sky glowed orange through the windshield. Even though I was in a van with three other people, I felt utterly alone. More alone than I'd ever felt in my life. I was in L.A., homeless, with the clothing on my back and forty bucks to my name. I blinked hard, turning away toward the window. If I was going to survive on my own, I was going to have to toughen up. There was no time for tears.

I turned to the girl. "What's your story?"

"He was gonna make me a movie star, but I think he was lying. He kept me locked in a room."

Movie star. The director's sick side gig.

"Did he put you in any movies?" I was relieved when she shook her head. I squinted my eyes, taking in the hollows under her eyes and the punkish pink streak in her hair. "How old are you, anyway?"

"Twelve."

Jesus Christ.

"Where do you live?"

"Wherever."

"Gnarly," the boy next to her said.

I chewed my lip, thinking about that.

"Where you girls want to go?" wetsuit boy asked.

"Al's Bar—downtown. For me," I added, sliding a glance at the girl.

"Union Station." Her voice was quiet. "It's downtown, too."

Even though she was just a kid, she sounded so sure. I did the math—she was a little bit older than my sister would have been. It only took me a second to decide.

"Actually, take us to the police station—downtown." I turned to the girl.

"No!" It was the loudest I'd heard her yet, and in that same stubborn voice she'd used with the director. "I'm not talking to the cops. I'm not going to a foster home. I'd rather die."

She crossed her arms across her chest.

"Where are your parents?" I asked.

"They don't care about me."

"Well, the cops can help you, maybe find you someplace safe to stay tonight or something. Someplace better than the train station." I tried to sound soothing but I wasn't even convinced myself. What I didn't say was that we needed to go to the police station because they would know what to do with a twelve-year-old homeless kid. Because I sure as hell didn't.

🌴 🌴 🌴

After stopping to ask for directions at a gas station and a few wrong turns, we made it to a police substation near Union Station. But it was dark, like the rest of the buildings in downtown Los Angeles. I got out and tugged on the door even though I knew it wouldn't budge. The surfers kept the van idling out front while they waited for me to make a decision.

"Take us to Al's Bar." I got back in the van and turned to the girl.

"I'm not dropping you off at Union Station by yourself. We'll figure out where to sleep and go to the cops in the morning, okay?"

She didn't answer, just looked down at her sneakers.

—CHAPTER—

3

A posse of homeless men ran up to the van as we pulled in front of Al's Bar in the warehouse section of downtown Los Angeles. They all spoke at once.

"Want me to guard your van, man?"

"Give me a dollar and I'll keep an eye on your ride."

"Watch your car?"

I cringed when one guy stuck his head in my open window. The girl and I lurched out of the van. After seeing the somewhat sketchy neighborhood with its graffiti-covered walls and hooptie cars, the surfer boys decided to bail. I stuck my head in the van's window to say thank you. When I turned around, the girl was gone. I caught a flash of her darting around a corner.

I raced after her, shrinking away from the homeless men trying to talk to me. I rounded the corner, whipping my head in both directions.

"Rain?" I said, half shouting. My voice echoed off the buildings. I waited. Shouted again. Counted to ten. Then to twenty. Then fifty. Empty streets.

I ran down to an alley half a block away and stopped, breathing hard. Also deserted. There was no sign of the girl. I paused, looking around at the dark streets. Making my way through the alley, I looked back over my shoulder every few seconds, feeling the hairs on my neck tingle. I emerged out of the alley onto yet another deserted street. Nothing. No movement, just long, dark shadows from the streetlights. A shiver raced down my bare legs. The girl had vanished.

Inside Al's Bar, it seemed like I'd stepped underground—in a musty smelling windowless cave with low ceilings and damp stone walls covered in graffiti and old music flyers. The band on the stage wasn't my friend's band.

A waitress told me my friend's band had already played and were on their way to their next gig in San Diego. Dread rose in my throat. I was out of ideas.

I pulled out a black bar stool and slid a twenty dollar bill across the scratched wooden surface. The bartender at the other end of the bar was bobbing his dreadlocked head in time to the band. I put my head in my hands for a few seconds, trying to get a grip on the rising panic.

I found myself moving my knee to the music. I looked up. They weren't bad. The lead singer's long bangs hid his face as he leaned out over the audience before throwing the mic down and tipping into the crowd. A platform of hands passed him around before thrusting him back on the stage. He sat on the edge, about to pull himself to standing, when a girl in a skimpy top grabbed his face and began kissing him. The crowd went wild. He looked embarrassed as he pulled away to sing the last chorus before falling into the drum set for the song's crescendo.

The dreadlocked bartender flashed me an infectious smile as he strolled over.

I nodded at the twenty. "Give me as much tequila as that'll buy." I hoped I sounded mature and confident so he wouldn't card me.

"What are you, fourteen?"

"I look young for my age." I scowled.

He raised an eyebrow.

"Fine. A Coke," I said, blowing my hair out of my eyes with a huff. Then added in a low voice, "And maybe some aspirin."

I hurt all over. My cheek hurt, probably from Chad's slap, my legs ached, and my ribs were bruised from my jump off the deck. I wondered if that girl had been hurt in the fall. And where she was. The bartender handed me my drink and a bottle of aspirin. I washed down four of the white pills with my soda.

"I'm Stuart," he said, and waited, raising an eyebrow. He wanted to know my name. I stared at a TV hanging from the ceiling. He cleared his throat. Oh yeah. My name.

"Um, I'm Ariel."

"Like the little mermaid?" He looked like he was about to burst into laughter.

"Yup." I looked away. But he was still standing there.

"Hey, I know it's none of my business, but who gave you the shiner?"

Instead of answering, I rummaged around in my bag for my camera and started taking snapshots of him. He put his palm up until I lowered the camera. I swallowed and closed my eyes.

"Jerk boyfriend. We broke up tonight."

He let out a low whistle.

And for some reason, I didn't know why, I told him even more. "He was the only person I knew in L.A. I'm not sure where I'm going to sleep now."

A huge grin spread across his face. Not the reaction I expected.

"Well, you're in luck. I manage the upstairs."

I gave him a blank look.

"The American Hotel?" he said.

"Never heard of it."

"You aren't from around here, are you?"

I shook my head.

In its heyday, he explained, traveling musicians and other performers stayed at the American Hotel when they were in town to perform. The drunken poet Charles Bukowski once lived there.

"When Bukowski died, his ex-wife came and we shut down the street. We had a funeral pyre and drank a bunch of wine," Stuart said.

When we read him in my honors lit class, I'd thought Bukowski was a woman hater so I wasn't too impressed by the hotel's credentials, but perked up when Stuart told me rooms upstairs went for two hundred and thirty dollars a month. And even better, that one was available.

"You gotta share a bathroom with everyone else on the floor." His eyes didn't leave mine as he said this.

"Fine." I arched one eyebrow. He thought I was some princess from the suburbs. That part of my life ended long ago, right about when they buried my mother.

Sharing a bathroom was a small price to pay to have a place to sleep. But then my heart sunk. "I don't have any money."

"We'll figure that out," Stuart said, drying some glasses on a bar towel. "Sadie—lives in four twelve—says they need a waitress where she works—Little Juan's. On First Street."

Relief filled me along with a sudden heavy fatigue. After I yawned for the third time, Stuart asked one of the waitresses to cover the bar for him and told me he'd be right back.

I stared at my reflection in the bar mirror. Would a restaurant hire me? My hair was ratty, and even in the dim light, the purple shadows of a black eye stood out.

I'd never had a real job in my life besides that one day as a movie extra when I met Chad. Nobody would want to hire me. I pushed back the fear and panic trying to settle in my chest.

A big black phone sat on the bar inches away from my fingertips. It would only take pressing a few digits to get my dad on the phone. Maybe he'd changed his mind. We hadn't spoken for two months. And our last words were ugly. But he'd been drinking. I wanted to believe it was the alcohol talking. I pushed the phone away and put my face in my hands. Part of me wanted to reach for that phone and part of me knew it would only end in heartbreak. I was so afraid that what I wanted, what I craved and longed for so deeply, couldn't be found on the other end of a phone line.

—CHAPTER—
4

The music had stopped. I didn't notice the boy beside me until the waitress behind the bar came over.

"Hey, Taj," she said.

"Eve." He drew out her name. I shot him a glance. It was that lead singer from the band.

"You guys rocked," she said, handing him a frothy beer. My eyes narrowed. There was no way *he* was twenty-one.

"There's more to come. We're saving the best for last." He ran his fingers through his hair so it stuck up everywhere. "A little song John wrote about his favorite waitress."

A pinkish blush spread across the waitresses face. She tugged on a stray curl of her afro and smiled sheepishly.

"Here's the big stud now."

A guy with a brown goatee leaned over the bar and kissed the girl. My fingers holding the camera itched to snap off a few shots of the two lovers, but I decided it would probably be rude.

"Hey."

It took me a second to realize the guy was talking to me. I peered sideways. Oh brother. He probably thought I was some groupie. My face warm, I pulled out a cigarette and was searching my bag for some matches when a lighter appeared in front of me. His hand brushed mine as he lit my cigarette.

"Thanks," I mumbled. I exhaled and then stuck my straw in my mouth, taking a sip so I didn't have to talk.

"Is that a…Coke?" It sounded like he was laughing. Now I regretted the maraschino cherries and grenadine that Stuart had stuck in my drink.

"No." Might as well own up to it. "It's not just a *Coke*. It's a Roy Rogers."

"Oh, pardon me—a fancy Coke."

I stared at his mouth. He had this slight gap in his teeth that was off to the side and only visible when he grinned.

He gestured at my camera resting on the bar. "Photographer?"

I shook my head and eyed his beer. "Fake ID?"

"I'm with the band." He winked as he said it, making fun of himself.

I tried to think of something witty to say. Before I could come up with anything that sounded halfway intelligent, a girl with perfect hair and eyebrows plucked into a permanently surprised arch thrust herself between us so firmly that I had to jerk my cigarette back so I didn't burn her.

"There you are!" She had a slight accent. "I came out of the bathroom—"

"Been here the whole time." He spoke in a monotone. Looking in the mirror, I was surprised to find him watching me. He gave me a slow wink.

"I don't really have time to deal with this tonight," the girl said. "I have a shoot tomorrow morning at a God-awful hour…"

"I told you…" And here his voice lowered and I couldn't make out what he was saying. Not that I wanted to. She muttered something I couldn't, thankfully, hear. Could I put my hands over my ears without looking obvious?

She turned to me with wide eyes, startling me. "Will you help us settle an argument?"

I shrugged.

"It's about what a word means," she said, looping her arm through the boy's and let loose with a brilliant smile. "It's not like it's a big deal that we don't see the same way about this one stupid word. It's not, like, a temperamental difference."

I blinked. Then got her drift.

"Um, you mean fundamental difference?"

"Yeah. Whatever." She flung her hair back over her shoulder. "Anyway, the word is passion. How do you describe passion?"

Band boy stuck his head around her body to address me. "Not describe. Define."

I chewed my lip. "Okay, well, passion is what makes you keep doing something when nobody is looking and nobody cares and everybody thinks you're crazy." I bit my lip and paused. "It's about losing yourself and finding yourself all at the same time. Like when you become so absorbed in something that when you look up, night has fallen and you've forgotten to eat…"

I trailed off. For a few seconds it was silent, so I almost jumped when the girl gave a noisy huff. Her eyes narrowed. "Come keep me company while I have a ciggie," she said to the boy, and stalked off, her hair streaming behind her. She didn't look back to see if he followed.

The band boy took a long pull of his beer with his eyes slanted sideways at me. He clicked his glass against mine. He made a big show of setting down his beer and turning to face me, his knees bent in my direction now. I lifted my camera and took a few shots of him staring at me. He lowered the camera until his eyes were only a few inches away from mine.

A group of guys walked up.

"Taj, my man," one said. "My friends here want a demo tape."

"Cool." The boy stood up, stubbing out his cigarette without taking his eyes off mine. "Gotta take care of business. Be back in a few. You sticking around?"

Before I could answer, he was gone, a slight breeze the only sign of his leaving.

The bartender returned, dangling two silver keys on a small ring and nodding toward the door. "We're all set."

I surprised myself by hesitating, thinking of how that guy had wanted me to wait. But right then, having a place to sleep was all that mattered. I slid off my bar stool, casting a last glance at the door to the backstage.

— CHAPTER —
5

Trailing behind, I followed the bartender, Stuart, up the stairs to the fourth floor of the American Hotel. Entering the wide hallway, I paused, mesmerized by a bank of windows that revealed a stunning view of the Los Angeles skyline a few blocks away. The soaring, glowing buildings filled me with a sense of wonder, the feeling that anything was possible in this city. I snapped off a few shots of the night sky even though I knew they'd only be blurry streaks of colored lights. Looking out at the city, I couldn't help but wonder where that girl would sleep tonight.

Stuart stopped at a doorway across from the windows—room four ten. I was a little disappointed my room faced the street and not the skyline. He handed me a rolled-up sleeping bag and a set of keys, saying I had two weeks to come up with this month's rent and started toward the stairs.

Before I could thank him, he rounded the corner, leaving me to unlock my new home by myself. The room was empty—a ten-by-ten-foot box with clean wooden floors, freshly painted white walls, and a long, tall window facing the building across the street. No closet. I kicked off my boots and tossed the rolled sleeping bag down, right onto the rectangle of orange streetlight stretching across the floor. No curtain. I turned off the light and crept to the window. I could hear and feel the rumbling of the band starting up again even though the punk rock bar was four stories below.

Across the way, the building housed lofts. In one window, a man stood and paced in front of a large canvas. In another, a group of people laughed and talked, holding cocktails. In a candlelit room on a floor below, long white legs ending in high red heels flailed in the air.

A slight noise on the street made me look down. I was surprised to see that guy on the sidewalk below. He was pacing, running his hands through his hair, making it stick up, and looking back and forth.

A door squeaked open and I heard the girl with the accent's voice filter up.

"Taj?"

"Just a second."

The door slammed behind her. He walked into the street and looked around. Before returning to the sidewalk, he glanced up at the building. I shrank back into the shadows of my room. The throbbing music stopped and the night grew quiet. Pressing my head to the cold windowsill, the only sounds were the cars passing on the 101 Freeway a few blocks away and the creak of the door opening again. "Dude, we're on."

The boy broke the silence. "Shit."

And then a door slammed.

I peered out. The sidewalk was empty.

My eyes adjusted to the darkness. Besides the blob of the sleeping bag, the only other visible shape was the silhouette of my combat boots. Stripping to my bra and panties, I folded my clothes and put them in a neat pile on the floor beside me. Shivering, I unfurled the cold sleeping bag and burrowed into it, the wooden floor uncomfortable beneath my head. I reached over and grabbed my leather motorcycle jacket and wadded it up as a lumpy, hard pillow.

The room was tiny, but better than the streets. I was alone in L.A. Loneliness was a familiar feeling, almost comforting at times, like a beloved old blanket, but now it was laced with fear and anxiety.

Things could be worse. I could be out on the streets like that girl. Or trapped in that house in Malibu. Or dead.

Reaching under my head, I unzipped an inside pocket of my jacket and pulled out a worn, soft picture of my mom and me. I held it up in the rectangle of streetlight falling across my bed. It was one of those automated pictures you buy at amusement parks. We sat side by side, coming down a steep part of a rollercoaster, our hair blown back and our arms up, giant grins plastered across our faces.

As I grew sleepy, memories of my mother and what would have been considered a storybook childhood popped into my head: a room with a pink canopied bed, loving parents, and ballet lessons every Saturday. I smiled in the dark. And then, before I could help it, like a train roaring into the station, a vivid image of the nursery in our Chicago home burst into my mind.

The mobile over the bed blowing in the breeze above the empty crib. The tiny coffin. A dark pall over our life. My mom's free fall into her own private hell.

Not every fairy tale had a happy ending.

— CHAPTER —
6

A silver-haired man not much taller than my five-foot-two-inches opened the heavy carved door of Little Juan's. I'd been pounding for at least five minutes.

"Yes?" He had a thick accent I couldn't place. One silvery eyebrow rose. He seemed annoyed. My nervousness grew.

I pushed my sunglasses to the top of my head. "Um, I just moved here and heard you need a waitress." I sounded like an idiot.

He looked me over, from my combat boots up to my wrinkled Catholic-girl skirt, black ripped t-shirt, and motorcycle jacket. His gaze lingered on my barely disguised black eye.

I'd tried to hide my shiner with about a pound of makeup. I'd also put makeup on my legs where I had other bruises from jumping off the deck. But bruises were nothing new. It was like that Sid & Nancy movie where Nancy whined, "I'll never look like Barbie. Barbie doesn't have bruises."

Barbie also didn't have a black eye from her boyfriend socking her because she didn't want to be in his porn flick. I didn't think she smoked either. And she probably had a mother who lived a nice long life baking cookies and attending PTA meetings.

Even I knew I didn't look like a promising job candidate. In contrast, not one hair on his head was out of place and the color perfectly matched his silver designer eyeglasses and pressed gray slacks.

I gave him a winning smile, but he frowned in response. "How old are you?"

"Seventeen." I pulled my shoulders back, lifted my chin, and brushed my bangs out of my eyes. I needed this job. Without a car, I needed work within walking distance of the American Hotel. I spoke fast, my words tumbling over one another. "I'll work really hard. And I'm a fast learner. I won't give you any problems, I promise."

I must have seemed desperate and pathetic, because his eyes seemed to soften. With a sigh, he said, "You have to wear your hair back, in a ponytail. And when you come in tonight, you'll have to put more makeup on that bruise."

I nodded eagerly, afraid to speak and jinx anything.

"I'm Amir. The manager. Please come in." He gestured to the dark interior. "You like coffee? Sit down. I'll be back in a minute."

I followed him in. I wasn't sure, but I thought I had a job.

I slid into the nearest burgundy vinyl booth, kicking my legs nervously. A long bar stretched along one wall near some swinging doors leading to the kitchen. It glittered with colored bottles on glass shelves. Giant Mexican-style murals of men with sombreros and burros covered most of the walls.

"*Buenos dias.*" A man appeared at my elbow with a cup of coffee, his lips curving in a smile under a tiny moustache. The loose back heel of his shoe flapped as he walked away.

Amir returned with a plastic-coated menu and a new, creased, white t-shirt that said *Little Juan's* across the back. "Study this. Be back by four. Sadie will train you. By the way," he said. "What is your name?"

"Nikki." The name didn't garner much reaction. The man nodded and walked away.

Veronica Black was the girl in Chicago. The one I kept close so she wouldn't get hurt anymore.

I gulped down my coffee and, remembering the bus boy's shoes, slipped my last twenty under the sugar container before I left.

I spent the day wandering around the neighborhood taking pictures. I got nervous every time a car drove by. I was pretty sure the Big Shot Director and Chad would never think to look for me in downtown L.A. I thought about that girl again and wondered where she had spent the night.

Worried I would be late, I got to the cantina fifteen minutes early, lingering in the doorway until a girl with long blond hair, haughty cheekbones, and regal posture came flying out of the swinging doors of the kitchen like a tsunami headed my way.

"You Nikki?" Her voice was brusque and there was no sign of a smile anywhere this side of the Mississippi.

I nodded, keeping my mouth shut. She threw a red half apron at me. "I'm Sadie. Put this on. You're going to follow me around tonight. Don't do anything but stand beside me and don't say anything. You're, like, invisible, okay?"

I recognized her name. She was the one who had told Stuart about the job opening. He said she lived on my floor. I actually owed her for this job, but I wasn't going to tell her that.

I watched her carefully, keeping a few steps behind her throughout the night. Her crap attitude seemed to work. Every guy in the place flirted with her, like they could be the one to melt the Ice Queen. She looked familiar, but I knew I'd never met her before. *She* could be Barbie, I thought, eyeing her.

Six hours and thirty bucks in tips later, I started my walk back to the American Hotel, feeling grateful both that Sadie had given me some of her tips and that this area of town seemed deserted at night. Halfway back to the hotel, a car stopped, making me jump, but it was only the Waitress Barbie. She rolled down her big-haired boyfriend's passenger side window and mumbled something about how only an idiot would walk home alone at night in downtown L.A. "Get in," she said, nodding at the backseat.

I got in. Although I didn't think Chad could ever imagine his spoiled, privileged Forest Lake girlfriend slumming it in downtown L.A., I had to be careful. That director was not messing around. I was pretty sure that if he'd caught me that night in Malibu, I'd be dead. And nobody would know.

—CHAPTER—

7

aitressing was a bitch. I woke up happy on my first day off in a week. It was a temporary break from my new status as the biggest screw-up at the restaurant. I was sure Amir was sorry he hired me.

Waitressing was definitely not the best gig for a klutzy girl. The other day I dumped a tostada on a woman's lap. Another day, I'd tripped, sending an entire tray of beer flying. Sadie had rolled her eyes. Nope. I definitely would never be Barbie.

The cooks in the kitchen made fun of me, saying things in Spanish and making faces when they thought I wasn't looking. Only that one busboy I had tipped generously that first day was nice to me.

Even though I had the day off, I decided I might as well do what I did every morning before I went to work—grab a coffee at the café downstairs and walk around downtown taking pictures. I wondered if I'd see that girl or if she were long gone, hopping a train to somewhere far away. I took several of the shopkeepers who paced the sidewalks outside their stores hawking their wares, cheap radios, Indian saris, and knock-off perfumes. That was my thing—unique portraits of people. More *National Geographic* style than *Vogue*.

Down Skid Row, homeless people lay or sat in nearly every doorway. A few of them would make unbelievable portraits, but my fear made me turn around, wincing, my heart ping ponging around inside my chest. Being in downtown L.A. felt like a different country compared to Forest Lake.

Around the corner from Al's Bar, two guys walked out of the café, talking and laughing. One was that goateed guy from the band who was locking lips with the waitress at Al's that first night.

"See you around, Big D," the goateed guy said, and walked off.

"Rock on," said the other boy, a slight, baby-faced guy with black eyes and smooth brown skin. He packed a box of cigarettes against the brick wall. Hearing the familiar, enticing sound, I paused.

"Can I bum one?" I'd run out the night before.

He offered the pack. I held my hair back, leaning toward the lighter he flicked open. He grinned at me between puffs of his Marlboro. I nervously bit my fingernails, trying to avoid looking at him. I was itching to photograph this boy with his black eyes, perfect skin, and blindingly white grin.

"Hey, man, what's your name?"

"I'm Delilah." It just popped out. I smiled to myself. I liked that name.

"That's cool," he said. "I'm Danny Mendez. I live upstairs. Fourth floor."

"Me, too. Four ten."

"I know," he said, bursting into cackling Mad Hatter laughter. "Stuart told me."

The bartender.

I hadn't really met my neighbors yet. I spent the mornings taking pictures and keeping an eye out for that girl and spent my nights at work. Did everyone here know one another? Weird. But maybe he knew band boy. "Hey, isn't that goateed guy in some band?"

"Yup. John. He lives on the fourth floor, too."

"Of course he does," I mumbled.

"He's got the big two-room place at the end. Lives there with Taj, the lead singer. Their band is the shit." The baby-faced boy smiled.

For some reason, I felt my face grow warm. The band boy lives on the *same floor.*

"Hey, man, we look like we're in a gang," he said, gesturing to our matching black motorcycle jackets. "Hewitt Avenue East Side. Yo." He made some awkward gang sign with his fingers and bent over cackling with laughter.

What was with this guy, anyway? Was he high? Why was everything so damn funny? But I couldn't help it—a tiny smile crept onto my face.

He eyed me for a moment, rubbing his chin. Then, as if he had come to some conclusion about me he liked, he grinned that Cheshire cat smile again. "Don't say much, do you?"

I gave a small smile, biting what was left of my ratty fingernails between puffs and looking up at the L.A. sky. It was sort of dirt colored at this time of day. I could smell the smog hanging in the air. The air was gritty, like inhaling a big whiff of dust and sand. Nothing like a Midwestern blue sky with big puffy white clouds. That was okay. I didn't care if I ever saw Chicago again.

Night had fallen and I was bored so I stripped down to my underwear and the big T-shirt I slept in, turned off my light, and sat down to watch people across the street in the lofts. One couple—the man with dark hair like my dad's and the woman with my mother's dishwater blond hair—always had their curtains open. I liked to sit and watch them, like they were a movie.

It was sort of what I'd always pictured my parents' lives would have been like if things had gone differently, if life would have been normal for our family. My parents loved city life but moved to the suburbs to raise me. They would have loved to live the life I watched taking place across the street, with bottles of wine, fancy appetizers, long bohemian dresses, all kinds of friends over for dinner.

Tonight, I held my mom's picture close to my chest as I watched. The man and woman were eating at their long table by candlelight. She was laughing at something when a small figure on the street below caught my eye. I sat up, spilling my ashtray.

It was that girl. She was walking quickly with her arms wrapped around her chest like she was cold. Looking at my boots and jeans in a neat stack on the floor, I calculated how fast I could dress and run down the stairs to catch up with her. Turning back, I leaned out the window to yell for her to stop, but she'd disappeared.

——CHAPTER——
8

Slamming the door of the American Hotel behind me, I ran, rounding the corner after the girl. Her small figure was a few blocks down the road when a sleek car turned onto the street. A jolt of panic surged through me. I instinctively shrunk into the shadows, pressing myself against a building. There was only one reason a car like that would venture over here near Skid Row. Chad and the Big Shot Director. Looking for us. My breath caught in my chest. Why wasn't the girl running and hiding? The car cruised slowly toward the girl.

To my surprise, she walked into the road and the car stopped. A tinted backseat window eased down. The girl leaned into the car, elbows on the window, talking in a low voice. I couldn't make out her words. After a few seconds, the car pulled away and the girl, clutching something to her chest, backed into an alley. I waited until the car rounded a corner and then ran down the middle of the empty street after the girl, my footsteps echoing in the silence.

I pushed myself, breathing hard, determined to catch up to her. Peering down the alley, I saw her at the end, turning onto a street lit with neon. Little Tokyo. I screamed, "Wait!" but it came out as a hoarse yelp.

I ran down streets teeming with people speaking Japanese and music tumbling out of the karaoke bars along with clipped, stilted voices singing Patsy Cline songs. I ran, heart pounding, until I was less than a half block away. I slowed to catch my breath and decided to tail her. I wanted to see where she was going and what she was doing. I wanted to know if that had been Kozlak and Chad in that car and if she had told them where I was.

She didn't know I was behind her. She wasn't in a hurry. She kicked a piece of trash—a can or something—that clattered along, propelled lazily by the toes of her sneakers. I followed her past the Little Tokyo mall, which was closed for the night. Whenever the girl stopped to peer into shop windows, I ducked into doorways and hid.

Seeing all the items in the shops made me realize how different my life had become. I was barely able to pay my rent. It was a far cry from shopping sprees on my father's Am Ex card when I was younger.

Passing a pay phone, I thought about what would happen if I called my dad.

The truth was the last few days I'd felt something—a sense of freedom and pride—that I'd never experienced before. I wasn't the fuck-up my dad thought I was. I *could* take care of myself. It was both a scary and good feeling.

I walked right past that pay phone. Soon, I had followed the girl into a less populated area. I had a feeling I was about to find out where she slept at night. Although Little Tokyo was vibrant, the rest of downtown L.A. was desolate at night. All the businesses were closed. The tall buildings cast long shadows across the circles of the streetlights and the only sounds were distant traffic and the occasional scuffle of a pigeon. Passing one dark street after the other, I got the feeling that

I could walk for blocks without seeing anyone else. I pulled my jacket closer.

The girl was now about a block ahead of me. I stuck to the shadows in case she glanced back. A bulky figure in a puffy coat emerged out of a dark doorway and followed her. I shrank back. She turned down an alley and the figure did, too. I ran to the mouth of the alley. At the far end, the girl was struggling with the man.

"Stop. Help. Leave her alone." My voice, small and hoarse and probably not loud enough for anyone to hear, echoed in the alley. "Stop," I said, racing down the alley. I'd tried to sound mean and as tough as I could, but even I could hear the waver in my voice.

But I must have startled the man because he bolted; leaving the girl huddled on the ground. My footsteps reverberated in the dark alley, which was lined with garbage cans and smelled like a toilet and rotten vegetables. When I got to the girl, she was curled in the fetal position, half lying in a puddle of something foul, clutching her stomach.

"He took my backpack," she said, sitting up. Fat tears streamed down her face. She looked around, head swinging from side to side and blurted, "My glasses!" She patted the pockets of her big flannel shirt. She pulled a pair of jeweled cat-eye granny glasses, but instead of putting them on, she clutched them to her chest and closed her eyes.

I crouched beside her. "You okay?"

She shook her head, her lank hair swinging in front of her eyes. "I need my backpack."

"I'm sorry. It's long gone," I said, standing and walking over to the end of the alley. The streets beyond were dark and empty. I was still jumpy, worried the man would return. I helped the girl to her feet, feeling her ribs through her shirt. When I put my arm around her, she winced.

"Are you hurt?"

"I need my backpack," she said, looking up at me and biting her lower lip with small teeth. Then she mumbled, as if talking to herself. "He's already gone for the night. He won't be back again until tomorrow afternoon."

She wasn't making sense.

"I need my backpack." She pulled at her hair. Her eyes darted around like a wild animal trying to escape. It reminded me of something. Or rather, someone. My mother. I yanked up the sleeve to the flannel shirt she was wearing as a jacket. Her arms were pale white—without a scratch.

"Do you smoke it?"

She looked down.

"Was that your dealer in the black car? Was it Kozlak?"

"He says after nine it's too dangerous around here." She squinted up at me, not answering my question. "There's a guy under the Fourth Street Bridge. He'll have something. I have to go there."

She scrambled to her feet. I got right in front of her. I waited until she looked up at me. "You need to answer me. This is very important. Was that the director in that black car?"

She gave me a blank look. "I need money. I need to go under the Fourth Street Bridge. Help me. Please."

I folded my arms across my chest. "I can help you, but I'm not going to help you get high. And not until you tell me if that man in the car is Kozlak, the movie director."

"Why would you think that old disgusting man is down here?" she yelled, spitting the words out angrily. She turned and stomped down the alley.

I knew I should let her walk away. I kept telling myself to run far away from this girl. *She's trouble.* But I knew I couldn't. I'd bring the girl home with me. But only for one night. I'd figure out what to do with her in the morning. Maybe not the police station, but something. There had to be some shelter or something she could go to. I ran to catch up to her. I took her arm and gently pulled her back.

"You're coming with me."

She didn't resist.

As we walked, I told myself again—it was only for one night.

— CHAPTER —
9

Back at the American Hotel, I heated a can of SpaghettiOs on a hot plate I'd found at the thrift store the other day. I'd also picked up two towels, a washcloth, and a few items of clothing.

The girl sat with her back to the wall and shoveled in big bites with a plastic fork. When she finished, she dug into my cigarette pack and lit one with an expert flick of her wrist. I decided to keep my trap shut. Smoking was the least of her issues right then.

I sent her down the hall to the bathroom with a towel, a large t-shirt, shampoo, and a bar of soap. While she was gone I paced. I'd been looking for the girl for days, but now that I found her I didn't know what to do with her. This was *such* a bad idea. Ripples of apprehension ran through me.

It wasn't like I could save her. I couldn't save anyone. I'd proven that. I couldn't save my baby sister from dying. I couldn't save my mother. I could barely save myself. I had no reason to want to save this girl. Deep down inside, I knew part of it was because she was the same age my sister would have been. Besides, letting her stay one night wouldn't kill me. Tomorrow, I'd figure out what to do with her.

I paced and smoked waiting for her to return. The sound of a motorcycle starting up filtered into my window. I peeked out. It was that band boy. A tall mini-skirted girl with a pixie cut was on the bike behind him, her arms wrapped around his chest. I stared until they turned the corner.

After more than thirty minutes, when I was starting to worry she had run off, the girl came back from the shower freshly scrubbed with the large t-shirt hanging to her knees. Cleaned up, she looked even younger than twelve. She was shivering. It wasn't just a chill from her wet hair. I wrapped my unzipped sleeping bag around her. She looked wary, ready to bolt any second. Easy questions first.

"Rain, how long have you been on the streets?" It was the first time I hadn't thought of her as "the girl."

She looked down, thinking, her nose scrunched. "A month?"

That meant she was living on the streets before I saw her at the beach house.

"What happened?" I said. "Where's your family?"

Stretching her legs out in front of her and staring at the wall, she told her story without any emotion, as if reciting something she'd memorized.

She'd lived with her grandmother for as long as she could remember. After finding her grandmother's body in their Santa Cruz home last month, she fled with her backpack and grandmother's glasses. Worried about being put in a foster home, Rain went looking for her parents. They were living with a bunch of other homeless hippies in an area of Santa Cruz dubbed Tent City because transients camped there and called it home. I asked Rain what her parents were like.

"They did their own thing, you know," she said, still not meeting my eyes. "Smoked weed...just chilled out most of the time. I kept asking if they could help me find a ride to school, but they kept forgetting."

I asked why she wasn't living with them anymore.

"They left. I was getting some firewood down by the river and when I got back, the tent was gone. Stan from one of the other tents said they took off to Cabo San Lucas or something."

She said it so matter-of-factly, without malice, that my heart broke right then and there.

The other people in Tent City raised enough money for Rain to buy a bus ticket to Union Station in downtown L.A. In her grandmother's old address book, she'd found an L.A. address for her mother's sister. But when she got to the house, she was told her aunt had died years ago. Not knowing where to go or what to do, she made her way back to Union Station and slept in the bus station that night and the next. During the day, she'd walk over to Little Tokyo and beg for money from Japanese businessmen.

One night the Big Shot Director pulled up to the bus depot in a limo, offering her food and new clothes and promises to make her a movie star. But when she got to his beach house, he kept her locked in a room. She never saw him, just watched TV all day. He would occasionally unlock the door and hand her a tray of food without saying anything except, "Eat up. Boys don't like skinny girls." The night I saw her, Rain had been there four days. She had escaped her room that night for the first time by jamming little pieces of paper in the lock mechanism.

"Let's go to the cops," I said. "They'll arrest that guy. You can't hold a kid prisoner. They can help you, help find you a place to live."

She drew her knees up to her chest and put her chin on them. "I'd rather die than go to a foster home. I'll run away and go right back to the streets."

She lifted her head, eyes unwavering. She was serious. Her lips were pressed tightly together and her arms were crossed. Her gaze never left mine. In the back of my mind, I knew going to the cops probably was a bad idea for me, too. Even though my dad didn't want me, I was technically a runaway, too. Maybe she was right. A foster home *would* be hell.

She started itching her arms and clutched her stomach. "I don't feel good. I need some more."

"When did you start smoking heroin?"

She shrugged. "When I got to Kozlak's house. He gave it to me."

Fury rose in me, making my hands clench into fists. With the anger came something else. The girl's desperation reminded me too much of things I'd pushed deep down inside.

"How'd you get it after that? Since we ran away? The guy in the black car?"

Wariness spread across her face. She eyed the door.

I stood and opened it for her. "I don't do drugs and I'm not going to let someone who does drugs stay with me." I raised an eyebrow and stood in the open doorway. "Either you try to kick or you leave right now."

I waited, watching as she picked at the blue polish on her toenails. Pressing her lips together, she nodded and scooted back against the wall.

"You've got five minutes to think about it."

I told her to wait and went down the hall to that guy Danny's room. His door was open and a sheet of paper was tacked to it.

My cheeks are numb
I've been drinking too much
My brain's numb
I've been thinking too much
My heart's numb
I've been loving too much.

I peered in the open doorway. He was pecking away at his typewriter. When I knocked, he gestured for me to come in.

"What you doing?"

He stopped typing.

"Poetry, man. Keeps me sane."

He looked at me, waiting.

I blurted it all out. "There's this girl. And she's twelve and homeless and hooked on heroin."

He swiveled the chair to face me.

"She's in my room. I told her she can stay the night but she needs to get off drugs. Some guy stole her stash. She said something about going under the Fourth Street Bridge to get more."

Danny nodded his head. "Under the bridge—that's where all the homeless junkies live. It's a goddamn miniature city. She can't go by herself. Shit, I wouldn't go there alone if you paid me. You say you want to help her off the junk, huh?" He stood and paced as he talked. "Takes about three days and it ain't pretty. You gotta basically babysit her the whole time. Make sure she doesn't get dehydrated and shit. Hold her hand and all that stuff. She'll freak on you. It ain't easy, my friend."

"Three days?" I turned to leave. "I barely know her. I can't do that. I have to work tomorrow."

"I guess you'd better kick her to the curb, then," Danny said, stopping his pacing and staring at me. "Unless you stay with her, she's gonna go find some more in the morning."

"Well, she can't. She doesn't have any money. She doesn't have anything. I told you she got mugged in Little Tokyo."

Danny's face grew serious. "There are other ways to pay for the junk, *chica*."

His words sent me spiraling back to the abandoned house with my mother's claw-like grip on my blouse, ripping it until my pink lace bra showed, her hoarse whisper in my ear, the frantic look in her eyes. I knew all about the other ways.

I could try to help this girl get off drugs, which could take more than one night, or I could send her back to the streets right then and there. I'd left my mother in that abandoned house. This time was going to be different. I had no choice.

"Will you sit with her for a few minutes?" I asked Danny. None of us had phones in our rooms so I'd have to walk to the restaurant to ask for time off.

Danny grabbed a deck of cards and we headed to my room. Before I left, outside my room, he grabbed my arm.

"Hey, home skillet. You said you don't really know this girl. And while it's cool and all, why are you helping this girl?" He didn't say it in an accusatory voice, more like a matter-of-fact, trying-to-figure-me-out way.

Danny watched me closely, eyes fixed on my face.

For a long few seconds we stared at one another. Finally, I shrugged and turned away. I couldn't possibly explain it to him since I didn't exactly know why myself.

— CHAPTER—
10

A girl with a huge afro and kohl-rimmed eyes sat sentry in front of my door when I got back to the American Hotel. When she gave me a shy smile I recognized her as that waitress from the first night at the bar—the one kissing on that goateed guy.

"Don't you work at Al's?" I said.

"Yeah, I work there a few nights and at the café in the mornings." She stuck out her hand. "I'm Eve. I'm keeping an eye on your girl while Danny runs to the store to get some Gatorade. Last time I checked she was sleeping. That's good."

"Thanks," I said, surprised this girl was spending her night helping a complete stranger.

"No worries," she said, smiling. Up close I could see a light dusting of freckles across her nose. It was just the thing that propelled her looks from pretty to stunning. She would be an amazing portrait subject.

"I heard you just moved onto our floor," she said. "I also heard you got at least two names: Nikki *and* Delilah. Now, I like them both, but I guess I'd rather have you pick one name for me to call you. Otherwise, it will be too confusing for me. I'm just a simple gal."

Heat flushed my cheeks. "How about Nikki?"

Her eyes crinkled with a smile. "Girl, you don't know how glad I am another woman moved in up here. Now there are three of us on this floor. You, Sadie, and me. I'm a couple doors down from you, in four oh five. I was starting to think the entire floor was going to be all guys because Sadie keeps talking about moving to the west side as soon as her boyfriend leaves his wife. We girls need to stick together."

Eve told me a little about Sadie. Even though Sadie's married boyfriend was a jerk, he'd fixed up Sadie's tiny box of a room nicely.

"She's got a fancy bed, bookshelves, a little desk, even an air conditioner in the window. It's like a little girl's room, all flouncy and stuff."

"Trippy." The Barbie waitress had her own mini dream house? I chewed on my lip trying to imagine that.

We talked a bit about the other people who lived on the fourth floor. I sat up straighter when she mentioned the boys in the band. They worked as bike messengers, Eve said.

"Wholesome farm boys from the Midwest. Whatever they feed those boys on the farm…whew. Let's just say they are the most enthusiastic boys I've ever met. I didn't go to bed last night. I haven't slept yet, if you know what I mean."

I was a little embarrassed. I wasn't sure if it was her candid talk about sex or if it was imagining the three of them in bed together. I got out a cigarette, offered her one, and tried to change the subject.

I lit her cigarette. "Can I take your picture someday?" She nodded, but it was her turn to blush.

"How did you end up here, in the American Hotel?" I exhaled as I asked my question.

"I'm just a girl from Inglewood. Nothing special. I'm hanging around here until I find the love of my life and then I'm going to move into a little house somewhere on the east side and have two point five kids and be a housewife." She smiled, looking down.

"No offense, but that sounds like hell to me."

"You're funny. I like you."

Danny returned with his electric guitar dangling from a strap around his neck like an oversized necklace and a cigarette hanging from his lips. His black eyes were somber.

"What'd your boss say?"

"He told me I couldn't save someone from themselves," I said, and rolled my eyes. "But he gave me the time off."

"He's right. It's bad, man," he said. "That girl is hurting. Too messed up to even play Crazy Eights with me. She puked at first and then stuff started coming out both ends. Eve barely got her down to the bathroom in time."

I gave Eve a grateful smile.

"I don't think that little girl's got anything else in her anymore," Eve said.

Danny handed me a bottle of lime green Gatorade and told me to make Rain take tiny sips every once in a while so she didn't get dehydrated.

Eve got up to leave. I swallowed a lump of something that seemed stuck in my throat. These two strangers had gone out of their way to help me.

Danny gave a lopsided grin. "Everything cool now? We're going to head down to Al's for a *cerveza*. Think you'll be okay? We can check back later."

I wanted to beg them to stay with me and tell them I was scared to go into that room alone and needed their help, but instead, I nodded. I waited until they disappeared down the hall before I cracked the door. A dark mass was huddled in the middle of my futon mattress. Someone had brought in a few candles, which flickered from the door opening and sent eerie shadows bouncing around the room. I closed my eyes. My feet felt heavy, as if it were impossible to take a step inside that room.

"Nikki?" Rain's voice was scratchy.

Her voice jolted me from my daze. I knelt beside the futon, brushing her hair back. "I'm right here."

She surprised me by grabbing the collar of my leather jacket and pulling herself up to a sitting position. She drew herself close to me, inches away from my face. Her eyes glittered in the candlelight, huge dark pools. I'd never seen such massive pupils in my life. They almost seemed to absorb all the white in her eyes.

"Please help me," she hissed. Bony arms clutched me, all the tiny blond hairs on her arm standing straight up. Sweat was dripping down the sides of her face and her nose was running. The way her tiny fingers clutched my arm and the haunted look in her eyes threw me back almost two years to the night I found my mom in that abandoned house.

Closing my eyes to shut out the memory only brought it spinning to the forefront: the dark clouds that day, the distant wailing of a baby, the stench of my mother's breath, her once manicured fingernails, now yellow and jagged, ripping the necklace off my neck, begging me for help. Telling me that only I could save her. That if I walked out that door, she would die. And then—how I turned my back and walked out.

The buzzing in my ears faded as I let the memory go. "I *am* helping you," I said as firmly as I could, prying Rain's hands away. I held her and stroked her hair for what seemed like hours as she fidgeted, kicking the covers off one minute and then pulling them up, shivering, minutes later.

At one point she jumped up, stomping her feet, saying it felt like ants were biting her. Another time, she bolted out of my arms, leaned over on her hands and knees, and dry heaved into a plastic bag, her back contorting in spasms. I rubbed her back, trying to soothe her. I lost all sense of time. Every once in a while, I drifted off to sleep for a few seconds before jerking back awake.

Long after the sun came up, seeping through the slits at the side of my makeshift sheet curtain, the soft sounds of snoring filled the room. Relief flooded through me. I huddled on the floor next to the futon and closed my eyes.

I woke to whimpering sounds. Rain was rolling around on the floor, clutching her stomach, crying and moaning.

"It hurts. It hurts so bad. Help me, please."

Her eyes were red and she looked around wildly, jumping at slight sounds. Panic zipped through me. Should I ask someone to call 911? Did people die from withdrawals? I didn't know. I grabbed her and held her, stroking her hair, trying to calm her. Slowly, she relaxed in my arms, her face wet with tears and perspiration. She slept for a while and then woke up, reaching for me.

"My granny said she wouldn't leave me, but she did." Her voice was small, like a child.

Last night the person in my room had seemed possessed, not like a twelve-year-old girl. This morning, I saw that girl again as she pleaded with me.

"Don't leave me. Please don't leave me like she did. Please let me stay here." She looked up, searching my face. "I don't want to do the drugs. Please help me. I don't want to be on the streets. I just want a normal life. Do you understand?" Tears were streaming down her face. "I just want a normal life."

I nodded. I just wanted a normal life, too. But it was too late for me. But maybe not for this girl. Although part of me wanted to run away and never look back, I took a deep breath and looked her right in the eyes. "Okay. I won't. I promise. You can stay with me. I'll help you stay off drugs, okay?"

Rain nodded, wiping her tears on her sleeve.

I meant it, too. My mother had begged me not to leave her, but I had. I left. And she had died.

By the third day, my room smelled like death.

My neighbors on the fourth floor had pooled their money to buy an extra futon and sleeping bag, so now Rain and I each had our own beds. I didn't know how I could possibly ever repay them for their kindness. Every once in a while, I thought about that band boy, Taj. I'd met most people on the fourth floor, but hadn't seen him since that day he was on his motorcycle.

My fourth-floor neighbors had also brought us water and food, though Rain never ate more than a sip or two of broth before she puked into the tiny trash can I'd washed out a dozen times already. I was most worried about her getting dehydrated so I tried to make her take a sip of water or juice every hour on the hour. As a result, I hadn't really slept for three days and it showed. My hair was tangled and smelled like throw up.

But that morning, Rain actually drank about a cup of soup and kept it down before she fell into a deep and seemingly peaceful sleep. I lay down beside her and was surprised when I woke and it was already night. I sat up and noticed the empty futon across the room. I jumped up, but a small voice behind me said, "I'm over here."

Rain was kneeling at the window with the sheet I used as a curtain drawn aside. Her shoulder blades stuck out from her back like little bird wings.

"How you feeling?"

"The people across the street are having a party," she said.

"Yeah. Those are the lofts. All the rich artists live there." I narrowed my eyes. "You hungry?"

She let the sheet fall and turned to face me. "I ate your crackers. Do you think I could get a Hershey bar?"

I nodded. She turned back to the window, pulling the curtain back open. The orange streetlight illuminated her. She was watching the neighbors, concentrating, with a wistful look on her face. Did she feel that same yearning and longing that I did watching the loft people living their vibrant, seemingly perfect lives?

——CHAPTER——
11

Rain bounded into our room, chased by Danny. Both collapsed in a heap on her futon, giggling.

"We raced all the way from the gas station and *I* won," Rain announced triumphantly, dumping a brown paper bag full of Hershey bars on the floor.

"Only 'cause this old man smokes too much," Danny said, panting and fake coughing.

"You owe me a poem. You promised!" Rain said, sitting up and ripping open a candy bar.

"Hey, don't you worry, *hija*, I'm a man of my word. I'll write it tonight. Oh, but I forgot, you have to give me all your candy bars, though," he said, reaching out toward them teasingly.

"No way." She erupted into laughter and shielded the candy bars with her body. She took a big bite of one bar and when she was done chewing, said, "You have to write the poem tonight and then you have to put on it that it's for Rain. And then you have to hang it on your door like all the others."

"Okay, okay, Miss Mini Drill Instructor," Danny said, saluting. "Now I need to take a nap. You wore me out." Danny buried his face in the sleeping bag. Soon, loud fake snoring noises sent Rain into another fit of giggles. "Get up, goofy." She pushed his shoulder, trying to roll him off the futon.

Rain had been living with me for a week. We had quickly established a routine. We spent the mornings taking long walks through downtown L.A., taking pictures, visiting the Contemporary Temporary Museum around the corner, or browsing the thrift store for books. When I was at work, she either read in our room or hung out with Danny playing Crazy Eights. I worried a little bit about leaving her alone—that she might go looking for that guy in the black car—but she promised not to leave the American Hotel without me. She wasn't telling me everything and it worried me. The other day, Danny and I had been smoking in front of the café when a black car turned onto our street and slowly drove past.

"It's him. The guy Rain knows."

"*Pendejo.*" Danny swore under his breath. "That guy is bad news. I feel it in my bones."

"Who is he?" I tried to see through the dark tinted windows, trying to spot a glimpse of a big white mane of hair. Rain claimed it wasn't the Big Shot Movie Director, but was she lying?

Today, sprawled on my bed, Danny gave up the fake snoring and was dealing a game of Crazy Eights when Eve came in bearing day-old bread from the café downstairs, a butter knife, and a jar of Nutella. We dug into the food and washed it down with instant coffee I made on my hot pad.

After everyone left, Rain and I moved out into the hallway near the windows so we could smoke sitting in the golden beams of sunset pouring across the wooden floor. I tried asking Rain once more about the guy in the black car.

She blew her hair out of her eyes and picked at her blue toenail polish. Finally, she looked up. "He needs to keep it secret because he's very important. He's famous, okay? I'm not supposed to talk about him. I told you."

Giving up, I asked Rain if she was angry with her parents for abandoning her at Tent City. She was quiet for a minute as if she was really thinking about it before she shook her head. "Not their fault. They're free spirits. They don't mean to hurt anyone else. They just do their own thing."

We sat there for a few minutes silent and smoking. Then she leaned her head onto my shoulder. It took a minute for me to realize she was crying.

"What's wrong, Rain?" I pulled back and tried to see her face.

She hid her face in her hair and shook her head.

"What is it?"

"Thank you," she said. "Thanks for taking care of me. Thanks for being the big sister I never had."

I looked away so she couldn't see my face. She didn't know. I'd never told her about my sister dying. I'd never told her that calling me her big sister might be the one thing she could say that would reduce me to a puddle of tears. I pretended to rummage around in my bag for another cigarette and my matches until I had gained control of my emotions.

We sat there tapping our feet, listening to Danny down the hall playing guitar with his amp cranked and his door open.

The sun had nearly set and shadows had grown long when the building's cranky old janitor appeared with his frown and bucket and mop. He talked to himself and was always glaring so I usually tried to avoid him. Today he charged over to where we sat, ferociously swabbing the wooden floor, not waiting for us to get up and move, but splashing gray mop water all over us as we scrambled to our feet.

"Dirty whores," he mumbled. "Don't you have homes? Go home. This is not your home."

I was about to tell him off when Rain jumped up and grabbed his hand with both of hers. My body tensed. But the man stopped what he was doing and looked down at Rain, who smiled up at him. "It's okay," she said quietly.

I froze, waiting for his reaction. He gazed off into space for a few seconds, but then shook away Rain's hand and quietly began mopping, this time slowly instead of frenetically.

Later that night, in our room, Rain was crying in her bed.

When I asked her what was wrong, all she managed to choke out was, "That poor man."

I had just started to reach for a bag of chips off a shelf at the gas station convenience store when I saw something familiar out of the corner of my eye.

Turning, I froze. I stared at the lean back and stringy blond ponytail just a few feet down the aisle. Chad had found me. I wanted to run, but my legs felt like they were stuck in cement. My face felt hot and then icy cold.

The man turned. It wasn't Chad.

But it was a reminder that I still had to be on guard. For the first few weeks I'd worked at Little Juan's, my heart would pound every time I saw the back of a blond or white-haired man in the restaurant. Walking through the streets of downtown L.A., I was constantly alert, darting into doorways whenever I saw familiar silhouettes.

But it had been a month. I'd started to relax a little

This was a good wake up call. I looked for Rain. She was flipping through a stack of magazines near the counter. She seemed to be doing it casually, but I noticed she kept casting sideways toward the clerk who was chewing gum and talking on the phone. Her behavior was so odd. I decided to wait outside and spy on her.

Outside, I found I could watch her by looking at a reflection from the window without her seeing me. She furtively looked around then shoved the magazine under her shirt. I had given her some money so she didn't feel like she had to ask me for everything. When she walked out, I asked if she'd bought anything. She looked away as she said no. If she was embarrassed to buy it, it was partly my fault. I mocked most magazines at the convenience store, telling her she'd be better off reading *The New Yorker* or something. Even though she always rolled her eyes, I felt like this was what a good big sister would do—steer her siblings away from trash and be a role model for intelligent reading.

Later, when she was in the shower, I searched through her stuff. Finally, I found the magazine lying flat under her futon. It was some celebrity gossip magazine. I wasn't sure why she was acting so weird about it. I flipped through it really quickly, wondering if the man in the black car, the famous one, was in this magazine or if she was just embarrassed to buy something that I found so clearly low brow and trashy.

The next day, we were standing in front of the American Hotel's door smoking when a big black car pulled onto our street. Instinctively, I pushed Rain inside the front door. The car—with its impenetrable dark windows—stopped at the end of the block, idling. I walked into the street and stood facing the back of the car until the ash on my cigarette grew so long it broke off and fell onto the sidewalk. It was the car. The one that had stopped for Rain.

It was like a standoff. I was holding my breath, waiting for something to happen. My heart was thudding in my throat and my legs were trembling. I didn't know whether to run over to the car and jerk the backdoor open or run inside the American Hotel.

Without thinking, I reached into my bag, took out my Nikon, and started walking down the middle of the street toward the car. Before I had even held it up to my eye, the driver gunned the engine and the car jerked away. My finger kept clicking the shutter release. I continued firing off shots, walking down the middle of the road until the car squealed around a corner out of sight. My heart was racing. I stood for a few seconds in the middle of the street, my chest heaving. I felt a strange exhilaration that I'd been able to scare off the car by myself. Well, my camera and me. Right before I tucked my camera back in the bag, I caught a glimpse of a pink-streaked head quickly ducking back inside the window of our room.

When I got upstairs, Rain was huddled in a corner, her arms wrapped around her legs, her face even paler than normal.

"Who is that man in the car, Rain?" I titled her chin so she would meet my eyes.

"I can't tell you." Her lower lip quivered as if she were trying not to cry.

"Is it Kozlak? Is it the director? I need you to tell me the truth. This is very important."

She shook her head vehemently. "I told you, it's not the director. I would never lie to you. I promise. You have to believe me."

"Why can't you tell me who it is?"

"He made me promise. I don't break my promises."

I believed her. Her honor code might not make sense to many people, but I believed her when she said she didn't lie. "What does he want? Why does he keep coming around? I thought you were happy you kicked. You don't want to get high again, do you?"

She shook her head wildly. "No!"

If the man wasn't her dealer, what was he? Maybe something more, something even worse.

—CHAPTER—
13

I t totally didn't feel like Christmas. For starters, it was seventy degrees out. I was used to a bitterly cold and white Christmas.

After waking, I stayed in bed and let myself think of my mom, something I usually didn't allow myself to do because my thoughts always turned nightmarish. Today, I tried to concentrate on the good memories, the early ones—my mother in her flowered flannel robe hugging me and smiling while I opened presents on Christmas morning. But even remembering that was too much. As soon as I felt hot tears forming, I pushed the memory deep down inside.

And yet for the first time in years, because of these new friends of mine, I was excited about Christmas. We were having a party on the roof later.

I left Rain with Danny so I could shop for presents. Of course, nothing was open on Christmas Day, so I headed to the gas station. I wasn't sure who was coming to the party. Danny told me that Sadie wouldn't be there. I was glad. She barely acknowledged I was alive at Little Juan's and walked right by me in the halls of the American Hotel like I was invisible. I hoped that band boy would be at the party.

Back at the hotel, I passed out my presents early in my room. That way I wouldn't feel bad if I didn't have presents for other people at the party. Danny loved the gunmetal-gray Zippo and kept flicking it open in different ways—between his legs, behind his back—being his usual goofy self. Rain was harder to shop for, but as soon as I saw a rack of backpacks, I remembered that man stealing hers in the alley. I grabbed a purple one and filled it with pink lip gloss, packs of gum, and a stack of Hershey bars. I also threw in a few gossip magazines. Because I felt guilty for making her embarrassed to want to read them. She immediately tucked her granny glasses into the outside pocket and hugged the backpack to her chest.

Down the hall, the padlock to the rooftop door was on the ground. Crawling up the small staircase, we emerged onto the roof in time to catch an ethereal sunset. The air was fresh for once. Instead of the heavy smog smell, an ocean breeze had snuck into downtown somehow, bringing with it the salty, briny smell of the beach.

"It's amazing," Rain said, staring at the sky.

The pinks, oranges, and fiery reds swirled across the clouds on the western horizon. I reached for my camera and was surprised that I had forgotten it in my room. Could I rush downstairs and get it? No. I'd miss this brief magical moment. So instead, I soaked it all in, willing myself to sear the image and this night in my memory forever.

Danny handed me a bottle of red wine and Rain a grape soda. I took a swig of the wine before handing it back to Danny. Rain started talking about getting a cat.

"I'll get you a little *gato*," Danny told her, ruffling her hair. "You stay off the junk until summer and I'll take you down to the animal shelter and let you pick out any little kitten you want."

I frowned at him. Why was he assuming she'd get back on drugs?

"Leave me alone," Rain said. "I don't want any more H. Why don't you guys just leave me alone? Otherwise, I'm going to bed." Her eyes blazed with anger.

"Okay, okay." Danny held up his palms in surrender. "Don't leave. I haven't even shown you my new dance moves. Plus, you gotta check this shit out. It's a bootleg copy of the new Beastie Boys album that's not out yet. I got me a friend at Capitol Records who gave me the hook up."

He pressed play on a ghetto blaster and began wiggling around, doing some old school break dancing on the tar roof, while Rain and I bopped around to the beat, our heads hung low and our hair falling over our eyes.

The sky turned violet and Danny left, saying he had a surprise for us. Rain and I stood looking off into the distance at the skyline. The sight of the tall, looming skyscrapers always sent a thrill of excitement through me that I couldn't explain.

A few minutes later, Eve's mammoth afro popped up from the stairwell. She was giggling like a schoolgirl. Right behind her was the boy with the goatee she'd kissed in the bar. Eve's round rear end was eye-level with him and he cupped it coming up the stairs, which earned him a playful punch in the shoulder from her. Behind them was the band boy, Taj.

Eve introduced the goateed boy as John. When she introduced Taj, we both pretended like we'd never met, which I guess we hadn't. Officially. She told me their band, Tell Me Lies, had just returned from a tour, up to Seattle and back. "They opened for X," she said, grinning and looping her arm possessively around John.

No wonder I hadn't seen him around. He was on tour with Exene Cervenka and John Doe's band. I was impressed, but tried to hide it. I peeked out from under my bangs. He was watching me, so I looked down, focusing on his Converse sneakers and the skateboard dangling from his arm. Rain came over to me then and Taj walked away. I realized that I'd never seen him talk to Rain. He hadn't been there the first few nights when she was sick and everyone had pitched in to help. And now, he seemed to avoid her altogether.

I was wondering about his weird behavior when Danny emerged from the stairwell juggling a giant platter of tamales and a plate of brownies.

"Merry Christmas, *gringos*," he said, cackling in his characteristic Mad Hatter way. "This is how we do it in East L.A., baby."

We sat in ripped lawn chairs someone had hauled up onto the rooftop and dug in, punctuating our bites with swigs of wine and beer

"Oh my God," Eve said, swooning and rolling her kohl-rimmed eyes back as she bit into her third tamale. "That's it. I know for sure now—I'm a Chicana trapped in a black girl's body. I'm going to become Catholic, marry an East L.A. boy, have ten kids, and eat like this every night. I swear it."

"It's too bad I like boys, *Señorita* Eve, or I would be your perfect man," Danny said, a grin spreading across his baby face. "You see, I'm a black guy trapped in a Chicano's body. I only wish I had the bootie to prove it." He stuck out his flat butt and started wiggling it around until we were all laughing so hard we were practically crying.

Despite her comment about marrying a boy from East L.A., Eve only had eyes for John. And he kept his arm around her the whole night. Every once in a while, I'd glance at Taj. He was practicing tricks on his skateboard, occasionally failing and landing smack on his ass. I tried to ignore him. But every time he caught me looking, he smiled that gap-toothed grin.

After the sun set, without intending to, we split off into two distinct groups—Taj, John, and Eve standing against the west wall with their backs to us, facing the city skyline, and Danny, Rain, and I sitting behind them with our backs pressed against the east wall, also taking in the view of the city. Danny and I polished off one bottle of wine and started on another. When Rain reached for a brownie, Danny grabbed it and stuck it behind him for a second.

"Now you see it, now you don't." With a flourish, his hand came back with a giant-size Hershey bar. "Got this especially for you, *niña*."

Rain reached for the bottle, but I told her to stick to soda.

"You're not old enough to drink either." She made a face. She'd been in a bad mood ever since Danny talked about her staying off the junk.

I couldn't argue with that. None of us were. Besides her, I was the youngest one there. Danny was the oldest at nineteen.

Then it struck me. These people were turning into friends. Real friends. Not like the ones I had in high school, the ones who whispered about me in the halls and stopped inviting me over to their fancy homes when my mom left us.

Looking around at the faces on the roof, a tremor of worry raced through me. What if I opened myself up to these people and they turned on me, too? Maybe it was smarter to keep them at arm's length—to keep my guard up.

But I had a feeling it was already too late.

—CHAPTER—
14

lose to midnight, an introspective mood seemed to fall across the rooftop. Night falling had brought a slight chill. It was nearly a full moon and big, puffy clouds kept floating past, sometimes briefly blocking the beams of moonlight shining down on the roof. The boombox in the corner was playing the Ramones, but at such a low level it was mellow background music.

John and Eve were off in a corner kissing and whispering. Taj stood off by himself.

I allowed myself all of five minutes to think about my dad, my mom, and my sister, and then shook the memories off. It hurt too much to remember what I no longer had.

I wondered if my friends, like me, were remembering families and friends who weren't here with us.

Maybe this was my family now. I cast a glance at Rain. She was off in a corner. I wondered if she missed her family. I walked over to her as she leaned over the wall and looked at the street below. She gave a tiny gasp. It was nearly inaudible, but I heard it. So did Danny, who was standing nearby. We both hurried over to the edge of the wall. A black car turned the corner.

"What's your home boy doing in this neighborhood on Christmas?" Danny sounded angry. Ever since he'd come back with the tamales, his body was stiff and tense, and although he was still goofy, it seemed like he had to force his smiles. There was a glint of something in his eyes I'd never seen before. Something dangerous and sad.

"Leave me alone. Mind your own business." I'd never heard Rain sound so nasty. Danny looked crushed.

"Hey," I said, grabbing her arm. "You're being rude. We all know that black car is trouble. Just because you want to keep your mystery man's identity a goddamn secret doesn't mean you have to act like an ass to us about it."

She whirled back, jerking her arm away. "Don't you dare tell me what to do. You don't understand anything at all. You can't tell me what to do. You aren't my big sister. I hate you."

I sat there for a second and then, when my words came out they were flat and cold as steel. "Why don't you get the fuck out, then? Why don't you just leave?"

My face burned as she ran away.

Out of the corner of my eye I saw Taj watching.

I was reeling from her words. Screw her. I had taken her in and tried to take care of her, and for what. Her hatred. But, immediately, guilt and horror filled me at what I had said.

"Oh my God," I said with a sob.

Danny touched my arm. "Hey, she didn't really mean it."

"The hell she didn't."

"Wait here, I'll go talk to her. I'll tell her you didn't mean it."

"Thank you, Danny. I'm such a jerk." I wiped away a mutinous tear that had escaped.

"Nah. She totally deserved that shit. She was being a shit teenager. We've all been there, right? Neither one of you meant it. I'll go fix it. I'm a good mediator. I'm good at that shit. God knows I've had years of practice with my old man and old lady."

I watched as the black car stopped in the middle of the road below us. What the hell was it doing?

"You'll keep an eye on her, right?" I asked Danny.

"Sure thing." He loped toward the roof door.

After they left, even in the dark I could tell that Taj was watching me. I was sure he heard our nasty exchange.

Blushing, I stretched and stood, walking over to get a better view of the city at night. Standing against the waist-high wall, the city loomed before me. Giant silver skyscrapers dotted with squares of white light sparkled against the night sky. A big cloud drifted lazily across the moon, making it dark. It was then I sensed him at my side.

"It doesn't even seem real, does it? It feels like you can reach out and grab a skyscraper, doesn't it?" His voice was husky.

Keeping my gaze on the city skyline, I nodded. I was relieved he didn't bring up the confrontation with Rain. We were both quiet for a moment.

"When I look at the city, it seems alive, like it has a life of its own," I said without turning. "It makes me feel like by living here, I'm part of that, you know, part of something bigger than my own life. I don't feel so small and alone." I immediately regretted my words. "That sounded kind of pathetic, didn't it?"

"No," he said, shaking his head, his voice rising in intensity. "It totally makes sense. I think of L.A. as a spirit sometime. Without getting too granola, it's like everything has a spirit, the trees, the animals—why not a city? It makes sense. Los Angeles has an energy unlike anywhere else. If there was ever a city that was alive, why wouldn't it be here?"

I nodded, a bit too enthusiastically, probably thanks to the wine. "This city makes me feel like there is nowhere else on earth I should be—that I'm exactly at the right place at the right time. Almost like I'm at the center of the universe. For the first time in my life I feel like I'm where I belong, where I'm supposed to be."

"Exactly," he said, staring straight ahead. "Like if I weren't here, I'd miss out on something—or everything."

I thought about what he said for a few seconds. Maybe I was drunk, but I knew what he meant. Every day at school after my mother died, I'd sat in that empty classroom, eating my lunch alone while everyone else in the school laughed and had fun and made plans for the weekend. The silence between us felt awkward, so I reached over for a brownie from the plate on the ledge and began nibbling.

In the moonlight, Taj's face showed something like surprise. "I didn't think you…"

I was confused. We watched as Eve and John parted for a second and she disappeared down the stairs.

"Oh, never mind," he said. "Hey, I was thinking…" His voice faltered. He seemed a little nervous and for some reason this made my heart race. "There's this song by the Red Hot Chili Peppers and it talks about what you said, about the city making you feel less alone. I got the tape in my room. Want to go down and listen to it? I think you'd dig it."

He moved closer and I was glad another cloud cast us into darkness because it hid the warmth I could feel spreading across my face. He was so close. His fingers were near my belly, grabbing the edge of my shirt and pulling me toward him. The heat of his fingers against my bare skin, gently caressing the soft area right above the waist of my jeans, made me catch my breath. When I looked up at him, searching for his eyes in the dark above me, I felt a little dizzy and didn't know if it was from being this close to him or from too much wine. His head dipped down toward me when the loud racket of a door slamming open startled us.

It was Eve.

"I can't find Danny," she said. "And the bathroom door is locked. Nobody is answering when I knock."

Rain.

I pulled away and raced for the stairs, feeling unsteady. For some reason the wine had hit me hard and fast like never before. As my boots squished across the warm black tar, it felt as if the roof was trying to suck me into it. In my peripheral vision, the night sky was blurry and filled with streaking stars and teetering buildings.

When I reached the staircase, the steps seemed to stretch and elongate under me. The voices behind me were distorted, including what sounded like Taj calling my name. But I kept going, clutching the wooden railing on the stairs when I felt like I was going to fall. Finally, after what seemed like forever, I was at the bottom. Down the hall, Danny's door was open, but his room was empty. I pounded on the bathroom door.

"Rain? Danny?"

Nothing. Meanwhile, the hallway began spinning. Taj and Eve and John caught up to me. Everything seemed to be tilting back and forth. What was wrong with me? I threw myself to the ground, peering under the crack of the bathroom door. Underneath, a big pair of men's bare feet blocked my view. They weren't moving.

I got up, pounded, and yelled again. I shoved my body against the door, trying to break it down. I barely noticed when Taj appeared beside me and knelt with something in his hands. A screwdriver. Within seconds the door handle was off. I shoved the door open and Danny woke up, cringing as the door pinched his toes.

"*Hijo de tu puta madre*," he hissed, his eyes scrunched up in pain.

My eyes searched the rest of the bathroom, including the shower stall. Empty.

"Danny." I leaned down to shake him. "Where's Rain?"

His eyes rolled back in his head. Taj and John silently helped Danny to his feet, supporting him. I sprinted to my room. Why hadn't I gone here in the first place? Something was really wrong with me. I was dizzy and couldn't see straight. I couldn't have been that drunk. The keys were dangling in the door to my room. I flung open the door and scanned the small space. Rain's purple backpack was missing. I ran back into the hall. Taj, John, and Eve were all looking at me.

Rain was gone.

— CHAPTER —
15

My vision was kaleidoscoping. Panic rose in my throat and my voice became shrill. I searched the faces in front of me as if they would give me the answer.

Just then, Danny seemed to realize what was going on.

"Rain's gone?" His words were slurred. "She was just here." He looked around and seemed confused. "I told her to wait right here while I went to the bathroom. We were gonna come talk to you, Nikki. That's no good, sister. Smack, once it gets ahold of you, it ain't gonna let you go easy. I know."

He started laughing.

"This is not even remotely funny, you asshole." In the sudden silence, I realized I had shouted the words, which echoed in the hallway.

Danny's baby face crumpled.

All the faces in the hall seemed unfamiliar. I turned to them. "What are we going to do?"

"Nothing right now," Taj said. "If she's still not back in the morning, we'll look for her. Give her a chance to come back on her own."

"Danny said that she went looking for drugs."

"That's not necessarily true. We don't know what happened," Taj said. He looked off to the side, biting his lip a little. "Danny's relationship with drugs is a bit…uh, complicated. Just 'cause he thinks she wants drugs doesn't make it true. He could be totally wrong. I think you should lie down. Maybe try to get some sleep."

Go to sleep? Frantic, I ignored him and headed toward the stairs. At the stairwell, I turned. They all stood there, exchanging glances. I didn't have time to figure out what that meant, but pounded down the stairs.

The walls seemed to be undulating, breathing in and out as if they were trying to close in on me, so I raced down them as fast as I could. It was like one of my panic attacks, but much worse. What the hell was wrong with me?

Finally, I hit the last step and flung open the front door, looked up and down the street. Nothing. Not even a homeless guy hanging around. I darted toward the café. As I rounded the corner, I saw something far down the road. Was it a car without lights? Two darker, smaller shapes were nearby. My vision was going wonky. It seemed like the yellowish street light circles were spinning and moving in and out. Shadows elongated, stretched, and then receded. I put one palm flat on the wall beside me for support because a wave of dizziness swarmed over me, making me feel off balance. I tried to keep my eyes on the shapes near the car, if it was a car.

I squinted hard, trying to focus. The smaller figure was dressed in white. It had to be Rain. We had bought her a white sweatshirt at the thrift store the other day. As I strained to see, the white figure merged with the darker shape at the same time a sound, a short, piercing cry rang out and then was suddenly muffled. I startled, taking a step as the larger dark shape, the car, disappeared around the corner.

"Rain!" I shouted, but then closed my mouth, knowing it was useless. Hearing a sound, I turned and found my neighbors standing there, staring at me. Eve had her hand pressed to her mouth.

"We've got to find that car. I think they took Rain." My voice sounded weird, more piercing and high-pitched than normal. I put my palm up against the wall again to support myself. Bile rose in my throat and I leaned over, worried I was going to puke. When I looked up, four faces searched mine.

"What car?" Eve said. She came up and put her arm around me, rubbing my arm, soothingly.

"There was a car. That black car was here. I swear it." Again, my voice was screechy.

"Come on, let's go inside." Taj took my arm gently, but I shook it away.

"Don't patronize me. There was a goddamn car and it took Rain."

"We believe you saw something, sweetie," said Eve. "But are you sure? Those brownie's Danny brought are pretty strong." Eyes narrowed, she shot a glance at Danny. "Especially for someone not used to it."

Brownies? Oh God, of course. That was what was wrong with me. There had been something in the brownies Danny had brought. No wonder he had told Rain she couldn't have any.

"But I don't do drugs." I closed my eyes for a second.

"Yeah, well, you just got a dose of liquid acid, sister," John said, his arm around Eve. "Are you sure you saw Rain get in a car?"

"I don't know," I said, and paced, stopping to kick the wall of the brick building with my steel-toed boot. Bad move, because it made me feel even more off balance and nauseous. "I don't know," I said again in a small voice as I slid to the ground, my back against the wall.

"Hey, it was probably Rain," Danny said.

I turned to him gratefully. "You saw it," I said. "Earlier, you saw the black car in this neighborhood, right? We both saw it together."

I waited, but Danny didn't say anything. Nobody said anything until Danny laughed and said, "I told you, *chica*, smack grabs ahold of you. Bammo. You need it. You go find it. That's probably what Rain did. Went looking for that *pinche culero* in the black car."

I swallowed back a sour taste. I stayed like that for a while—crouched on the ground with my back to the wall, staring off into the darkness, hugging my knees and shaking my head.

—CHAPTER—
16

Sometime later, after I finally threw up a few times, I lay on my futon praying for the spinning and hallucinations to stop. When I closed my eyes, I had a complete song and dance show on the back of my eyelids. Mickey Mouse in tails and a top hat dancing to imaginary music in my head.

Did I really see Rain in her little white hoodie being tossed into a big black car? If so, it was my fault. I told her to leave. I told her I didn't give a shit what she did anymore. She was only doing what I said. I'd basically kicked her to the curb. My head hurt thinking about it and the drugs weren't helping.

Good God, I'd never touched anything stronger than alcohol before. Could taking acid make me see something that wasn't even there? When would it wear off?

Whenever Mickey Mouse took a break from his routine, my mind kept replaying what I had seen on the street. It was so dark and the car was far away. But then again, why would a car drive around without lights unless they were up to no good?

What if Danny was right? What if Rain got into that car on her own, either because she didn't think she could stay with me or because she wanted drugs? I didn't know what it felt like to be addicted. I only knew what it had done to people I loved.

When I was fifteen and my mother chose drugs over her husband and daughter, I swore to myself I would never get high. And here I was lying in a residential hotel in Los Angeles, waiting for the liquid acid to get the hell out of my body.

I was sure my Radcliffe-educated mother didn't choose what ended up being her destiny either—having a stillborn baby, getting hooked on drugs, and overdosing in a crack house.

Her choices tore our little family into pieces. After her death, my dad began drinking heavily and falling asleep in front of the TV every night. One night, more than a year after my mom died, I was trying to pull him off his armchair to get him to bed when he started crying. Deep inside, I already knew he blamed me for my mother's death—I'd seen it in his eyes when he looked at me. And he was right. But he'd never come out and said it until that night in front of the TV. "You could've saved her, you know." His voice was low and slurred, but to me, every word seemed as if it were yelled through a megaphone. I knew he was talking about my mother, but at that moment, it felt like he was also talking about my baby sister. Two people dead because of me.

The next morning, I packed a bag with a few items of clothing and my camera. I spent the next month crashing on people's couches and trying to drink myself to death. One day I was sitting on a curb hungover, with deep black circles under my eyes and knots in my hair. I was smoking a cigarette and picking at a hole in my tights when I noticed a car had stopped in front of me. It was my dad's sleek Jaguar. The window slowly rolled down.

"My clients…they're all gone. The house—poof, probably gonna be gone, too. This car? A matter of time." My dad's voice was tinged with fury. He was drunk. Maybe the drunkest I'd ever seen him. His eyes seemed to be looking right past me, as if he couldn't even focus. "My life is shit, Veronica. Utter shit. My wife is dead. Dead." He choked on a sob, staring at the windshield. "And my daughter, sitting on the curb like a crack whore. You're dead to me. Don't bother coming home."

His car lurched away from the curb, fishtailing a little, kicking back a few small pebbles and sand that hit my shins. I blinked rapidly, trying to understand what had just happened. Not wanting to believe it. When his words finally sank in, I sprang up and, standing in the middle of the street, began pulling things out of my bag, a book, my makeup bag, a full water bottle, and began chucking them in the direction of the car, which was now several blocks away.

"I hate you! I hate you!"

I slumped to the ground, tears streaming down my face. I knew he thought it was my fault my mom died. I'd have to live with it forever. But crack whore? I'd never done drugs in my life—not even smoked pot. And I was a goddamn virgin. Right then, I made plans to change that as soon as possible. I met Chad the next day.

Now, my face pressed into my futon at the American Hotel, I waited for the drugs to wear off so I could feel normal again. I was tired of this new life. I was tired of everything.

Finally, around dawn, I fell asleep. By noon I pulled myself to the bathroom, hoping I wouldn't run into anyone in the hall. My jaw was achy and stiff and my entire body was sore, but I wasn't seeing strange things anymore.

I'd been foolish to think I could help Rain by letting her stay here with me, by trying to be a big sister to her. What a fool. I hadn't been able to save her.

The man in the black car had taken her. I didn't care what anyone else said—I'd heard her try to scream. Even high on acid, I knew what I'd heard. Rain had tried to scream for help. She hadn't wanted to go with him.

The police might believe me, though. I'd get dressed and head to the substation I'd gone to that first night with the surfers. That would be my first stop. I'd tell them she'd been kidnapped. If only I knew the man in the black car's identity.

I yanked Rain's futon up. The magazine was still there, pressed flat. I flipped through the pages, analyzing each celebrity face. Who was her mystery man? He was always in the backseat, rolling down the dark-tinted window. You had to be rich to have a car with a driver, right? She'd said he was important, famous.

I quickly flipped through the pages until I came across one that was carefully dog-eared. *Here we go.* The page contained articles about three men.

Andy Martin was a thirty-year-old Los Angeles comedian who was going through a messy divorce after his wife caught him sleeping with the nanny. He was good looking in a nerdy way with big, black Elvis Costello glasses and a sensuous mouth. His shtick was performing at comedy clubs and producing sexy plays attended by bachelorette parties.

Rex Walker was the most famous of the three, starring in a series of blockbuster action flicks. He smiled out from the photo like a superhero with his sculpted cheekbones, perfect black hair, and Dudley Do-Right chin. He was in his early forties and married to a British stage actress with her own busy acting career. He split his time between L.A. and the London house where his wife stayed with their two children.

Matt Macklin, in his late twenties, was the bad boy of the bunch and the best looking with his shoulder-length strawberry blond hair and scruffy five o-clock shadow. His hatred of paparazzi gave Sean Penn a run for his money. He was from Ireland, but the article said he was staying in Los Angeles. He was a notorious drunk and womanizer known for bar fights and destroying hotel rooms.

I ripped out the page and taped it to my wall. I paced and looked at the men in the pictures, wishing they could talk.

I was coming back from the bathroom when Danny loped up to me with his usual loopy grin and guitar strap strung around his neck.

"Hey, home girl. Rain back?" He seemed so sure and hopeful that she was in my room, sleepy from her adventures but safe.

"No," I said, my eyes narrowing. "I asked you to keep an eye on her. But you decided to get high instead."

Even as I said it, I knew it was wrong. It was my fault Rain was gone. I had no right to blame it on Danny.

Danny mumbled something about only being in the bathroom a few minutes. "And sorry about the brownies, man, I thought you knew."

I tuned him out. He was right. I was so naïve, I deserved to have eaten his stupid brownies. I didn't say anything more, just slipped inside my room and softly closed the door. I hated myself so much that I couldn't bear to see his kind face. He should hate me, just like Rain did.

"Damn," he said from the other side of the door. I was leaning back against it, listening. It was silent on the other side. A few seconds later, the squeak of his sneakers told me he'd headed back toward his room.

My insides wrenched and knotted with guilt. I didn't want—or deserve—anyone's friendship right then. It hurt too damn much to have friends and care about people. I had started to really care about Rain—foolishly thinking of myself as her big sister—and now she was gone.

I straightened up and grabbed my bag. I had to find her. It was my fault she left. I told her to leave and she ran out in the street and that guy in the black car grabbed her. Because of my temper. It was my job to find her. But I'd have to do it on my own.

The only person I could count on was myself. When would I ever learn? Once upon a time, a girl named Veronica Black had cared about other people, had relied on other people, and look what happened. As far as I was concerned, Veronica Black was dead. Just like my dad wanted her to be.

—CHAPTER—
17

The woman behind the desk at the police station on East Sixth Street wrinkled her nose when I told her why I was there.

"How old are you anyway?" she said, loudly cracking her gum and patting her tight gray curls. "Aren't you supposed to be in school?"

"I graduated early."

"Well, you look like a teeny bopper. Go ahead and have a seat. You know, I got a niece looks young like you. Hates it. She's treated like a little kid and she's got kids of her own now."

The door slammed open and a skinny man wearing a hoodie came in, wildly looking around. When his glance fell on me his eyes grew wide and he crossed to the other side of the room, standing in a corner behind a fake potted palm like he was trying to hide.

The clerk rolled her eyes.

"What is it today, David?" she said, drawing out her words with a long sigh.

The man cast me a fearful look and ran out the door, mumbling something I couldn't quite understand, but that sounded like "white devil."

"Don't take it personally," the woman said. "David thinks if you aren't black, you're out to get him. We only have one white officer here at the substation and if he wanders by the front desk, David runs away. It used to be sort of entertaining. Now, it's just tiresome. It's not really his fault. He says it's because of the radio the government surgically implanted in his head. That's what happened when Reagan kicked all crazies out of the institutions and onto the streets. Made our life more interesting, I guess. At least that's one way to look at it."

The tiny lobby had one chair, a mint green vinyl one, next to a small round coffee table with magazines and the *LA Times*. I pushed aside the fashion magazines and picked up the newspaper.

The front-page story was about some cops on trial. Last year, four L.A. cops had pulled over this black guy, Rodney King, and hit him more than fifty times with their metal batons. My eyes grew wide reading it. A bunch of cops stood around and watched the other cops beat the crap out of this guy and didn't even try to stop it.

Thinking back, I sort of remembered something about it on TV last year. At the time, sitting in my Forest Lake bedroom with neighbor's driving by in Range Rovers and Porsches, it seemed like something happening in a third world country, sort of like the surreal coverage of the Persian Gulf War.

The grainy black-and-white home video the news kept showing of the guy getting beat up had sickened me. I finally changed the channel when they showed a photo of the guy with his bloody eye nearly swelled shut and his face so disfigured that his moustache drooped down by his jaw. I knew it was awful and wrong, but it didn't seem real. It didn't seem like anything that could affect me in my life.

But now, reading the *L.A. Times*, it became clear that my childhood had sheltered me from the reality of the outside world. Even though the horror of my mother's drug addiction and death had marked me forever, I still hadn't known what it was like to live in a world not shielded by extreme wealth and privilege.

Until now.

Reading about the Rodney King beating now didn't only make me sick, it made me furious. What the hell was wrong with people? When that crazy man, David, hid from me and called me a white devil, I'd felt a flush of shame at my privileged upbringing as a white person, even though feeling ashamed about it was just as ridiculous as him calling me a name like that.

As I read more of the story, I realized that at least one decent person in the world had taken a stand. Thank God for the guy who woke up, videotaped the beating, and had the guts to take it to the news station when the police department wouldn't answer his questions.

I sat back and thought about that—the impact that one person could have against an organization as powerful as the Los Angeles Police Department. I read on. After an FBI investigation, a grand jury returned indictments against four officers who beat Rodney King. The trial was supposed to start in a few weeks.

Thirty minutes later, after I'd read most of the paper, the door to the back offices opened and a police officer came out.

"Come on back." I followed his broad straight shoulders back to a dingy office. He sat down, leaning forward, his fingers splayed in a "church temple" stance on the desk. His tight, neat crew cut, starched uniform, and intense demeanor made him seem more like a drill instructor than a cop. "You want to report your friend missing?"

I told him about Rain and everything that had happened the night before, leaving out the part about ingesting a drug-laced brownie and the part about meeting her at Kozlak's house. For some reason I was afraid to bring up Big Shot Director's name. When I finished, the police officer sat back, his lips drawn back in a thin line.

"So your friend—who is twelve and a minor and a homeless junkie to boot—up and disappeared during a party last night after you guys got in a fight. And for some reason, you think she was kidnapped, taken against her will by some celebrity or something in a big black car? Did I get all that right?"

"Yes. I heard her start to scream." I was pissed off that he dismissed Rain so easily as a "junkie." My anger was growing the more he said.

"Is that your story?" he interrupted.

"Yes, but you're making it seem like she took off on her own. She didn't. She screamed." My voice rose and I gritted my teeth.

"Do you have any proof she didn't leave on her own volition? You guys were in an argument, right? Maybe she just needed some time to cool off." He raised both of his eyebrows.

I was starting to get angry. "She wouldn't have left without saying something first."

He scanned a piece of paper on the desk. "So, you don't even know her last name? And her first name is…what, Rain? Are you even sure that's her real name?"

"Yes." I rolled my eyes. "I told you. Her parents were hippies. That's her name."

"And her parents were also homeless in Santa Cruz? And she has no living relatives other than her parents who ran away to Mexico? So, in other words, she's a runaway who should be in the foster care system instead of living in some residential hotel in downtown L.A.?"

"Yes," I said dully. He was not going to help me. He didn't take me seriously at all. I was relieved I hadn't mentioned Kozlak and Chad in case he decided to get in touch with them about Rain.

"I'll take down a report, but I'm going to warn you there isn't much here to go on. I think you're out of luck. The most you can hope for is that she gets sick of being homeless and on drugs and comes back to you. But I'll tell you right now—that never happens."

It was almost what the Chicago police had said about my mom. I stared at him without blinking.

"And," he said, holding his door open for me, "when she does come back, you need to bring her down here. She should be in a foster home and in school."

When I stood and he saw how short I was, he raised an eyebrow. "How old are you anyway?"

"Eighteen. I moved here the minute I turned of age."

He looked at me for a second as if he didn't believe me. I stood and walked out before he asked to see my ID.

I raced out of the police station, slamming the glass door behind me. The cops were useless. What had I expected? L.A., Chicago, they were all the same.

The shadowy streets of downtown L.A. were dirty, strewn with cigarette butts and litter, and cast in deep shadows by the surrounding skyscrapers. But unlike at night, during the day they were alive with people. Walking back from the police station, I found the alley where that man had attacked Rain. If I was wrong—if everyone else was right—then she hadn't been kidnapped and had gotten into the black car on her own. If she'd gone with the man to get more drugs and had been let out a few blocks away, she might still be around.

Keeping an eye out for a pink-streaked head, I nearly ran into a homeless woman pushing a shopping cart. She smiled and it gave me courage. "Have you seen a girl with pink hair around?"

The woman nodded vigorously.

"I did see that girl." She eyed my bag meaningfully. I took out a five dollar bill.

"Where did you see her?"

The woman plucked the money out of my hand. "She was here the other night and then I saw her under the bridge. Yup. That's where she is now."

I hurried away, casting a last glance down Skid Row, which suddenly seemed darker than the surrounding streets. That night I found her in the alley, Rain kept talking about finding someone under the Fourth Street Bridge.

Pounding up the stairs to my room, it was clear what I had to do, but every inch of me screamed against it. It seemed like fate wanted me to retrace my footsteps and tread the same path I had trod trying to find my mother. I only hoped it wouldn't end the same way.

I collapsed on the floor, leaning against the wall with my eyes closed. My heart was racing, thudding up in my throat. My breath came in short gasps and I was gulping for air. I put my head down between my knees and tried to regulate my breathing, but every time I thought about where I was going and what I had to do, my pulse began pounding in my ears, drowning out any other sound. It was a panic attack. Not the worst one I'd ever had, but still.

Entering a homeless camp, even in the middle of the day, seemed impossible to me. Ever since that day I'd found my mother, I'd had an irrational fear about homeless people. But I needed to do this. Once I calmed my breathing and my heart rate seemed to return to normal, I remembered the promise I'd made to Rain as she went through her withdrawals—*I won't leave you.* I had told her to get the fuck out and now my job was to bring her home.

As I sat there, steeling myself to get up, my neighbors passed by outside in the hall, their voices carrying as they laughed and joked. Probably on their way to grab a beer at Al's. A small part of me wondered what it would be like to open that door and ask them for help, but I shook my head, knowing once more I was on my own. My freak out the night before had ruined everything. I stood, taking a deep breath. The sun was growing lower in the sky and there was no way I was going to go under the bridge at night. I wasn't the naïve, sheltered girl with the pink bedroom anymore. That night, long ago, when I went to find my mother, I'd foolishly traipsed into that abandoned house in a pretty flowered dress and ballet slippers.

I've worn steel-toed combat boots ever since.

I looked around for a weapon. I shoved a small paring knife I'd bought at the thrift store into the zippered pocket of my leather jacket. Maybe I couldn't stop a bunch of homeless guys attacking me, but I could go down fighting.

CHAPTER
18

The Fourth Street Bridge was a few blocks away from the American Hotel. Besides housing a small homeless city underneath, the only thing I knew about the bridge was that Danny had told me it was one of several bridges crossing the dry L.A. River bed connecting downtown with East L.A.

When I first stepped underneath the bridge, the sun was starting to dip closer to the horizon, coating everything in glowing gold light. The first arch under the bridge was empty, a dirt lot. I let out a big breath I hadn't even realized I'd been holding. Maybe there wasn't a homeless camp here after all. But when I rounded the second wall of concrete, I stifled a gasp.

A small village lay before me. I shrunk back against the wall.

In a space the size of a baseball infield, at least a dozen cardboard shelters had been built against the colorful graffiti-covered walls under the bridge. Ratty rugs were placed in front of some of them. Broken chairs held drying clothing items and books and canned food were stacked on other boxes and crates. It was like a band of crows had collected shiny things and scattered them everywhere in the camp, which made it oddly colorful and cheery.

Several men stood huddled around, warming their hands over black metal trashcans with smoke pouring from them. One man sat in a corner cross-legged, unscrewing a jar and singing some old Johnny Cash tune my dad used to like.

A horrid stench drifted over to me—the combined smell of unwashed bodies and urine and feces. I realized I was standing right by a small garbage can used as a toilet, so I scrunched away a few feet.

My legs were shaking. Part of me wanted to run away and never look back. But I owed it to Rain to try to find her, apologize, and bring her back home.

Besides, while part of me was irrationally terrified by the homeless camp, a small part of me—the photographer in me—was intrigued and wanted to document this small city that lay beneath the bridge, hidden from passersby. But today I had to leave my camera in my bag. Instead, I took in the small hidden world before me. Somewhere along the line, maybe because I was so intent on taking in the scene before me, I forgot to be afraid.

Then someone noticed me.

It grew silent. The men nudged each other and looked my way. Menace filled the air. My instinct was to bolt, to turn and run as fast as I could. But I steeled myself. I needed to ask about Rain. The shadows were growing longer and I wanted to be far away from here when the sun set.

"I'm looking for my friend," I said, my voice shaking and too loud in the silence. "Her name's Rain. She's twelve."

The whites of more than a dozen eyes stared at me in the silence.

I stood straighter and tried again, making my voice sound more confident, even tough. "If anyone knows anything about her, I can make it worth their while." One man snickered. I worried my words would be taken the wrong way, that they would think I had cash on me right then. "I can get money for you later. Please tell me if you've seen my friend."

Again, nothing. My blood raced, but I fought the urge to run.

One guy with a dingy scarf looped around his neck took a step my way. I shrunk back as he got closer. "Maybe you should ask the guys farther down under the bridge. Maybe they know sumpin' about your friend."

Everyone sniggered. I hesitated. If I hurried, I could check it out before nightfall. I started to walk toward the other side of the concrete wall that separated this part under the bridge from the next. My neck hairs tingled as the men watched me. When I was nearly to the wall, a man stepped out of the crowd. I braced as he approached, ready to kick and scratch, but when he got closer, a glimmer of kindness in his eyes confused me and then relaxed me at little.

He spoke in a quiet voice. "Young lady, you need to leave. Everything is different now because of Rodney King."

That guy who got beat up by the cops. My eyes widened. "Because I'm white?"

He shrugged. "And because this is no place for a young lady like yourself. You shouldn't be down here alone unless you have a gun."

The man's voice was that of an orator, like the kind you'd hear reading eulogies or telling family stories. It was precise and clipped, yet also deep and languid as if he had spent a lifetime reading poetry out loud. I didn't know if he was the only clean homeless guy under the bridge or whether my nose had gotten used to the odor, but he didn't smell, seemed clean, and didn't frighten me. He was more like someone's grandpa. And his face—it was striking. I kept my distance, but couldn't stop staring at him. He was old. Really old. He had soulful eyes and the most magnificent wrinkles crisscrossing his mahogany face. My fingers itched to photograph him, maybe in the late afternoon, using the long shadows to highlight the contours of his face.

The man in the scarf yelled, startling me out of my thoughts. "If she ain't gonna go down there, then she needs to get the hell out of here. I ain't gonna tell her twice."

The older man said to me in a low voice, "Go on now. It's time for you to go back where you came from."

"Tell her to turn around and keep walking until she sees all white people," someone yelled, the words sending a ripple of laughter through the crowd.

"I can't. I have to find my friend." My voice let me down. I stuttered with fear. "You said yourself it was no place for a young lady."

"She's not down here," he said.

The men were now moving around and I could hear arguing and heated voices. The older man lightly touched my elbow, only for a second, but I still cringed. I was ashamed of this reaction. But he didn't seem to notice. He leaned in, his voice low and urgent. "Where might someone find you if they possibly had information about your friend?"

The way he said it gave me hope. I started to answer. The other man with the dirty scarf was heading our way. The man in front of me saw him, too.

"The young lady was just leaving," he said with steel in his voice.

I only had a few seconds. I didn't want this stranger to know where I lived so at the last second I blurted in a whisper, my voice so low it was like an exhaled breath, "I work tomorrow night at Little Juan's."

He gave a small wink. He'd heard me.

I race-walked out from under the bridge toward the street, looking behind me every few feet. Nobody was following me. The man with the kind eyes and mahogany skin give me a nearly imperceptible nod as he warmed his hands over the fire in the trash can, keeping his gaze on me. After seeing I was safe out from under the bridge, he took a step back into the shadows, disappearing.

—CHAPTER—
19

The dark streets were full of ominous shadows and strange noises as I walked back to the American Hotel, making me glance back behind me at every block. Thinking about Rain—out on the streets, maybe hooked on heroin again just like my mom—filled me with a heavy dread and overwhelming guilt.

With a ferocity that surprised me, everything that had happened since that night in Malibu hit me like a shock wave, flooring me, stopping me in my tracks. My new life was exhausting. Waitressing itself was tiring—not only being on my feet for hours, but smiling at assholes so they would leave me a tip. Simple tasks necessary to survive, such as buying toothpaste and feeding myself, seemed overwhelming. I wanted to be a normal seventeen-year-old worrying about pimples and who was going to ask me to the prom. Not thinking about paying rent and having clean clothes and food to eat.

The sob that rose up into my throat also made me weak in the knees. I sank to the curb and put my head between my hands. I missed my mother so badly it was hard to breathe. I wanted everything to go back to the way it was before. I didn't want to be in L.A. anymore. I wanted to be back in my bedroom in the suburbs with the smell of lasagna wafting upstairs as my mom called me down to dinner. Having that nursery full of coos and giggles and life and my mom laughing and folding and stacking baby clothes. Instead, two small headstones on a grassy hill had shattered that dream.

I was fooling myself if I thought I could survive in L.A. on my own. I thought I was tough, but I was wrong. I was playing a game, and now the jig was up. I didn't think I had it in me anymore to go on. I sat there for a moment with my head in my hands until a noise startled me and I stood, brushing myself off.

What was I thinking by taking in Rain and making promises to her? The truth was I could barely take care of myself. I went through the motions, but terror raced through me late at night when I was alone in my room. I wanted my dad. I wanted him to tell me that everything was going to be okay. I wanted him to take care of me. I wanted the man he was before my sister and mother died, when he was sober. I wanted him to tell me he loved me. I turned toward the gas station where the payphone booth was lit up like a beacon. I listened as the operator asked him to accept my collect call. His voice rose as he answered yes. We spoke at the same time.

"Veronica?"

"Dad?"

"Thank God." He sounded sober. A sharp intake of breath and whispering. Was someone else in the room with him? It had to be midnight in Chicago. Was it that woman from his office? My stomach hurt imagining them together.

"Veronica? I was so worried. I thought you were dead, just disappearing like that."

Guilt swam over me and I closed my eyes. "I'm sorry."

"Where are you?"

"California."

"Oh, for Christ's sakes." He whispered something to whoever was in the room with him. "Listen, are you okay?"

My body filled with relief. He hadn't meant what he said.

A homeless guy eyed me as he passed. I kept my eye on him as he walked into the gas station. I swallowed hard. "Dad, I'm sorry."

"I know." He exhaled loudly.

It wasn't what I expected him to say. I wanted him to apologize back and tell me he loved me and missed me.

"Listen, can we talk later? This isn't really a good time. I'm glad you called to say you were okay."

"Dad? I think I need to come home now."

No answer, just the muffled sound of voices, as if he was covering the phone with his hand. "Um, yeah, listen, Veronica, that's not really an option now. I don't know if you heard, but I lost my job. But it's okay because things are getting better. I'm in AA and NA and Julie and her kids moved into the house. I'm trying to get my act together, but the thing is…there's not really any room here for you."

My heart sank. I closed my eyes. What had I expected? A heart-warming reunion? A plane ticket waiting for me at the airport?

The homeless guy came back out of the gas station. He stood, staring at me, drinking his booze out of a paper bag.

"Veronica? Are you there?"

I didn't answer. I glared at the creepy homeless guy.

My dad kept talking. "I mean, maybe in a few months I can get some money and if you give me your address, I can send it to you to help or something, but right now I'm really struggling to just survive day to day. I'm working the program, you know, going through the steps. I'm glad you called. I was worried…"

The homeless man wandered off, casting me a last look. I'd been foolish to call my dad. It had been a mistake.

"Veronica?"

"I'm here."

"Okay, then," he said. "Call back in a few months. I should have a job then and can send you some money. Okay?" More voices and noises in the background. "Listen, I gotta go now."

"Okay. Bye," I said to the sound of a dial tone.

Gently, I placed the receiver in its cradle. That was it. Up until this moment, I'd always, in the back of my mind, thought that if things got really bad, I could swallow my pride and go back home to Chicago. Now, I knew that was not an option.

I'd have to take care of myself.

I angrily swiped away a few tears that were mutinously leaking from my eyelids. I closed my eyes tightly. No more crying. I took a deep breath and slowly let it out, squaring my shoulders as I opened the payphone doors. It was up to me now. I was on my own.

—CHAPTER—
20

The next day I slept in. I didn't leave my room until I had to get ready for work. Right when I was about to open the bathroom door, it swung open. The band boy stood before me half naked in the doorway. A few drops of moisture still clung to his abdomen right above the white towel wrapped around his waist. A fleck of shaving cream clung to a spot near his ear.

I instinctively backed into the hall. I had bedhead, smudged makeup, and morning breath that could drop a T-Rex to its knees.

"Hey." He grinned. I could barely meet his eyes. He was practically naked. When I looked down to avoid his gaze, his towel slipped a bit and revealed a sharp slice of hipbone. A sprawling tattoo curved around his ribcage—an angel with a lifelike face that I was sure had been copied from a photograph.

"Nice towel," he said.

"You got something against seals?" I'd bought it at the thrift store down the road because it reminded me of going to the zoo with my mom when I was little and how she'd always wanted to watch the seals for what seemed like hours.

"Nah, love them."

"Me, too," I said, and then for some reason, maybe because I was nervous, I blurted out something I would normally never tell a stranger. "My was crazy about seals. She had this little ratty stuffed seal she'd had since she was a kid. It was all matted and one eye was missing. One night when I was scared, she gave it to me."

"I always liked dolphins but my mom was crazy about seals. When we went to the zoo, she would squeal and get all excited like a little kid. If it were up to her, she'd have stood there for hours watching the seals, but I always wanted to move on and see the orangutans."

As soon as I said it, I could feel my face grow warm. But he smiled so I continued. "She had this little ratty stuffed seal she'd had since she was a kid. One night, I was really scared and couldn't go to sleep so she gave me her seal to sleep with, to keep me safe. It was all matted and one eye was missing. 'He'll keep you safe,' she said. After that, seals became my favorite animal, too."

I finished and clamped my lips together tightly, surprised I'd shared all that with a stranger. It was not normal. Not for me. Even though I had spent a month with Chad, I'd never told him about my family. I'd never volunteered anything personal about myself. Nothing. All I'd said was I'd had a screwed-up home life and wanted to leave Chicago as fast as I could. And he obliged. I'd never really had a real boyfriend, so it never occurred to me that his overwhelmingly lack of interest in me and my past wasn't normal. At the time, it was convenient. Only now did I realize that Chad never wanted to know a single thing about me because he didn't give a crap. I was a pawn in his sick child porn plans. I stared at my bare feet, now feeling totally awkward.

"You still have it? The seal?"

I shook my head. "I was in a hurry…I left it behind. I tried to get it back once, but all the locks on the house were changed."

He didn't ask me why I couldn't get back into my own house.

"That sucks." His eyes grew darker. "By the way, have you heard from your friend? That kid?" He stared past me.

I swallowed and shook my head.

"Sorry about that," he said, still not meeting my eyes. "I'm sure she'll turn up."

I didn't answer. I was growing antsy, eager to have him leave.

"Listen, I should probably take a shower so I can get to work on time."

He nodded, frowning slightly for some reason, and started toward his room. I stood in the doorway and watched him leave. He stopped and turned. He smiled when he saw me still looking. "Hey." His voice sounded less cocky and maybe even a bit uncertain. "You doing anything Friday night?"

His question made my mouth go dry. I had Friday off. I managed to shake my head.

"Cool. I still want to play you that song by the Red Hot Chili Peppers, but today I got this CD that will blow your mind. It's from a Seattle band called Nirvana. It's their first album. They played Al's last year."

I waited a moment before answering. It would be better than sitting alone in my room, worrying about Rain. Better than spending another night like last—pacing and smoking in my room, trying to figure out where she went, pausing every time there were footsteps or voices in the hall.

I'd managed to avoid everyone on the fourth floor the past few days, especially Danny. My stomach bunched into knots when I thought about him. Maybe he would also be at Taj's and we could talk, I could apologize. It wasn't Danny's fault that Rain disappeared, but I'd had no problem blaming him. And in front of everyone. It was my fault Rain was gone and about time I admitted it to everyone.

"Okay," I said, which prompted a huge smile from Taj.

"Cool. Friday. My room. Eight?"

I nodded and closed the bathroom door. It would be fun to hang out with him, even if he didn't believe that someone had taken Rain against her will. Because although I didn't want to admit it, a tiny sliver of doubt had crept into my own mind about whether she really had been kidnapped. I told her to leave. She only had one option to do so. That black car.

Maybe she had asked to get in and I had imagined the scream as something ominous. Maybe it had been a happy laugh or playful scream. It was so hard to know for sure whether what I saw that night was real. It had been dark and I had been high on acid, of all things. Me, the girl who didn't do drugs. How could I be sure of anything that night? With every hour that passed since Christmas, the less certain I was about whether Rain had willingly got into that car or been forced to get in.

The only thing I knew for sure was that it was my fault.

—CHAPTER—
21

The surfer boys were dead.

I found out skimming through the *LA Times* before work on Thursday. The small news item made my heart leap into my throat.

Two USC Students Found Slain in Malibu

The article said Jonathan White and Charles O'Donnell were found in what "appeared to be a gang-style assassination"—bullets to the head. They were found in a VW bus parked in a Malibu beach parking lot. A young boy walking by the van had asked his dad why the van's window was splattered with red Kool-Aid.

I leaned over and dry heaved into a plastic bag I kept in my room for the trash. Sweat poured down my hairline. My hands trembled uncontrollably, making the paper shake and rattle noisily as I read on.

The article said the students had been reported missing after they didn't show up for college classes. Police were investigating whether it was a drug deal gone bad, since a small amount of marijuana was found in the vehicle.

Oh God. My stomach crunched into a painful knot. It wasn't a drug deal gone bad. I put my head in my hands and tried to regulate my breathing, which had gone wild. My heart was beating double time and I couldn't catch my breath. I put my head down between my knees, feeling tingly and dizzy.

The boys had been found in that parking lot where they surfed. Where Big Shot Director's Jeep had seen us drive away. He had found the surfers and killed them or had someone kill them. Had the surfers told him where they had taken me? Of course they had. It was only a matter of time before Chad and Kozlak found me.

I had a few hours before work, enough time to visit the police station one more time. I should tell the cops that Kozlak killed the surfer boys. But I had no proof. And I had practically zero faith in cops. They hadn't helped me when my mom was gone and they hadn't helped me when I told them about Rain. But I didn't know where else to turn. I needed someone wise in the ways of the world to tell me what to do.

I knocked on Sadie's door.

It was a gamble since she'd only started acknowledging I was alive this week, but I didn't know who else to turn to.

After I knocked a second time, I heard a faint, "Come in."

I pushed open the door. She was lying face down on her queen-size bed wearing only a silky nightgown. Her room smelled like expensive perfume and baby powder. She didn't look up. I stood by the door uncertainly. On the floor was a tiny suitcase upside down, its contents—frilly lingerie and perfume—scattered. It was the first time I had been in her room. Eve was right, it was like a little girl's fancy bedroom. She had a tiny white desk with a light green chair pulled up to it. Above it, there was a small shelf with books such as *Black Beauty* and *Treasure Island*. Her bed had white coverlets, bedside tables, and a canopy.

She sat up, sniffling a bit more. Her eyes were red and puffy.

"I thought you were going out of town," I said, eyeing the dumped suitcase on the floor. She had taken a few days off work saying she was going away for New Year's Eve, which I then realized had been the night before. I'd spent the night alone in my room with my curtain closed tight and my nose buried in a book. Happy New Year's to me.

Standing, Sadie briskly made herself busy, picking up the clothes and hanging them on a big rolling rack next to a small dresser. "Something came up."

That "something" was probably her married boyfriend flaking on her. I'd heard her complaining to another waitress about him the other day.

"Listen, I need your advice."

"Shoot." With her back turned to me, I told her about the surfers and Kozlak and everything. When I finished, Sadie had turned and was staring at me. She didn't like me much, but I hoped she would at least give me some advice.

"You think I should go to the cops?"

"Forget the cop shop." She stood and held her door open for me to leave. "They won't do jack. They find out you're seventeen; they'll stick you in a foster home. You were lucky that didn't happen last time you were there."

Despite Sadie's advice, I needed to do *something*. I needed to something to help stop the guilty feeling crawling across my arms and scalp and making my stomach hurt. I scraped up a few quarters from a jar I kept my tip change in and headed to the gas station payphone. Looking around furtively, I shoved in a few quarters and dialed 911. I spoke fast, worried they could trace the call, which was a ridiculous fear.

"9-1-1. What is your emergency?"

"I know who murdered those two USC boys, the ones in the paper. A movie director named Dean Kozlak. Kozlak. Go investigate him. He did it."

I hung up before the operator could say a word.

The police had let me down before, so I didn't expect much, but maybe somebody would take it seriously. It wasn't enough. The guilt was still there, gnawing away at my insides.

—CHAPTER—
22

All night at Little Juan's on Thursday, I was a nervous wreck, jumping every time the big, heavy, oak front door opened, expecting Kozlak's big white mane or Chad's thin little blond ponytail. I was sure that before he killed them, Kozlak had got the surfers to confess they'd dropped us off at Al's Bar. And if Big Shot Director knew I was in the neighborhood, what would stop him from visiting all the businesses in the area to look for me? What would stop everyone at the American Hotel from just giving me up, telling the director where I worked?

I was also anxious for that homeless guy to walk in the door with information about Rain. I'd told the man under the bridge that I'd be working Thursday night. And as much as I tried to push back the gruesome image I had of the dead surfer boys, it was there just below the surface. The restaurant was crazy busy, with groups of people wandering around out front, waiting to be seated. The chaos was amplified when the karaoke machine was brought out and a bunch of old guys took turns crooning *Mack the Knife* and *Bennie and the Jets*.

A group of men at the bar started getting rowdy, hooting and hollering and snapping their fingers at Sadie to serve them. One guy, with thinning hair and a bushy moustache, had drunk so much he kept slipping off his stool, catching himself before he fell on the ground. I'd seen him before even though Sadie was always the one to wait on him. He was always falling down drunk and at the bar nearly every night. Tonight, I was delivering some nachos to a guy at the bar when the guy with the moustache started getting obnoxious.

"Hey, Sadie, how's about those chips?" His voice was slurred and his eyes bloodshot.

"Told you, Ernie. Aren't ready. Nothing I can do about it."

"How's about if I show you this? What then? Can I have chips then?" He unzipped a fanny pack sitting on the bar wide enough to reveal the shiny silver handle of a gun. He started laughing with all his friends, who were slapping him on the back.

"No," Sadie said, unfazed. "But if I tell Amir what you did, he's going to eighty-six you."

"Aw, I was kidding."

I followed Sadie into the kitchen. "Oh my God, that guy had a gun."

"That's just Ernie," she said over shoulder, surprising me by answering. "Total moron when he's drunk. Unfortunately, he's always drunk. Him and his friends at the bar are all LAPD."

"LAPD? They're cops?"

Sadie clipped a new food order up on a metal shelf and scooped a paper-lined basket deep into some steaming tortilla chips the cooks had dumped into a huge bin.

"Here, this is for table four," she said, handing me the chips and muttering, "The idiot cops cause more problems than the gangbangers."

Gangbangers? I'd been here for a while and had never seen any gangbangers. At least I didn't think I had. Before I could ask more, Sadie launched into a story about Ernie and some bar fight he got into with another cop—a woman detective. They were both drunk and screaming at each other. Ernie tried to leave, but the detective followed him into the men's bathroom. She clocked him in the face and he fell, hitting his head. There was blood everywhere. Amir called 911, but Ernie bailed before the ambulance got here. The bar was dead for a week except for two men in suits who were from LAPD internal affairs, investigating the fight. The female cop got off scot-free. Ernie was still on probation.

"Everyone knows Ernie's just a drunk screw-up," Sadie said.

"Doesn't that bother you, having to wait on drunk cops who show you their guns when they want something and get in fights?" I was so surprised she was talking to me, I was almost afraid to ask her anything.

"No, as long as they tip me," she said. "You haven't been around much, have you?" She barreled out of the kitchen, balancing four burning hot plates. "Besides, I've seen worse than that."

"Like?"

"When I lived in New York, some guys broke into our penthouse and tied up my boyfriend and me. Thought I was a goner, but they bailed when they found our drugs."

"Oh," I said, trying to digest that. She misread my look.

"I don't do any of that shit now. I'm clean as a whistle. In fact, I've been straight for sixteen months now."

"Did you live in a bad area of New York?"

"Only if you consider Fifth Avenue a bad area," she said, and walked away. I let that sink in before scrambling to catch up to her.

After being a bitch and ignoring me for the past few weeks, Sadie had finally warmed up. Go figure. And boy, did she have a lot to tell. By the end of the night, I learned that Sadie had once been a cover girl. No wonder she looked familiar. Her face had graced magazines around the world and her rich suitors thought nothing of chartering private jets for her Parisian shopping sprees. I could see traces of that one-time beauty with her long legs, carved cheekbones, and pouty full lips. But now she had dark circles under her eyes and a grayish, tired pallor to her skin. She told me she was twenty-two, but she seemed older.

I asked how she ended up at the American Hotel, which seemed like such a slummy slide from a Fifth Avenue penthouse.

"Shit happens. But I'm not sticking around here long. I'm saving my money. My boyfriend and I are moving to the west side. Waitresses there make thirty grand a year."

I kept thinking about what Sadie said about Ernie. Did "drunk screw-up" equal crooked cop, someone who might help me find Rain by unorthodox methods?

So, for the rest of the night, when I wasn't keeping an eye out for Kozlak, Chad, or that homeless guy, I steeled myself to approach the cop. Finally, he got up to use the bathroom and I cornered him in the hall. He turned. I stood frozen, unable to form four little words. He was about to turn away. It was now or never.

"I need your help." I stuttered a bit, but somehow made a complete sentence.

He looked at me out of the corner of one eye as if he were suspicious I was going to ask him to do something untoward.

"My friend. She's missing. I'm worried…" I paused. This was the part I had been afraid to say out loud or even admit to myself. "I'm worried she's dead somewhere—her body unidentified in some morgue—and no one will ever know. You can check stuff like that, right?"

The words tumbled out with a sob I hadn't known was there. I swallowed hard and looked down. When I looked up, Ernie's eyes seemed less bloodshot and more focused.

"What's her name?" He stroked his bushy moustache and ran his hand back over his thinning hair.

"Rain. She's twelve, only about this high, and has pink streaks in her hair."

He nodded with his lips pressed together and made his way past me into the men's room. I sat there, dumbfounded, as the door to the bathroom swung shut behind him. Was he going to help or not? Looking around, I pushed open the door to the men's bathroom, keeping my eyes on the floor, "So…are you gonna help me or not?"

There were a few seconds of silence before he gave a loud sigh.

"I don't know yet."

I let the door slam closed.

Ernie left shortly after. I still jumped every time the big, heavy, oak front door opened. Right before ten o'clock, as we were cleaning up and preparing the restaurant for the next day, I spotted a figure standing outside the front door. I hurried outside. This man was a different one than the older guy I had spoken with under the bridge. I reared back. This guy had a stocking cap pulled low, hood pulled up, and jacket zipped up to his nose, big eyes peering out at me.

"You looking for the girl?"

I nodded. He seemed skittish, glancing over his shoulder every few seconds as I spoke to him. He seemed more scared of me than I was of him.

"Do you want to come in and have something to eat? I was about to eat my dinner."

He shook his head. "I don't want nobody to see me here."

"Okay. Hold on. I'll be right out."

Inside, I grabbed the food I had bagged for my next day's lunch, added a few more tacos and an extra load of chips and headed out front. I handed him the bag, "This is for you and your friend."

"Frank?"

That must have been the name of the older guy with the mahogany wrinkles.

"Yes, Frank. What's your name?"

He ignored my question. "Let's go over here," he said, walking over to an area in shadows. I was still a little nervous so I stayed under the circle of the streetlight a few feet away. The smell of fresh tortilla chips in my bag was making my mouth water. I didn't know how often this guy ate, but I was surprised he hadn't torn into the bag right away. Instead, he sat the bag down on a low wall beside him. "I seen your friend," he said in a stage whisper. "I seen her lots of times a few weeks ago."

I came closer. He leaned over and whispered louder. "Yeah. I seen her the other night. She was talking to that dude in that big black car that's been cruising around downtown. You know the one?"

"Yes," I said in excitement. "Do you know who that car belongs to?"

He looked over his shoulder again before he said something I didn't hear.

"Excuse me?"

Again he looked both ways before answering, a little louder this time. "I said, that dude is bad news."

My heart sunk at the same time I felt a surge of adrenaline. He knew the mystery man. "What do you mean? My friend got in that car. Who is he?" I searched his eyes, but the shadows hid his expression.

"When girls get in that car, they don't ever come back." He stared at me as he said it.

"What do you mean? I don't understand."

"I hear things from my girl who works the streets up on Sunset. She say they into some evil, deranged shit."

"They? Who are they? What do you mean 'they'?" My voice grew shrill.

A car passed and its lights flickered over us, sending the man cowering deeper into the shadows. I followed, afraid myself until I saw it was a small sedan with a crushed fender and Bondo on it, a vehicle that neither Big Shot Director nor Chad would be caught dead driving.

"I gotta go. Thanks for this," the man said, and picked up the bag of food from the small stone ledge he'd been sitting on.

"Wait. Do you want some money? Is that why you won't tell me? Here's twenty bucks." I thrust the money toward him, but he ignored it. "How can I find them? Who are they? Please, you have to help me!" I was begging, but he kept walking. "Can't you give me any more information? Anything? At least tell me your name?"

He didn't turn around. The people in the beat-up car must have been lost because they did a U-turn and started heading back our way. Momentarily blinded by their headlights, I put my hand up to shield my eyes. When I turned back, the man was gone—he had dissolved into the shadows.

I kicked the curb in frustration. Then I noticed something on the ledge where the man had picked up the bag of food. It was a book with a picture of a super nova exploding on its cover. The book was called *Insights*.

—CHAPTER—
23

Right before eight on Friday, I stood poised to knock on Taj's door, staring at my hand raised in the air. I didn't know why I was so nervous. It wasn't a big deal. We were just going to listen to some music.

I was also nervous about whether Danny was inside that room. Every time I thought about how I had spoken to him, my stomach hurt.

I double checked my jacket pocket to make sure I had my cigarettes and finally rapped on the door.

"It's open." Taj's voice sounded very far away.

I twisted the knob. A hodge podge of old candles lined the hallway before me. One room lay to my right then the hallway appeared to open up into the second room at the end. "Back here." He sounded distracted. Maybe eight meant eight thirty or something.

The first room, which must have been John's room, had a Mexican blanket crumpled on an old mattress and a poster of Jim Morrison taped to the wall. A display of various bongs—red, blue, and yellow—

lined the floor under the windowsill. Clothes and overflowing ashtrays covered every other inch of the bare floor. The whole apartment smelled like guys—like spicy aftershaves and cigarettes and stale coffee.

It was quiet. I followed the trail of dripping candles that led into the back room. Taj was alone.

He sat at a small desk in the corner near the window, scribbling into a black sketchbook. His messy hair stuck up even more than usual and I soon saw why as he forcefully ran his fingers through it. He looked up and seemed confused why I was there, which made me squirm.

"Where are John and everyone else?" I asked.

"Huh? Oh, they're all at Eve's smoking some new bud from Amsterdam or something." He seemed distracted, half turned toward me, but his eyes kept wandering back to his sketchbook. He kept writing in the big black book. I could see from across the room that his handwriting was neat and precise. A skateboard and a baseball bat were propped against the wall near his desk.

"How come you didn't go to Eve's, too?" I half turned back toward the door, ready to leave.

He smiled. "I try not to get high much during the school year. It screws with my concentration. That's why I didn't eat the brownies."

For a second I wondered if he was making fun of me.

"I've wanted to apologize about that," he said. "I would've warned you, but I thought you knew they were dosed."

"Totally my fault for being so naïve." I winced, remembering how clueless I had been.

"Listen, have a seat. I'm sorry, I'll be with you in a second…need to finish this—it's homework. If I don't, I'll be lost when I sit down again tomorrow, okay?"

I nodded hesitantly. He turned back to the table, but I stayed standing. Where was I supposed to sit? Besides his chair and desk piled with books and a mini frig, there was no other furniture in the room except his bed. The queen-size futon was on the floor and covered with Indian print pillows and colorful blankets. I stood there, uncertain.

He scribbled for a few more seconds. With a flourish, he stood up and put the pen away in an old coffee tin full of pens and pencils.

When he noticed I was still standing, he glanced down at the bed and saw my confusion.

"Sorry, my bed has to serve double duty as a couch. Hope that's okay."

"You're in school?" I said, easing myself down on one end.

"Kick off your boots. You'll be more comfortable."

I hesitated. I'd worn boots ever since that day I'd found my mom in the crack house. They were my talismans. To most people, they were footwear, but to me, my Doc Martens sent a message—*I can kick your ass if I need to, so don't even think about messing with me, I've got a brand of crazy you've never even heard of.*

But it would be awkward trying to sit on the bed with my feet sticking over the edge onto the wood floor the entire evening. I reluctantly unlaced my boots and tucked my legs beneath my black skirt in an attempt to hide the hole in one of my black-and-white-striped socks. Without my boots, I felt more naked than if I had stripped off my top and was sitting there in my bra. Ridiculous, I know.

"Just junior college. It's all I can afford right now. I mean, you probably go to USC or something."

I bit my lip. I couldn't even afford junior college right now. I pulled my mashed pack of cigarettes from my jacket pocket and lit one by leaning over a nearby red candle. My hands were shaking and I hoped Taj didn't notice. I wasn't usually this nervous. Maybe it was his intensity—the way he looked at me. The way he bent over that notebook concentrating. The way he sang on stage, pouring every drop of emotion into the words. It seemed like he wasn't afraid to feel deeply and intensely and show this nakedness, this vulnerability, to the world. I wondered what that would be like.

"What's your pleasure?" Taj leaned over a small refrigerator. "I've got beer or wine."

"Wine's good." I tried to sound cool and causal and flippant, but I worried I seemed nerdy. And young.

Taj handed me red wine in a coffee cup. He pressed play on a small silver ghetto blaster perched on top of the mini fridge before plopping down on the bed, nearly into my lap. He lay down with his head right near my hips, staring at the ceiling as he took a drag off his smoke. If I moved my leg even slightly, it would touch his head. I had to stop myself from either totally scooting away from him or grabbing his head and putting it in my lap.

"This is that new band I was talking about—Nirvana," he said. "They kick ass."

The music started with a heavy beat so loud it startled me. Taj began bobbing his head to the throbbing, contagious rhythm. He looked at me and grinned, revealing that gap between his teeth that suddenly seemed incredibly sexy. I looked away and sunk back into the pillows, closed my eyes, and felt the music course through me while I moved my own head to the deep rhythm. The singer's raspy voice was perfectly filled with angst.

The song abruptly ended.

"That was…incredible," I practically whispered. My praise sounded lame, but it was all I could come up with

"I know!" Taj said, sitting up beside me, his intense eyes even brighter than usual. One of his long legs in his faded black jeans was now pressed tightly against mine. I was afraid to move. He lit a cigarette and handed it to me, which seemed intimate. The next song was a bit mellower and I closed my eyes again. I felt Taj's warm breath near my ear.

"Mmm, you smell good." He deeply inhaled.

If I turned even slightly, our mouths would meet. His fingers were in my hair, stroking it and then tucking it behind my ear. "I knew your hair would feel like silk," he whispered into my ear, his hot breath sending a shiver through me. Then his mouth was on my neck.

His fingers twined through the back of my hair and turned my head softly so my mouth met his. He gently bit my lower lip and kissed me in a way that made me aware of every inch of my body. I'd never been kissed like that before. He pulled me onto him and I felt how bad he wanted me. I arched into him and moaned, an animal sound I'd never heard come out of my mouth before. I felt out of control, a feeling I always tried to avoid, one of the many, many reasons I didn't want to do drugs. But I let myself go, feeling instead of thinking, letting Taj's fingers work over my body, allowing my body to follow its desire.

But then I remembered Eve saying the two Midwestern boys keeping her up nights and seeing Taj with a different girl a few nights apart. He was a player.

I pushed him away and reached for my bag. I started rummaging around, unearthing my camera. Without meeting his eyes, I fiddled with it, snapping off a few shots of him looking dazed and flustered. He seemed confused for a second, but then he brushed back a stray wisp of my hair that had fallen into my eyes. "Sorry," he said. "I got carried away." His eyes were so soft I had to look away. A new song started and he leapt up to crank up the volume.

"This one's my favorite." He started singing the first lines of *Come As You Are* as soon as it began.

He smiled as he danced and crooked his finger at me to get up. I didn't hesitate. I put my camera down and stood, grabbing his outstretched hands. We held hands and he spun me around and we laughed and danced until the song ended and we both plopped back on the bed, out of breath.

The wine was making my cheeks hot. I snuck a glance at Taj, who had settled back onto the cushions with his eyes closed and a grin on his face. I grabbed my camera, kneeling and taking close-up pictures of him with his eyes closed, his dark hair spread on the burgundy pillow behind him. He squinted and peeked out of one eye.

"You looked…so happy." I knew it sounded lame.

Carefully he unwound the camera strap from around my wrist and set it gently on a nearby table. I tried to reach for it but he grabbed my hand and began lightly stroking my palm with his fingertips. "Heard you're from Chicago. What brought you to L.A.? What dream have you come here seeking in the City of Angels?"

Maybe the wine had loosened me up, or maybe it was just the affect he had on me, but I wanted to tell him, to share myself, to talk to him about anything and everything.

"A foolish dream I guess," I said, pulling away so I could light another cigarette. "I was hoping to become a photography intern. I met this guy on a movie set in Chicago and he said he could hook me up out here. He ended up being a royal loser."

As soon as we got to Chad's place in Venice Beach, I knew I'd made a mistake. He ignored me. It was clear he was no longer interested in me as a girlfriend. He slept on the couch and left me alone for days on end while he was off shooting commercials in different cities. My feelings were hurt but I filled my days exploring and taking pictures. I wasn't interested in the stereotypical Venice Beach photos of fire jugglers or Rastafarian men on roller skates playing the ukulele. Instead, I photographed people like the little girl in traditional African garb sitting on a curb feeding a small dog bites of her sandwich or the pair of junior high school kids with mohawks eating cotton candy. But all that film was undeveloped, back at Chad's place in Venice. Gone forever.

Taj asked what my parents thought of me coming to L.A.

"My mom passed away." I didn't want to talk about my dad. I folded my arms across my chest.

"My dad died a few years ago," Taj said.

The two statements hung in the air. It was obvious neither one of us wanted to say anything else about our parents. Taj changed the subject.

"Where's he now?" Taj asked. "The movie dude?"

"Dead, I hope."

He chuckled for a minute. My glassy stare shut him up. "Wait? Is he the one who gave you that shiner when you first got here?" His eyebrows furrowed as he stubbed out his cigarette. "That guy needs his ass kicked."

I was bored talking about me and reached for my camera again. He gently blocked my arm. "How come every time I start to bring up something you don't want to talk about, you reach for your camera?"

"What were you working on when I came in?"

He went with it. His eyes gleamed and his voice raised a notch as he spoke faster. "Finishing up a song I'm writing. You actually inspired it."

"I thought you said you were doing homework," I said, trying to ignore the part about me inspiring a song.

"I did. I'm studying music at L.A. Community College. If I get the grades and get a scholarship, I can transfer to UCLA next year. I didn't grow up dreaming of moving to L.A. and being a bike messenger."

"Of course not." I was embarrassed for some reason and hid my face in my hair, leaning down to stub out my cigarette. I also felt intimidated. Even though he was ashamed of going to a junior college, it was still college. Something that seemed an impossible dream for me was his life. I bet he went to school with that girl who was on his motorcycle. A flash of jealousy surged through me.

College seemed like something I had planned in a past life. What was once a reality for Veronica Black was a mirage for Nikki Black—something she could not reach, no matter how hard or how long she tried because she was too busy bringing tortilla chips to drunk cops and saving her measly tips to buy cans of food at the gas station convenience store.

"The song I'm writing is about what we were talking about on Christmas. It's called *City of Angels*. I'll play it for you when it's done. Right now I've got some of the lyrics and need to work on the melody."

Christmas was the night Rain disappeared. Remembering her made my stomach flip. Although hanging out with Taj had been a good distraction, the worry that had been gnawing at my insides had come back with a vengeance.

"You haven't asked me about Rain."

Had I imagined it, or had he swallowed hard?

"Yeah, sorry about that. I don't mean to seem like an insensitive prick, but…"

The CD had ended a few minutes ago and the silence seemed heavy and awkward.

"But what?" I prodded.

Taj cleared his throat. "Maybe Danny is right. Maybe it wasn't a kidnapping. Maybe Rain didn't want to live here anymore. Maybe she wanted more drugs."

What the hell? My mouth opened, but it took a few seconds for any words to emerge. "I'm not sure exactly what happened that night, but I did see something and I did hear her scream. I was tripping, not unconscious. You really don't believe me either, do you?"

"I didn't say that..."

"Yeah, but that's what you meant. Screw this." I jammed my camera in my bag. "You act weird around her anyway. What did she ever do to you?"

He stood up and his eyes glinted. "You don't understand."

"You don't like her and you don't care that she's gone and maybe lying in a gutter dead somewhere."

Taj clenched his fists by his side and seemed like he was about to say something. His nostrils flared and he looked right through me. "You. Don't. Understand."

"You're right. I don't." I yanked on my boots. "I don't know what I'm doing wasting my time here. I should be out finding her right now."

Thoughts of my mother and her crack-fueled hell increased my rage. My throat felt like it was closing up and my chest grew tight, making it harder to breathe. Screw all of them. They had no idea what they were saying. I scooped up my jacket. Right then, the CD started blaring some hidden track on the album, an industrial heavy chaotic beat with possessed-sounding shouting, making me jump.

"Hey." Taj tried to grab my hand but I jerked away from his touch.

I pressed my lips together. I gave my laces a violent tug and stood.

"You know what your problem is," he yelled over the thumping music. "Your problem is you're scared."

That stopped me dead in my tracks. Without turning around, I said through gritted teeth, "I'm not afraid of anything or anyone." Which, of course, was a lie. In an instant, he was right behind me. I could feel him before he spoke again, this time softer and in my ear.

"Yeah, you are. You're afraid that someone might actually get to know you and you can't handle that. You'd rather be alone and small and miserable. That's why you hide behind the lens of your camera. You feel sorry for yourself. You want to keep everyone at arm's length so they don't get to know the real you, Nikki." He drew out the name. "Or whatever your name is."

His words felt like a slap. I turned, wide-eyed. He let go of my hand. He stared at me with something in his eyes that was both passionate and sad and angry all at the same time.

For a second, I stared back. Then I whirled and stomped away. Slamming his door and running down the hall to my room, I ignored the wetness on my cheeks.

— CHAPTER —
24

Sitting in my tiny room, I once again paged through the book, *Insights*. At a glance, it was dense reading. Had the homeless man left it for me? Or had a customer forgotten it outside the restaurant while waiting for a table? The cover claimed in bold type that the book was "America's #1 Advice Book." On the back was a picture of a guy who was a dead ringer for the skipper from *Gilligan's Island*. The blurb on the back said people who read the book had the power to overcome any obstacle they faced in life. I flipped through it page by page in case the homeless man had hidden a note inside or written something on one of the pages.

Nothing.

Rain had been gone a week and I was no closer to finding her. The homeless man's words haunted me—girls who got into that car never came back. Every morning before work I wandered the downtown streets, hoping to spot Rain. No luck.

The day I'd read about the surfer's deaths, I'd told Stuart, the bartender, about Chad and Kozlak, saying they wanted to kill me and might be able to trace me to Al's Bar.

"They couldn't beat it out of me, sister. You're cool. Relax. You're a wreck," he said, pouring me a shot of tequila. I didn't tell him it'd be much worse than a beating.

Every day I race-walked to work, keeping to back streets and ducking into the bushes every time a car came near. I was acting crazy, but I didn't want to take any chances.

And every time the restaurant door opened, I still jumped, worried that Chad and Big Shot Director would walk in.

One morning, someone yelled my name. Poking my head out my apartment window, I saw a guy I barely knew, Steve, sticking his head out his first-floor window.

"Stuart wants to talk to you," he said, and ducked his head back inside.

We didn't have a doorbell at the American Hotel, and I didn't think anybody had a phone line. People on different floors leaned out their windows and yelled at one another, like that game show, *Hollywood Squares*. People coming to visit stood in the middle of the street and yelled until someone tossed a set of keys down. It was the normal routine. But it was the first time someone had yelled for me. I didn't even know that guy on the first floor knew my name.

The bar was dark. Stuart's dreadlocked head was bent as he fiddled with some musical equipment on stage.

"Hey, girl. Dude came looking for you last night."

He described a skinny guy with a stringy blond ponytail. Chad.

"Told him, sure I remembered you 'cause you looked like you were in elementary school so I carded you and kicked you out."

I grinned.

"Told him you took off with some frat boys from Long Beach."

"Thanks." I leaned over and gave him a quick, embarrassed hug.

"No sweat."

Relief flooded through me. They'd be searching for me in Long Beach. Chad would never believe I could survive in this gritty part of town. For the first time since that night in Malibu I felt like I could relax. I finally felt safe.

That night at work, I found out that the cop, Ernie, had come through.

He stopped me in the bathroom hallway and told me no bodies of minor Jane Does were found in L.A County over the last week. I was relieved and a little surprised that he'd actually checked.

I walked home from work to find a line in front of Al's—people there to see a band called Jane's Addiction. I wanted to go, but couldn't spare the ten bucks cover charge. I was fishing for my keys in my bag when I saw Taj. With yet another girl. He was toward the back of the line that wound around the building, his arm around a tall redhead wearing a funky hat and thigh-high boots. She looked like a model. Or college girl. The girl nuzzled his neck. I couldn't stop staring. The line moved and they scooted closer to the door. The redhead started walking backward, holding both his hands. Even from where I was, I could hear her low-throated laugh.

Taj glanced over at me. His hands dropped to his side and he moved away from the girl. It didn't matter. I knew where I stood. And it wasn't in that college girl's league. I flung open the door and ran up the four flights of stairs to my room without stopping, telling myself it didn't matter, ignoring the disappointment I felt.

Back in my room, I pretended I was at the show downstairs by sitting on the floor, bobbing my head. The band was amazing. I tried to shut out the image of Taj and that girl. Later, I turned out my light and spied on my neighbors across the street again. It was like watching a movie set to a hard rocking musical sound track.

I couldn't stop looking at the couple in the loft—the one that reminded me so much of my parents—as they did the most mundane couple things. I sat there and smoked half a pack of cigarettes watching them. They laughed and talked as they cooked a late dinner party after some fancy event. They answered the door to women in fur and men in tuxedos. They and their friends sat at a massive wood table, toasting something or someone with crystal-cut wine glasses, laughing and talking. I kept smoking and sat there, holding my mother's picture, until my legs fell asleep under me. Finally, the couple stood in their doorway saying the last goodbyes to their friends. They put their arms around each other and retreated to their dark bedroom.

—CHAPTER—
25

The next morning, the golden sunbeam filtering through my window lifted my spirits. For no good reason I felt a tiny glimmer of hope, a small sense of peace tamping down the desperation clawing at my insides since Rain disappeared. Stuart had sent Chad on a wild goose chase. I needed to believe that everything was going to be okay, that I was safe and Rain was safe, too. I pushed back thoughts of the two surfer boys and the memory of Taj with that girl.

I leaned against the wall in a patch of streaming sunlight, closing my eyes and feeling the sun's warmth beat down on me until someone knocked. Last night at work, Sadie, in what I assumed was some odd gesture of friendship, had said she was going to drop by this morning to give me some old clothes she didn't want any more. I told her I pretty much would take anything as long as it was black—the only color I'd worn since my mom died.

"Come in."

The door opened. It was Taj. For a long moment, we stared at one another. I scrambled to my feet and started straightening my hair, which was sticking up.

"You should've stayed like that," he said, and slowly smiled.

I stared at him. It was his turn to have a shiner and there was a small cut across his nose. I gestured to his face.

"Some losers were bugging Eve at Al's last night." He shrugged.

I had forgotten that Eve also filled in as a waitress at the punk rock bar. "Is she okay?"

"She's fine." He came over and stood against the wall, running his fingers through the dust swirling in the sunbeam. His knuckles were covered in newly formed scabs. "Jerkoff skinheads needed to be taught some manners. Making cracks about jungle love. John took on the lot of them. I was only backup."

Skinheads? Jungle love? Oh. Because Eve was black and John was white. My face grew hot thinking of anyone saying anything cruel to Eve. My hands clenched into fists and adrenaline surged through me, making me want to kick the wall. How could people be such assholes?

"They won't be around this neighborhood anytime soon." He paced my room, running his fingers through his hair. A few times he started to say something, but stopped. I raised my eyebrows but he closed his lips tightly. A golden beam of light lit him from behind, giving me an idea.

"Take off your shirt," I said over my shoulder, rummaging around in my bag.

He turned around with a grin. "I think you got the wrong idea. I wanted to talk, but if you insist." He flung his t-shirt across the room and stood smirking at me. For a second, I couldn't talk, and then my photographic instincts took over. The light would be gone soon.

"Go sit in that sunbeam. Right now."

"I didn't know you were into guys with black eyes or I would've gotten one weeks ago."

I ignored him, loaded a new roll of film and, perched on my knees, starting snapping off shots.

"No, no, no. Don't look at *me*. Light a cigarette. Look out the window. Like you're thinking of something important."

He sputtered out a laugh. He was so startling beautiful sitting on my wooden floor with his bare chest and bare feet in faded jeans that I quickly went through an entire roll. He took a deep drag, eyebrows drawing together as I dug for another roll. Damn. I was out of film. I sat back on my legs and made a face.

"The light's almost gone anyway," he said, moving so close to me I inhaled sharply. He pulled me up by one hand and wrapped the other around my waist, pulling me closer. He leaned down and his warm lips were so urgent on mine, I pulled away.

"About last night…that girl you saw—" he started.

I cut him off with my mouth. The next moment we had sunk onto my futon. I rolled over so I was on top of him, kissing his jaw and down his neck, his groans encouraging me to go on, farther down. When I got to his tattooed angel, it brought me up short. Who was this girl he loved enough to tattoo on his body? I ran my fingers down his side, tracing the tattoo. His eyes were softly slit.

"Who is she?" I said it quietly.

He sat up, sending me teetering to one side and slowly pulled on his t-shirt without answering. Standing, he kept his back to me. His sudden coldness stung. He started toward the door. But then paused with his hand on the doorknob.

Then he opened my door and walked out.

—CHAPTER—
26

Dark clouds whirled in the sky overhead, bringing with them the hopes of rain to break up the endless days of heat and sun. It felt like the city was alive, throbbing, simmering with rage and violence, ready to boil over. I sat at the bar at the restaurant, sipping a soda and smoking, watching the news on the TV screens hanging from the ceiling. The restaurant was dead. The heat zapped any motivation to go anywhere. Nobody wanted to move.

Even the news people talked about the need for rain to cool temperatures and tempers. They said something needed to happen soon to stop the violence bubbling up in the ghettos.

Reporters talked to police officers who said that murders, robberies, and calls about crazy people rose during heat waves like this, especially when the Santa Ana winds swept through L.A.

Sadie told me the winds were a legend in Los Angeles. The TV showed shop owners sitting outside their business, fanning themselves with newspapers, bored. Stores had sold out of fans, popsicles, and sprinklers long ago. As night fell, the clouds grew gentler and drifted close to the ground, shrouding downtown in misty fog. With it came gusts of cool, fresh ocean air. It wasn't the rain everyone had hoped for, but it was something.

The mist even had a name, Sadie said—the Santa Ana Fog. It sometimes settled over the city when the winds died down. As if by an arranged signal, people poured into the restaurant full of energy and laughter. I ran from table to table and left that night with more tips in three hours than I usually made in two nights.

When I ended my shift, a man with a stocking cap pulled low approached me as I walked out of the restaurant. The cap hid most of his features. All I had was a fleeting glimpse of a plaster-white face poking out of a torn puffy coat. He didn't say anything, handed me a note, and disappeared into the fog.

In tiny, neat letters, Frank asked me to meet him at the gas station the next morning. I was excited that he might know something about Rain. It had been more than a week since I'd talked to the other homeless guy.

I began walking home, yawning and running what the note said over in my mind. What was Frank going to say? A slight breeze blew my hair into my eyes and sent a chill across my bare legs. A sound behind me made my heart race and then the crunch of running footsteps was close and loud and fast. I whipped my head around to peer into the darkness behind me but couldn't see anything in the fog. Icy fear rippled across my scalp as the sound grew louder. Walking backward now, my eyes searched the soupy grayness. I turned and started to run when a figure emerged from the mist.

A man in a ski mask. Reaching toward me. My body jerked backward as he yanked on my bag. A startled scream escaped me, but unless someone drove by, nobody in this deserted warehouse district would hear me. I tried to scream again, but nothing came out except a choked eek.

The man, who wasn't much taller than me, kept jerking the strap on my messenger bag, which was looped over my shoulder and across my chest. Terror racing through me weakened my legs. Even if he let go, I wasn't sure I would be able to walk. Running was out of the question.

In the chaos, I wondered why he wasn't trying to drag me into the bushes to rape or kill me. It must be a plain old mugging. He'd take my money and leave. My thinking cleared slightly and the panic subsided a tiny bit. Cash. Money. Tips. As he yanked on the strap, which chafed against my neck, I managed to dig into the front pocket of my jeans and thrust a wad of cash at him.

"Here," I said, panting. "My tips. All my money. Take it, please."

The man hit my hand away, sending the money flying and the coins tinkling onto the sidewalk "Give me the bag, bitch." He said it in a menacing low growl.

His words sent fear shooting through me again. He didn't want my money. He kept groping for my bag. He tugged on my bag and some of its contents spilled, a lipstick, a pen, a book. He jerked on the strap harder.

"Stop. Stop. Here, you can have it." I tried to untangle the bag's strap from my hair and jacket collar but my hands were shaking so bad I couldn't get it off. The man grabbed a hunk of my hair and yanked it back so hard I cried out.

"Hurry up."

No matter how hard I tried, I couldn't untangle the strap. I pulled and tugged and it seemed to get tangled even more on my body. I was sobbing. "I'm trying," I choked out.

The man punched me in the gut and sent me sinking to my knees on the ground, woozy. My vision started closing in on me when bright lights blinded me. The jarring sound of screeching tires sent the man scrambling away. I groped and felt my bag still on me. A familiar girlish voice echoed through the mist.

"Where you going, motherfucker? You scared of little old me? You want to mug my friend? I don't think so." It was Sadie. "That's right, run, you fucking slime ball!"

In the chaos of the moment, my mind stuck on one thing—*my friend*. Sadie had called me her friend.

Through the mist, I saw Sadie standing in the headlights of the car, legs spread, in her black miniskirt and Little Juan's t-shirt, gripping a huge gun with both arms outstretched. With the fog surrounding her and the headlights illuminating her silhouette and mane of long blond hair from behind, she looked like an avenging angel.

— CHAPTER —
27

The homeless guy who had left me the book was dead.

His name was Chris. Frank and I were sitting behind the gas station in a dirt lot strewn with used condoms, beer cans, and cigarette butts.

I sank to the ground. The rocks and debris cut into my bare legs, but I barely noticed. The stink of gasoline and the nachos the gas station sold made my churning stomach heave. Bile shot into my mouth and I swallowed it, making a face.

"What did Chris tell you when you met him that night?" Frank's voice and face were stern, but his eyes were red.

Shaking, I related my conversation and how Chris had talked about "they," not "him," when he mentioned the black car, but hadn't explained further. Frank listened with his face scrunched, then nodded.

"What happened?" I asked. "I mean to Chris. How did he…" I wanted to know but was also afraid of what he would say.

"He was found behind the car wash with his tongue cut out."

I slumped back against the gas station wall, my heart pounding.

"I don't understand." I couldn't process what Frank had said. He wasn't making sense. "His tongue cut out?" I finally managed to ask.

"My dear, haven't you watched any mob movies?"

"No. I mean, yes." I lifted my head and stared out at the dirt lot. I could feel my chin quivering.

"Then you must know they cut out your tongue when they think you've said too much."

I shook my head. "That's impossible. Nobody saw us talking or heard our conversation." Then I remembered the car that had passed, briefly shining its lights on us as we spoke that night. "Oh God, someone did see us. A car. And it did a U-turn. Oh my God."

A man was dead because of me. For talking to me. How many more people would die because of me? My vision started closing in and I couldn't get enough air into my lungs. With my head between my knees, I opened my mouth and concentrated on gulping in air. *Pull yourself together. Tongue cut out.*

I leaned over and threw up the coffee I had downed on my way over. Frank reached down and patted my back awkwardly. Even though he was homeless, I didn't shrink away from his touch and I was glad.

"I'm so sorry." I blinked and wiped my mouth.

Frank nodded. He pressed his mouth together. "He was a good man. He was a little out there, but he always meant well."

I covered my face with my hands.

"Now, now there. Chris would've never met with you unless he thought it important." Frank paused. "He must have told you something. Something important. Think hard."

I stared down at the broken glass and cigarette butts near my boots. I realized what he meant. If someone was dead because they talked to me, it must mean they killed him for something he said. It had to do with the black car. What was it?

"I told you everything we talked about."

"Think," Frank said. "Is there anything else that happened?"

"I found a book," I said. "After he left. It was on the ledge. I think he left it for me. It's called *Insights*."

Frank's eyebrows drew together, his wrinkles crinkling around his eyes, and his teeth worked the inside of his lip.

"*Insights*, huh? That's a very disturbing book. It claims to be an advice book, but it is much, much more than that."

"Like what?"

"It is all about controlling other people."

"How do you know so much?" I was embarrassed, worried I might be insulting him by stereotyping him as an ignorant homeless person, but I had to ask.

"I minored in religious studies."

I raised my eyebrows and he continued.

"My dear, I know it's hard to believe but this old man holds a master of fine arts from UC Berkeley. Once upon a time, I lived in San Francisco with the beat poets. We held gala poetry readings in Golden Gate Park and probably did a few too many drugs." Here, Frank chuckled, but then his face grew grim. "Unfortunately, my own personal devil was the bottle. I loved it much too much. I loved it more than anything else in this world. More than my job, more than my house, more than my wife, and more than…" He looked at the sky and murmured, "…my kids."

"I'm so sorry," I whispered. My mother loved drugs more than she loved me.

Frank shrugged. "It's not a unique story. I'm not special. Same story as most of the fellas underneath the Fourth Street Bridge. But I got one thing going for me that they don't."

He waited until I asked, "What?"

"I'm clean and sober." He fished out a small gold medallion and rubbed it between his fingers. The worn medal glinted in the morning sunshine. "Thirty-six months now. I go to AA meetings five times a week. I'm going to find a job soon. I'm moving out from under the bridge."

I really hoped so. Frank radiated peace and calm and something I couldn't put my finger on it. It wasn't his melodic baritone voice that lulled you. It wasn't the goodness gleaming in his eyes. It was all that and something more. Something I never dreamed I would ever see or find in a homeless person. Not after the day I found my mother in that abandoned house surrounded by homeless addicts.

I stood and fished out my smokes. Frank lit my cigarette for me.

"I don't know why I'm encouraging this. You're too young to smoke. It's bad for you."

I cupped my shaking hands around his to shield the flame and my eyes met his in gratefulness. It was the first time I'd ever touched a homeless person. And it felt okay. Good, even. I thought about the first time I'd met him and how he'd been so protective of me.

"What did you mean the other day when you said things had changed now because of Rodney King?"

"The people are preparing. You don't want to be some little white girl in this city when that verdict goes down."

"Preparing?"

"For the uprising."

On the walk home, I counted back in my head how many days had passed since I'd spoken to Chris. A week. And I was still no closer to finding Rain. I didn't even know where to start. She had been gone now for more than two weeks. Since then, besides my two encounters with Taj, I'd been avoiding everyone on my floor. I was still so angry they thought Rain had run away.

Lying in bed that night, I remembered what else Frank had said to me before I left him that morning, urging me to leave Los Angeles. I told him I had no other place to go.

"You be careful, then." He said it with a look so penetrating I couldn't meet his gaze. "L.A., you may think she's a queen worthy of all your devotion, but don't forget that L.A. is a selfish woman. She will woo you with all her charms, which even I admit are quite considerable, but then she will turn on you in an instant. Like that." Here he snapped his fingers, startling me. "The mistress of angels only cares about herself. Don't fool yourself into thinking otherwise. She likes nothing more than to take innocent young ladies like yourself and your little friend, use them up, and then spit them out."

— CHAPTER —
28

Rain had been gone for one month.

Any time I had to be in the hall at the American Hotel, either coming home or using the bathroom, I would hurry, hoping to avoid anyone, especially Taj. He hadn't come to see me since the day I took his pictures. I even started taking showers on the third floor, sneaking down the stairs with my towel and bathroom stuff. I'd ruined everything with Danny and Eve the night Rain disappeared. At least Sadie still spoke to me at work. None of them believed—like I did— that Rain had been taken, so I didn't need them anyway.

That was fine. I'd prove them wrong all by myself. Screw them. I didn't need them. I didn't need anybody.

One day, I was so sick with a bad cold that I couldn't even lift my head off my futon. Luckily, it was my day off, because I didn't even know how I would've let Amir know I wasn't coming in. I was weak and dizzy. I slept until the afternoon, rolling around, having feverish dreams. I crawled over to one of the small purple crates I used as shelves and ate an entire sleeve of crackers before lying back in bed, exhausted by the effort. As I lay there, I wanted my mother so badly it took my breath away. All I wanted was her cool hands on my forehead, tilting my head up to sip some broth, and soothing me with her melodic voice, telling me everything would be okay.

When it sank in that nobody was going to take care of me, I cried, feeling sorry for myself and ashamed about it at the same time, burying my face in the vinyl slipperiness of my sleeping bag. Nobody cared. Not only that, but nobody even knew I was sick. I could die right there and nobody would know.

🌴 🌴 🌴

I woke the next morning feeling better, but with a knot of anxiety in my stomach. Rain was just like me. Nobody cared about her either. I was the only one searching for her. If I forgot about her, she would disappear into nothingness, discarded like a cigarette butt.

I sat on my futon, staring at the magazine picture of celebrities I'd taped to the wall. Which one was Rain's mystery man? The black car had not been around our neighborhood since thev night Rain vanished. I went over everything I knew about Rain's disappearance. Somewhere in the scraps of information lay the answer, the clue that would lead me to her.

Words floated through my mind in big black letters.

Black Car. *Insights*. Tongue cut out. Young girls. Disappearing. Never seen again. Attempted mugging. My bag.

The mugger didn't want my money. It didn't seem to be random. My bag contained a small makeup bag, a journal and…my camera. My camera. I usually kept my camera in my bag. That must have been why that guy wanted my bag and not my money. They—whoever they were—had sent him to get my bag with the camera inside.

I had taken pictures of the car in front of the American Hotel. The windows were too dark to see inside, so the only pictures I got were of the car's exterior. Did they know I couldn't see inside? They must have known. There must be something else in that picture they didn't want me to see. Then it hit me and I stood up and started pacing with excitement. Oh my God. I might have the car's license plate number. I sat up, but then I slouched back down on the ground. So what? Even if I had the license plate number, how was that going to help me? If I was a cop, I might be able to trace the owner through the license plate. But I wasn't. I was a dumb kid. Or at least that's what the cops thought—that I was some stupid teenager and that Rain was a junkie. They wouldn't take me seriously.

I put my head in my hands, closing my eyes tight. *Think. Think. Think. Who could help me?* My eyes popped open wide. The downtown cops might not help me, but maybe someone else would. Maybe a cop who wasn't so by the book. Like Ernie. He helped me before. But this was a bigger deal. Maybe if I made it worth his while.

I walked over to a small photo shop in Little Tokyo and handed the clerk my rolls of undeveloped film. It would cost me several days' worth of tips to develop them. The idea of seeing those pictures of the surfer boys made my chest hurt. But I also had some of Rain that I could show people when I looked for her. The people at the photo place deflated my enthusiasm when they told me it would be a week before I got my pictures back. But I had to do something. I couldn't sit around and wait for the answers to come to me.

Maybe I could find out more about the three celebrities in back issues of magazines. I walked the eight blocks through downtown to the Los Angeles Central Library. The library arched high into the L.A. sky, a stone, square, monolithic fortress topped with a colorful pyramid at the pointy triangular top of the building.

I spent an hour scanning back issues of magazines for articles on the three celebs. They were the closest things I had to any suspects. I wanted to see if any of them used a chauffeured black car, but I didn't see anything helpful other than a small blurb about the comedian, Andy Martin, starting a three-month gig at a comedy club in West Hollywood.

I walked out of the library empty handed but full of hope. I wasn't even close to ready to give up. I raced down the steps of the library and out in the L.A. sunshine, taking the steps three at a time. I leaped, skipping the last few steps, flying high in the air and landing with my legs spread wide, feeling invincible. I was on to something. I knew it. I wasn't quite sure what it was yet. But it was there. Now, there was no turning back. I wouldn't stop until I knew what happened to Rain.

—CHAPTER—
29

The next week, I got to work early and waited in the parking lot behind the restaurant for Ernie. Earlier, I had flipped through my newly developed pictures, trying not to glance at the ones of the surfer boys, until I got to the shots of the black car and found one that showed the license plate number.

I tucked that picture into my inside jacket pocket as I waited, pacing along the perimeter of the ten-foot high fence surrounding the restaurant's parking lot. The smell of deep fried tortilla chips and carnitas tacos seeping out of the restaurant made my stomach growl so I lit a smoke to stave off the hunger and calm my nerves.

More than once, I decided asking Ernie for help was a terrible idea and started to head into the restaurant. One time I even had the back door open before I turned back around. I needed his help. I didn't like it one bit, but if I hoped to find Rain, I was going to have to be smart. Ernie could tell me what I needed to know.

When I saw I was already late to work, I yanked my hair back in a ponytail and wrapped my apron around my waist, so when I walked in late Amir would think I had already been there a while and ducked outside for a smoke.

Forty-five minutes after I was supposed to be at work, Ernie finally arrived in a big, rusted-out, four-door sedan. I felt a little sorry for him seeing his crappy car. Sadie had told me the other day about how Ernie had gone downhill after he found his wife having an affair with a daytime television producer. She bailed with his two kids and moved to the producer's Hollywood Hills house.

Today, Ernie's thinning hair was combed back as if he'd just showered and his bushy moustache was trimmed, but he still looked like he had been through the ringer—weary, beaten down. It wasn't only the red veins snaking out from his nose or the dark bags under his eyes—it was the look in his eyes, as if he'd seen it all and was done with it. Seeing him like this somehow made it a little easier to ask for help.

"I got a problem." My voice was wavering.

He gestured toward my cigarette. "You know, smoking's bad for you."

I looked at the lit cigarette stuck between his lips and rolled my eyes. He turned and eyed the door to Little Juan's, seemingly eager to get started drinking.

"Wait. Remember that girl I asked about? My friend?" This time my words came out more steady. Almost calm.

It took him a second, but he slowly moved his chin up and down.

"She was taken by someone in this car." I tried to hand him the photo that showed the license plate number on it. My hand was shaking. He briefly glanced down at the picture, but wouldn't reach out to take it. Instead, he shoved his hand into the front pocket of his jeans.

I tried to sound assured. "I need to know who owns this car."

Ernie glanced around the parking lot. "I can't run this plate for you. It's against the law."

"I'll make it worth your while." I stared at him. He wouldn't meet my eyes. His shoulders dropped and a small smile twitched the corner of his lips. I was talking his language.

"Fifty bucks."

He looked off into the distance, squinting as if there was something to see besides big gray buildings.

"Please take it." Now I was begging and I didn't care. He waited a long moment. I reached up and pressed the photo into his palm, bending his fingers closed over it. Our faces were so close I could smell his aftershave. I looked into his eyes, only inches away. "Please."

He didn't answer, only turned and walked away, slipping the photo into his shirt pocket.

—CHAPTER—
30

fter that night, Ernie stopped coming to Little Juan's. Sadie said he went back east to care for his dying mother. Just my luck. I had a hard time believing he was unselfish enough to care for a sick woman unless maybe there was a lot of booze in it for him. He was probably waiting for her to kick it so he could collect on the will or something.

Rain had been gone for two months now.

I'd never been so lonely in my life. I sat in my room sometimes with my back against the door and listened to other people walking by, laughing, having fun.

One time, I heard the footsteps stop and could sense someone on the other side of the door. I waited, holding my breath, then someone said, "Come on, dude, just forget about it," and the footsteps faded away.

I was disappointed and relieved at the same time. But my goal was to find Rain. That was all that mattered. I spent my mornings before work walking through downtown L.A., taking pictures and keeping an eye out for a pink-streaked head. I also spent hours at the library, checking out books and browsing the magazines for articles about the three celebrities. I'd read the book *Insights* and still didn't know if it was a clue left for me or just a book some customer left on the ledge.

One day at the library, I was flipping through the magazines when a stack of *Time* magazines caught my eye. The latest issue of the magazine was on top of back issues. The cover story was about the high cost of college tuition and how some kids couldn't afford to go. Um, yeah, that was me. I scanned the article and was about to put it with the others when the issue beneath it caught my eye.

The cover of the May 6, 1991 magazine had a blue and purple exploding super nova, just like the cover of *Insights*, except up close the super nova was comprised of people's eyes. Creepy.

I flipped to the article inside. Within four paragraphs, a name jumped out at me: J. C. Hoffman. I paused. Why was that name so familiar? I was late for work, so I stuffed the magazine in my bag, promising myself I'd return it to the library later.

🌴 🌴 🌴

That night, in my room after work, I realized why the author's name J.C. Hoffman had seemed so familiar in that magazine article. He was the author of *Insights*. I scrambled on all fours over to a stack of books and magazines in the corner. Yep. J.C. Hoffman. Same guy, all right. The article was about Hoffman founding a religion called The Church of the Evermore Enlightened. The church was really big in Southern California, apparently. It even had a special "star" center for its celebrity members.

Rain had said her mystery man was famous, important. *A celebrity*.

What if the man in the black car was a member of the church? That would make sense. It would explain why Chris left that book for me since the guy who wrote it founded the church.

But there was no mention of The Church of the Evermore Enlightened in *Insights*. I flipped to the back of the book. The word enlightened wasn't even listed in the index, although it did list words like aberration and fetus and hypnosis and zombie. The next day, I visited the library and smuggled out three books on The Church of the Evermore Enlightened. I didn't want my library card connected to checking out those books.

I wasn't sleeping well. I looked like shit. My eyes had dark circles under them and I had lost so much weight I had to fold my work skirt over at the waist and my jeans hung down around my hips. Rain was out there with some creep in a black car that really didn't care about her. If I didn't try to help her, nobody would. She would be another lost and forgotten girl swallowed up by L.A.—just like Frank said.

In some ways I felt like L.A. was swallowing me up as well. I barely spoke to anyone outside of the restaurant. I missed Danny. I wanted to be friends with him again. One night, when I was feeling especially heartbroken and lonely, I tried.

On my way to the bathroom, I found him standing in front of his door, guitar on its strap around his neck, fumbling with a giant wad of keys, trying one key after the other in his lock. I hadn't seen any new poetry tacked to his door for weeks.

At first, I'd been tempted to walk by without saying anything, but he'd looked so forlorn and pathetic that I'd stopped. Sighing, I took the keys from him and after a few tries, unlocked his door for him. He was bleary-eyed as I led him into the room. I missed his grin and cackling laugh so much it hurt. But maybe it was too late to apologize. It seemed like ancient history. The damage had been done.

"Thought you hated me," he said softly, and stared down at his feet.

I pushed away the urge to hug him and instead felt a surge of anger that he was high again.

"What's up, Danny? Why are you doing this to yourself? What about your poetry?"

He ignored my question, threw his guitar on the ground where it bounced a bit, and plopped on his bed. "Some fucked up angel dust, man. Gotta lay down."

I left, turning out the light and gently closing the door behind me. Seeing him like that and his poetry abandoned, brought back a familiar feeling in my stomach, one of grief and loss.

Every night I worked, I hoped Ernie would return, but figured even if he hadn't permanently moved back east, there was no way after all this time he would have remembered to run the license plate for me.

🌴 🌴 🌴

One night, Sadie sat a group of five young men—all dressed in pressed black slacks and crisp white t-shirts—in her section. They had slicked-back hair and flashing diamond rings on their fingers. The oldest one probably wasn't old enough to drink. I gawked, frozen, holding a plate of tamales, unable to stop staring. Sadie winked as she swept past.

The youngest one, the runt of the litter, held his two fingers up to his mouth and stuck his tongue through them making an obscene gesture. The one who was clearly the leader of the group smacked him on the head. The older boy crooked a finger at me. My eyes widened. I dropped plates off at my table and walked over, wary.

"Excuse me, miss. Sorry to bother you, but Freddy's got something to say to you." He jerked his chin toward the scowling skinny youth who couldn't have been any older than Rain.

The younger boy's eyes glittered dangerously. "Sorry." He mumbled it so low I could barely hear, but could tell it was laced with venom.

The older one, who was very good looking up close, smacked him again. "Say it like you mean it."

The younger one scowled and looked down at the table for a moment. The veins in his neck and forehead pulsed and his face grew darker, purplish. It was a dangerous moment, but the older boy only smiled at me. The four other guys at the table ignored the show down, unfolding their silverware from the napkins. I would have bet money that under that table all five of them had guns.

But after a few seconds, the younger boy swallowed. "I'm sorry," he said, a bit more sincerely, but his eyes looked like they would cut me into a thousand pieces if given the chance. This little shit who I could probably beat at arm wrestling was actually the only one at the table who frightened me. He obviously had something to prove. Even so, I itched to photograph him, scowl and all.

The older kid, who was poised beyond his years, smiled so widely and charismatically I couldn't help but smile back. "Thanks for taking time to come over. I apologize for Freddy. It won't ever happen again. Tell Amir that Carlos said hello."

I hurried off to Amir's office.

"Hey, I think Sadie sat a bunch of gang members out there. And they said to tell you hello." I was still a little breathless after my odd encounter with them.

Amir looked up from his paperwork and glanced at the video screen that captured the restaurant's interior with security cameras. What he saw made him smile. "Oh, yes, those are my friends. They get free refills on their soda."

"Your friends?"

He nodded. "Do you know where I am from?"

I shook my head. I was anxious to get back to work, thinking of my customers waiting for me.

"I am from Iran. Do you know about the political history of my country?"

I was embarrassed that I didn't.

"My people have only known a life of fear. They live each day not knowing whether, on a whim, someone will arrest or kill their brother. Or mother. The government tells the school children what schoolbags they may use, what television shows they may watch, and what to read."

I stopped swinging my leg against the desk when I saw the glint in Amir's eyes.

"They drag little girls by their hair out of their beds, shoot them dead for nothing. For nothing." Amir spit a little and began pounding his fist on his desk.

I jumped back, startled by his words and sudden violence. He lifted his clenched fist off the desk and closed his eyes, but not before I saw the tears glistening there.

"Amir?" I said. "I'm sorry." I didn't know what else to say.

When Amir opened his eyes, the tears were gone. He stared in front of him, seeing nothing. He was back somewhere in his mind, maybe back in Iran. "I will tell you more another time, but you should know that in my country we grow up with the knowledge that authority is almost always corrupt. The right thing to do has nothing to do with what the government or law says."

I nodded. I wasn't a big fan of the law or government either. They hadn't done anything for me lately, especially by not believing me when I told them Rain was kidnapped.

"Let me tell you a little story," Amir continued, his eyes behind his silver-framed glasses once again focused on me. One night, Amir said, when the gang members came in, Ernie stomped into Amir's office. "You can't serve them. They're known gangbangers."

"I can serve whomever I want," Amir had told Ernie. "If you don't like it, you can leave."

"I'm not leaving. They are."

A few minutes later, a squad car pulled up, and some uniformed officers filed into the restaurant, staring the gang members down. Some gang law prohibited known gang members from fraternizing in public, or at least that was what the officers told Amir, who, sensing this wasn't the time or place to wage his battle against authority, asked the gang members to leave, apologizing profusely and saying it was out of his hands. However, as they walked out, Amir slipped the leader of the gang a slip of paper with this on it: 546 JKT.

A license plate number. Like I had given Ernie.

After he'd run off the gang members, Ernie kept drinking until closing time and then had stumbled off his bar stool and into the parking lot, but couldn't find his car. It was gone. Stolen.

When they eventually found his car, a week later, it was in a riverbed, burned to a crisp.

"Now," Amir said, rubbing his manicured hands together and smiling at me. "You might wonder how a group of teenage boys got one over on a veteran cop."

Although this conversation was riveting with its glimpse into Amir's life, I was anxious to get back to my tables before they decided not to tip me. But Amir continued.

"It's because Ernie made the mistake of thinking he was invincible. He never thought a group of teenage boys could ever threaten him, a big, tough cop. That feeling of power was his Achilles heel. He felt untouchable and that was the chink in his armor. He never thought for a second that a punk kid, a child, would have the audacity to steal his car. And yet, that is what the boy did, isn't it? Ernie's mistake was overestimating his power and importance and underestimating the little guy. Don't ever underestimate the strength and willpower of the oppressed."

When Ernie and his bushy moustache walked into Little Juan's one night, my heart jumped into my throat. I'd worried he was never coming back. I could barely keep myself from accosting him, bringing him chips way too often, but trying not to seem obvious. He placed his food order over his shoulder before turning back to his friends. I spent the night staring at the thinning hair on the back of his head, willing him to turn and look at me. He asked for the check and the disappointment settled like a stone inside me. He wasn't going to help me find who owned that car.

I ran his credit card and handed the bill back to him in the black leather folder. I sat at one corner of the bar, sipping a soda, taking drags off the cigarette I had resting in the ashtray, and staring at him as he got ready to leave.

He and his friends were nearly to the door when he said something to them and returned, reaching for the black leather folder. He opened it, scribbled something, gave me a meaningful look, and left without a backward glance.

As soon as the outside door shut, I sprinted over, scooped up the folder into my apron, and sprinted for the bathroom. My heart racing, I locked myself in a stall and opened the black leather folder. I breathed in deeply, preparing to discover the name of Rain's mystery man, at last.

Inside, Ernie's scrawl at the bottom of the check said, *Car registered to The Enlightened Star Center on Sunset Blvd.*

The Church of the Evermore Enlightened Star Center.

Proof that Rain's mystery man was a member of that church. That was why Chris had left me that book. Was he telling me Rain was at the center? And what exactly was the Star Center?

A stack of books about The Church of the Evermore Enlightened was on the floor in my room. So far, I'd only read two of them. The *Time* magazine article described The Church of the Evermore Enlightened as "a highly successful racket that stays afloat by using mob tactics to bully, not only those who criticize it, but also its own followers."

Frank told me that the murderers had cut out Chris's tongue in a Mafia-like message. Also, my attempted mugging seemed to fit into scare tactics of a group run like the mob.

One of those three celebrities on my wall had to be a member of that church. All I needed to do was find out which one. I was relieved I didn't have to work the next day and could spend time figuring out how to do that.

I stayed up until four in the morning reading about The Church of the Evermore Enlightened. Again, like so many things in my life, there was a drug connection. The church was against using even prescription drugs—with psychiatric drugs being especially taboo. But at the same time, many of the followers had past stories of heavy drug use.

Followers also believed that they could obtain "superhuman" abilities that would allow them to do magical things, such as change the color of traffic lights, have flawless memories, and travel outside their bodies.

It was also supposed to allow them to do other, scarier things, such as cut someone in half with their mind, shock them or poke out their eyes with mind control alone. *Freaks.*

The next morning, I scrounged up as many quarters as I could find in my room and headed to the gas station pay phone. I dialed 411 for information and scribbled the number of the Star Center on a page I ripped out of the yellow phone book. I plugged in a dollar's worth of quarters and dialed.

"Do you have a list of members?"

"We're not allowed to give out that information over the phone," a woman's clipped voice told me.

"What if I come in person?"

A car left the gas station revving its engine, making it hard to hear.

"That is private information."

"Okay…can you maybe answer yes or no if I give you some names?" I didn't wait for her response. "Is Matt Macklin a member?"

Silence.

"Or how about Andy Martin, you know, the comedian?"

Dead air.

"Maybe Rex Walker? You have to know who he is. You know, from that movie, *Dead or Deader*?"

"Hold, please."

Abba music started piping through the phone line. Was she checking the names for me? A male voice got on the phone.

"May I help you?"

Right then the phone beeped and I plugged in four more quarters. "Yeah, I'm trying to find out if some celebrities are members of your organization."

"May I ask your name?"

Images of Scooby Doo trying to solve a mystery flashed into my mind. "Velma."

"Okay, uh, Velma. What names are you interested in finding out about?"

I reeled off the three names. The man remained silent.

"May I ask why you are interested in this information?"

"Well, I'm sort of looking for a man I think might know my friend," I said. "I think she might be with him and I need to get a message to her."

Two angry drivers in a road rage honked at each other and squealed as they roared by the gas station right when the man said something.

"Sorry about that. I couldn't hear you," I said.

"I asked, what is your friend's name?"

Little alarm bells were ringing in my head. I worried I had said too much, but had to tell the man something for him to help me.

"Her name's Rain. She's twelve." The phone beeped again. Boy, was this an expensive call. What was it, a buck a minute?

"Rain. Twelve." The man repeated as if he were taking notes. "And is there a number where I can reach you?"

"But you haven't even told me if any of those men are members. That's why I called."

An older woman with a scarf over her head started knocking on the glass door of the phone booth glaring at me. I glared back and held up my finger. "One minute," I mouthed to her.

"So, are they members?" I said.

"I will see what I can find out. Where can I reach you?"

I paused for a minute. "I guess you can leave a message at Al's Bar. I don't have the number. I'm sure it's in the book."

Long pause. The woman in the scarf was glaring at me. I smiled back.

"Okay, then. I'll see what I can find out."

And before I could say anything, the man hung up.

When I brushed past the woman outside waiting to use the phone, she rolled her eyes at me and I was pretty sure whatever she said in Japanese was not thank you.

— CHAPTER —
32

By the end of the week, it got to the point where I would walk into Al's Bar and Stuart would shake his dreadlocked head from across the room. No messages for a Velma. Maybe I was foolish for even thinking that guy at The Church of the Evermore Enlightened Star Center would want to help me.

After two weeks, I took a bag of quarters back to the payphone. This time I told the receptionist to take a message.

"Tell the guy who helped me last time that I'm still looking for my friend, Rain. She's twelve. I think she's with one of your members. My name's Velma." I reeled off the number I had copied down from the phone at Al's Bar.

That night, Sadie came to my room to tell me she was staying home sick from work. Even feeling ill, she had perfect posture, and, if anything, looking wan brought out her haughty cheekbones. Standing in my doorway in a baby doll nightgown clutching a tissue box and sniffling, she told me her boyfriend, Tony, would stop by the restaurant at closing to give me a ride home. Although I usually only saw her at work, she had been very sweet to me lately. And overprotective ever since the night the guy tried to mug me—letting me ride home with her and her married boyfriend whenever we worked together.

I waited inside the restaurant after work for Tony to come. Usually when Sadie worked, he sat at the bar having a drink until her shift ended. There was no sign of him tonight. Maybe he was late.

I re-stocked the sugar containers, folded the big red napkins, and paced, smoking and drinking a Roy Rogers until finally I gave up. Tony had flaked. That guy was a tool anyway. I didn't understand what Sadie saw in him. Shrugging on my leather jacket, I grabbed my bag and yelled goodbye to Amir, who was still working in his office.

The heavy oak door swung shut behind me. I yawned, looking up for stars, which rarely appeared in downtown L.A. Instead, the normal orange haze filled the sky. A big van that had been parked across the street started up and did a screeching U-turn, heading my way. I froze, wanting to step back into the restaurant, but unable to do so, paralyzed by fear. The van pulled right beside me. The only thing I could focus on was a big gun inches away from my face. My entire body turned cold and time seemed to slow. My vision narrowed until all I saw was the barrel, not the person holding it, not the driver, not the van. In the back of my mind I knew I should run, or duck, or scream, but I couldn't move. Then, the metallic click of a trigger echoed in the silence.

"Bang. Bang." The words were slow and drawn out and monotone.

My vision started closing in more until only a tiny circle of light stood out from the blackness. Through the roaring sound of blood pulsing in my ears I distantly heard a raspy voice growl, "Back off, bitch. Or the next time the gun's loaded."

As the van screeched away, I started shaking uncontrollably and my legs grew weak. I collapsed onto the bench out front until the headlights of an approaching car spurred me back into the empty restaurant.

I slumped into a booth near the door, dizzy and panting. Tinny ringing filled my ears. Then I noticed Amir standing across the room staring at me. He sprang into action, hurrying over to me so fast that his usually perfectly coiffed silver hair jostled slightly out of place.

"What happened?" he asked with his thick accent.

"A van…a gun…in my face."

"Good God." He raced to the door and yanked it open. A few minutes later he returned. "They are gone now."

His eyes behind the silver frames scanned my face and he said, "Sit. I'll be right back."

He went behind the bar and grabbed the tequila bottle off the top shelf. He poured the liquid amber into two tumblers.

Handing me one, he sat across from me.

"Drink. You are in shock."

I raised the tumbler and somehow slopped some into my mouth. I gulped and felt the warmth slide down my throat into my belly. My shoulders slumped back into the seat and with shaking fingers I dug into my jacket pocket and pulled out my cigarettes. I felt a drop of sweat dribble down my hairline. It took me three tries to light a match.

I spent the next fifteen minutes telling Amir everything—my theory that someone involved in The Church of the Evermore Enlightened had taken Rain.

A glimmer of something I couldn't name flickered across his face. I asked him if he'd heard about The Church of the Evermore Enlightened. He nodded, his jaw set tightly. "They are very powerful. More powerful than you realize. They will not take kindly to you…looking around. I think that is what the gun was about."

"But I don't have a choice," I said, stubbing out my cigarette and downing the dregs of my drink. I felt better, more alert, and instead of feeling frightened, I was beginning to get angry about what had happened.

"Even so. I think maybe you should let it go."

"What?" I was surprised. "This coming from the man who lectured me about throwing off oppression?"

"Part of the quest for freedom involves knowing how to choose your battles," he said, standing. "You are only one girl. One person. You will not be able to fight them. This is not a battle you can win."

I felt anger spread through me, replacing my fear. He didn't know if I could win or not. He'd talked about people throwing off the mantle of dictatorship and here he was equating a religious group's power with something like a government?

"What about your whole lecture on not underestimating the little guy?" His passiveness disappointed me. He wasn't so tough after all. "That story you told me about Ernie. Remember?"

"I remember," he said, a smile pulling at the corner of his lips. "It is not the same."

Yes, it is. But I kept quiet.

Amir drove me home, waiting in his car until I waved at him from inside the glass front door. Arguing with Amir was a waste of time. I would have to prove him wrong.

— CHAPTER —
33

"That motherfucker," Sadie mumbled, throwing clothes around her room and not meeting my eyes when she heard about Tony flaking and the gun. I'd gone to Sadie for advice. At this point, she was my only friend, if you could call her that. She was usually so busy working and hanging out with her boyfriend I hardly ever saw her. But she was loyal as hell. And fierce.

"I'm taking the day off work," she said. "We'll go to that Star Center together. Someone is trying to send you a message and I got my own message for them." She reached into a drawer of her dresser and took out a gun.

I gave her a look.

"I got more than one." She turned her back and threw around some more clothes.

She didn't want to talk about it anymore, and I felt too stupid to ask where the guns had come from. Sadie lived in a different world than me in so many ways.

It took a few minutes, but I talked her out of coming to the Star

Center with me, saying I would be safe alone since it was the middle
of the day.

"Thank you. But go on to work. I'll see you later."

She gave me a skeptical look, but finally agreed and put the gun
back in the drawer. I tried not to show how relieved I was.

Sitting on the city bus, I couldn't tell if it was the smell of sweat and
gasoline or the old man smell of the guy beside me that was making
me sick, so I got up and moved. I ended up sitting across from a young
guy with scrawling tattoos up his neck and a teardrop tattoo near his
eye. He kept staring at me, so I glared at him. He made a face back,
but it was such a goofy one I couldn't help but burst into laughter. He
did, too, and yanked the cord for the next stop. As he got off the bus,
he stuck out his tongue as he passed me, but I just rolled my eyes in a
friendly way.

Now bored, I almost wished Sadie had come along, just to keep
me company on the long ride. Finally, it was my stop. It had taken two
transfers to get to the Sunset Boulevard stop. The bus pulled away with
a burst of nasty exhaust, and when it cleared, the Star Center was a
block away, soaring above the palm trees like a giant French castle. It
seemed as impenetrable as a heavily fortified stronghold, too. A stone
wall bordered the sidewalk, then a larger wooden fence, and behind
that, eight-foot high hedges in front of a line of palm trees. It was if
they were trying to soften the impression of a fortress. Maybe Amir
was right. Maybe I was in over my head.

As soon as I stepped foot onto the sidewalk in front of the center,
a security guard wearing dark sunglasses and riding a bike appeared
out of nowhere and stopped a few feet away. He got off his bike and
muttered into a walkie-talkie. I slanted my eyes at him sideways, glad
my sunglasses hid my gaze. He was heading my way. I lifted my camera
from where it hung around my neck and put my finger on the shutter

release.

"You need help finding the Hollywood sign?" he asked.

Even I knew we were nowhere near the sign.

I shook my head, my long hair wildly swinging. I wasn't going to dignify his stupid question with an answer. Ignoring him, I snapped off a few pictures of the hedge in front of the center, trying not to show I was intimidated. But he wasn't leaving. I tucked my camera back in my bag and crossed the street to a coffee shop, hoping he would think I was leaving and go away himself. He stood there with his arms crossed over his chest, waiting until I was inside the coffee shop before he turned and walked around the corner. I'd wait a few minutes and go back.

Inside, I plopped on a purple velvet couch near the front window, smoked a few cigarettes, and downed two Americanos without taking my eyes off the hedges fronting the fortress across the street.

Thirty minutes later, shaking a little from the caffeine and nicotine, I crossed the street. I was sure that big bozo with the walkie-talkie would come shoo me away again, but I had to try. This time no one came out so I headed toward the driveway. Despite the imposing walls, it was easy to walk down the driveway and right up to front door. The reception desk was smack dab in the center of a gold-wallpapered lobby. A woman with a bun and secretary glasses had her head dipped over a stack of papers.

"Excuse me?" I said. She barely looked up. I raised my voice a notch, clearing my throat and spitting it out in a nervous rush. "Can you help me? My name is Velma. I called asking about my friend, Rain. She's twelve. Do you remember talking to me? Are you the only receptionist who works here?"

She gave me a blank look, so I continued. "You transferred me to a guy who said he was going to help me. Who was that?"

"I'm sorry, we get dozens of calls here every day." She turned to the side of the desk and began shuffling through some papers. She was right. How stupid of me to assume she would remember my call and me.

I walked up to the desk now and leaned over. "I need your help."

She kept her gaze down.

"If someone called and asked about your members, who would you transfer them to?"

Again, nothing.

"Please listen. Do you have kids? I need your help. It's about a girl. She's missing." My voice trailed off. She was not going to help me.

"You're going to have to leave now." She picked up the phone and spoke quietly into it, looking up at the ceiling. I followed her gaze. Security cameras hung in each corner. I walked around the desk, keeping my eyes on the cameras. With a small whirring sound, they rotated to follow my movements.

"My name is Velma," I said into the cameras. "I need to talk to someone about your members. I think one of them knows my friend. Her name's Rain."

Two men in suits appeared out of a panel in the wall I hadn't even realized was a door. At first I thought they were going to help until they grabbed my elbows and pointed me toward the door. I struggled but they were holding on tight.

"Ow. Let go of me, you big gorilla. You're hurting me."

"Come along, miss."

The doors slammed behind me. I jerked around. The two security guards stood on the other side of the glass with their arms crossed over their chests. I flung open the doors and was greeted by a solid wall of flesh.

As I walked down the steps, I turned. The two beefy men were still standing there with blank expressions.

🌴 🌴 🌴

The next day, I was back in front of the center. I planned on standing on the sidewalk until someone came out to talk to me. Or I had to leave for work. I'd been waiting for about thirty minutes and nobody had come out, so I took out my camera and began taking pictures of the center. It took about thirty seconds before a guy wearing mirrored sunglasses and a walkie-talkie came.

"Can I help you?'

"Yeah. I need to talk to someone inside about your members and a missing twelve-year-old girl. Named Rain."

He said something quietly into his walkie-talkie.

"Have you seen her? Blond hair with pink streaks? I just want to talk to somebody. Anybody. Please."

"Time for you to leave."

Just then, a man in a mask came running up. "I don't think the young woman needs to go anywhere."

Another man in the same type of mask—a smiling guy with a small goatee and thin moustache—ran up holding a video camera to his face. "The last time I checked this was a public sidewalk," he said.

The masked cameraman recited some law while the polo-shirted guard tried to get away from the camera.

"Do you believe that humans are descended from aliens from another planet?" one of the masked men shouted at the guard, who was walking away, holding his hand up to cover his face. Pretty soon, the masked men were chasing him up the driveway.

A few seconds later, the two men returned. One guy stuck out his hand. "I'm Incognito. Pleased to meet you."

The cameraman offered his hand. "Incognito here, too. Nice to meet you."

I backed away. What kind of game were these guys playing? I wasn't going to shake their hands or tell them my name. I backed away.

"Don't be afraid," one guy said.

I squinted at him. "Why are you wearing masks?"

"Haven't you heard? These guys like to retaliate. They like to make sure anyone who films them or criticizes them is punished."

I'd taken a picture of the black car and was horrified by a sudden thought. What if they had taken Rain to punish me?

"I think they have my friend," I said, trying to see any expression behind the mask. "Do you think it was because I took a picture of one of their cars?" I swallowed hard.

The man in the mask must have seen I was on the verge of panic because he laughed.

"Nah. You've got to do more than that. You've got to harass them a lot—like we do," he said. "Why do you think they have your friend?"

The other man had stopped filming and the camera was hanging by his side. He seemed bored, as if he were just waiting for his friend to finish talking to me so they could leave. I told the man about Rain's disappearance. He was quiet. Again, I wished I could see his expression.

"How old are you?" he asked.

"Seventeen."

He seemed to file that way. "And how old did you say your friend was?"

"Twelve."

He made an exasperated sound. "And I suppose you went to the police and they brushed you off, didn't they? Not a big surprise." He swore. "Speaking of the police, here's L.A.'s finest to scare us away."

Two officers were headed our way. He started to walk away, but before he did, he leaned down to whisper, "Whatever you do, don't trust the cops. Some of them—a great many of them—are crooked and working with the church. Don't trust *anybody*."

I followed him. "Please. Stop. Tell me what you know. Why did it matter how old she was?"

He kept walking. I tugged at his sleeve, but he kept walking. I ran in front of him and put my hands up to this chest to stop him. "Please, you have to tell me. I can handle it."

But he brushed by me and walked on. "I'm sorry," he said again.

I stopped. He wasn't going to help me. The police officers stood blocking his way with serious expressions. Behind me, the other man in the mask came up and brushed against me. It took me a second to realize he'd tucked something into my hand. I stuffed it in my pocket. I crossed the street and headed for the café. The police escorted the two masked men to their squad car and drove away with the men in the back. As the squad car passed, one of the men turned my way, the mask looking at me as if imploring me to help.

🌴 🌴 🌴

In the café across the street from the Star Center, I sat with my knees pulled up to my chest, reading the pamphlet the man had slipped into my hand. A group called Incognito put out the brochure. All its members wore masks to protect their identities and didn't carry wallets with identification. What had happened to the two men I had seen? Could police put someone in jail for standing outside the star center? It didn't make any sense, but sent a chill down my spine. The brochure claimed that the church was a front for black magic.

Then I read something that made me spill my coffee.

The group claimed that some followers believed in killing kids to get magical power. It all sounded so far out, but with what I had learned about the church, anything could be possible. If they believed they could cut someone in half through mind control, they would probably believe anything. No wonder the man in the mask had grown grim when I told him Rain was twelve. And that homeless guy, Chris, knew all of this, or at least suspected it—that the man in the car was a member of The Church of the Evermore Enlightened and was taking girls who were never seen again.

That was when I knew.

Rain was probably dead. Or if she weren't already, she would be soon.

—CHAPTER—
34

The next morning, sick of avoiding the café downstairs—and all my fourth floor neighbors who hung out there—I decided to stop in, even though Eve was working the counter.

Maybe I went because I knew Eve was there. I was so lonely that every time I thought about my neighbors my stomach ached. They were only down the hall from me, but the distance seemed impossible for me to travel. I'd stop in for just a minute and talk to Eve. It wouldn't hurt anything. I still cringed every time I thought of her and John being harassed at Al's for being a bi-racial couple.

And after yesterday's revelation that The Church of the Evermore Enlightened believed in child sacrifice I didn't want to be alone. I was a little nervous when I pushed open the glass door, but Eve had a huge smile for me like I'd visited her the day before.

"Girl, let me tell you about last night." She idly tugged on a spiral curl that hung down from her huge afro.

I stared at the counter. I hadn't forgotten her comment about the Midwestern boys keeping her up nights. I wasn't into that kinky kind of stuff. And thinking of Taj still stung.

"If it's about having sex with Taj and John, I don't think I can handle it." As soon as I blurted it out, I knew it was a mistake.

She looked at me with surprise. "Whoa, girl. Under different circumstances, I wouldn't kick Mr. Taj out of bed for eating crackers, but I'm with John. He's my man. We're committed, you know?"

I blushed with shame. Anybody else but Eve would've been insulted. And rightly so. "I'm so sorry," I said, and stuttered a little trying to make amends. "I misunderstood…I thought when we first met…you said the two Midwestern boys kept you up all night…I guess I made an assumption."

"I'll say you did." Her black-rimmed eyes were wide. "Sure, I was hanging with both those boys, but John was the only one who got to put his feet on my rug, you know?"

I closed my eyes in embarrassment, but Eve put her hand on mine.

"Let me tell you something about Taj," she began. I tried not to seem interested and began folding my napkin into tinier and tinier triangles. "All the girls love Taj. They all fall for him. Like dominoes, you know. But here's the thing, he never feels the same way for them. It's sort of sad when you think about it."

Was she warning me away from him? She needn't. She continued, "But you know what I think? I think that he just hasn't found the right girl, yet. He's got his own problems to deal with. Like the rest of us. He probably just needs to meet someone he trusts so he can work all that shit out, you know?"

I stopped folding and listened, surprised. What "shit" did Taj have to work out? He seemed so alive and so open and passionate and unafraid. Except when it came to that tattoo. So what? What was the big deal? So what if the girl tattooed on his chest had broken his heart, big whoop. If that was the worst of his "shit," he had good problems.

We all had shit to deal with of our own.

"If he met the right person," Eve paused, giving me a meaningful look, "one who he could trust himself with, he'd be a great boyfriend."

When I didn't answer, Eve changed the subject, telling me how she and John were going to see U2 next month at the L.A. Sports Arena. Everyone had been talking about the show for months.

"No way. How did you get tickets?"

"Last summer, some friends and I pulled an all-nighter. You gotta get to Tower Records at, like, nine p.m. so you're first in line when they open in the morning. You bring beer, blankets, munchies, lawn chairs, and stuff. It's totally cool. Like a tailgate party before the show. Sometimes you've got to sweet talk the guys at the front of the line or the show will sell out before you even get inside. I just flashed them my dimples and the next thing I knew I was fifth in line."

I burst out laughing. She's right. Nobody could resist those dimples. Talking to her felt so normal and good. I'd missed her more than I realized. I suddenly felt shy. "It's really good to talk to you again, Eve."

She smiled back before slapping the counter, startling me. "I just thought of something," she said, eyes bright. "John bought an old Caddy last week. Maybe you and I can go for a drive. Have a girls' night out?"

I wanted to go so badly that it hurt, but something stopped me. Eve looked at me expectantly, waiting for me to answer.

I exhaled loudly. "Um, I'm not sure."

Eve's smile faded slightly and she started busying herself stacking some coffee mugs not meeting my eyes. My stomach twisted as she tried to hide the hurt expression that flickered across her face.

"Eve?" I waited for her to look up. "I meant to say that would be really great. I'd really like that."

Her grin returned full force. We sat there for a moment in silence, me nursing my coffee. She lit a cigarette and put her hand on her chin, smiling at me.

"Did you hear about the janitor?"

I shook my head.

"Cops were here last night. Led him away in cuffs. He threatened to kill his shrink yesterday."

Rain had felt so sorry for the grumpy curmudgeon. "That's sad."

"Get this. We walked by his room after he left. Door was wide open. Big stack of flattened boxes he used for a bed. Gallon jugs of water lined up against all the walls. And guess what else he had in his room?"

I shrugged.

"Nothing. Nothing else. That was it. Trippy, huh?"

"That's weird," I agreed.

I also remembered that Danny was also really nice to him one time despite the janitor screaming at him. Maybe Eve could tell me what was going on with Danny.

"Eve, I saw Danny the other night. He said he took angel dust. He was really messed up," I said. "He didn't seem like such a druggie when I met him."

Eve's brow instantly furrowed. Her eyes got shiny and she blinked. "Yeah, he's always struggled with drugs," she said, and pressed her lips tightly together, blinking some more. "But he really went off the deep end when they told him he was HIV positive."

"What?" I choked out the word, stunned. "When did he find out?"

"Remember on Christmas when he went by his sister's house to get those brownies and tamales?"

Oh God, how could I forget? I nodded and a sour taste shot up into my mouth.

"Well, his ex-boyfriend was waiting for him there. Told Danny he had AIDS. Merry Christmas, huh? They'd been together four years but homeboy had been getting it on the side the whole time. Danny got tested the next day, but he knew before they told him."

I closed my eyes. I was a total asshole.

Every time I heard footsteps in the hall that day, I opened my door a crack and peeked out. Once it was Sadie on her way to the bathroom. Another time, my heart sank to see John's and Taj's back as they walked by with some friends, including a blond girl in a miniskirt who was walking awfully close to Taj, gazing up at him adoringly.

Finally, I heard a jingle of keys. I raced down the hall, surprising Danny in front of his door.

"Whoa." He jumped back a bit. He seemed stone cold sober. One eyebrow rose over his black eyes as he waited for me to say something.

"Can I talk to you for a sec?"

"Sure." He held the door open for me. Inside, a seven-foot high wooden cross with different colors of wax dripping down it leaned against one wall.

"Cool."

"I been working on that at night." He paused. "Instead of writing. Hadn't had much to say poetry wise. Guess I'm still gathering my thoughts about some stuff."

He looked sheepish. He was talking about being HIV positive and I wanted to talk to him about that, but I had something to say first.

He sat on his wheeled office chair, swiveling back and forth. I took a deep breath and plunged in. "Danny…I've been such a jerk. Will you ever forgive me?"

A broad smile spread across his face. "Yeah, totally. Of course. I've been here for you the whole time. I'm your friend. Do you know what that means?"

I choked back a sob. "No. No, I really don't. Maybe you can help me learn what that means. Because I really want to know."

He jumped up and wrapped me in a hug. He held me for a long time with his head resting on mine. I mumbled into his soft flannel shirt. "I'm so sorry. I know you miss Rain, too. It was so unfair of me to blame you. I'm a terrible person. I'm a terrible friend. I'm so, so sorry."

"Shhhh," he said, rubbing my back. "It's okay, Nikki. I love you."

I stiffened and he pulled back, and out came that loud, goofy, cackling laugh I had missed so much. "Relax. I love you like a sister, home girl. You know, if I were straight, I'd marry you in a second."

"It's not that." I looked away. I wasn't convinced my own father loved me. I met his eyes. Seeing the warmth in them and his Cheshire cat grin did something. A hard and dark knot lodged deep inside me broke free.

"I love you, too."

It felt strange but exhilarating to say it. When was the last time I had told someone I loved them? Maybe my mother? But long before she became an addict. I bitterly regretted not telling her I loved her the last time I'd seen her. But now I focused on Danny and how good it was to make up with him. I had missed him so much. I sobered, remembering what Eve had told me.

"Danny...I heard about...what you found out...you know."

"You mean that I'm HIV positive?" He said it so matter-of-factly.

I nodded, pressing my lips together tightly.

"Yeah. At first, it really fucked with my head. I thought if I did enough sketchy drugs, I'd just do myself in and wouldn't have to deal with it. *Problemo* solved. But I'm a little better now. I'm not saying I won't still turn to that shit, but I'm better about it, smarter. I'm doing it to escape now, not to die. You see, here's the thing, I been meeting other guys who are HIV positive and it doesn't have to be a death sentence. Maybe that's what will happen to me, you know?"

I nodded.

"And the thing is, with all this shit happening, I realized I'm not really that afraid to die. It's okay."

I sniffed and he cupped my chin in his hand, his black eyes so full of life it made a sob rise into my throat. "No, really. It is. It will all be okay."

I just closed my eyes. Of course it wouldn't be okay. It seemed inevitable—maybe my curse—that everyone I loved would die.

—CHAPTER—
35

Voices and noises in the hall outside woke me the next morning. Shivering, I pulled my leather jacket over the long t-shirt I slept in and cracked my door.

Everyone from my floor was gathered in the open space in the hall in front of my room. They stopped talking and turned when my door creaked open. Through their legs, I glimpsed what they were standing around. A big, shiny black coffin. I blinked. The lid was off to the side. Good God. Was there a dead body in it? I shrank back against my door.

Taj turned, gave me a look I couldn't read, and gestured for me to come closer. "Better come over here."

In my socks, I crept over to the coffin, wary. Everyone parted to let me closer. The coffin was lined with red satin and empty except for one thing—Rain's granny glasses, the ones she never let out of her sight. The only noise was my heart thudding in my ears. My legs grew weak. Right before I collapsed, I felt arms around me. Not just one. Several. I was held up on all sides. Everyone spoke at once.

"It's not what you think."

"They're just trying to scare you."

"Everything's going to be fine."

I couldn't distinguish who was saying what. My legs were Jell-O. But my friends were holding me up. I clutched the arms supporting me and closed my eyes, trying to catch my breath. It felt like my throat had closed. I gasped, my mouth open, but couldn't get enough air in. My palms grew clammy and a wave of dizziness overcame me.

I was having a full-fledged panic attack.

Someone helped me into my room. I sat with my back against my wall and put my head between my legs, gasping for air. The sound of my heart pounding in my ears drowned out my friend's voices. I panted, trying to get more air into my lungs, but it felt like I had a sheet of plastic across my mouth, blocking the air. My vision had narrowed to a pinprick of light at the end of a long black tunnel.

I felt hands on my back, rubbing gently, and murmured voices. Finally, my heart slowed and breathing became easier. I kept my head down. After several deep breaths, I started to feel normal again. I peeked out through my hair at my friends. A circle of concerned faces surrounded me.

Eve crouched down and lifted my chin, concern filling her kohl-rimmed eyes.

"I'm okay. I get panic attacks," I said, trying to smile, but feeling like my lips made a goofy grimace instead. "Worst one in years." *Since my mom died.*

Eve threw her arm around me and drew me into a hug.

"It's okay, baby. You're with us. We won't let anything happen to you."

This time a real smile spread across my face. Eve knelt down beside me.

"I owe you an apology," she said. "You were right. Someone took

Rain. I'm so sorry I didn't believe you."

There were a lot of mumbled apologies. The sight of all the caring in the faces surrounding me made me feel happy, but guilty. I'd already wasted too much time. I was the one who needed to apologize. I needed the help of these friends even though the idea went against everything I had come to believe the past few years about taking care of myself. But after seeing that coffin, I couldn't do it on my own. If I was going to have any chance of finding Rain, I needed to ask for help. It was also time to admit that I wanted these people in my life. I not only wanted them, I needed them. They were the closest thing I had to family and I didn't want to let them go.

"I've got something to say." I took a big breath. "It won't take long. I need to apologize. I'm sorry. I've been a jerk. I need your help. I think I might know what happened to Rain, but I need your help to find her."

"Bitch, all you had to do was ask," Danny said in a super snotty girly voice. We all burst into laughter. He tackled me in a big hug and pretty soon we were all piled on one another laughing and hugging. When we finally disentangled ourselves, John cleared his throat.

"First off, what are we going to do about that?" He gestured toward the coffin in the hall.

Hearing him say "we" sent a surge of happiness and relief through me. I wasn't going to have to tackle this on my own.

"Why don't we let Nikki fill us in on what she knows and we'll make a plan," Taj said.

With everyone piled into my room, I told them everything I'd learned about The Church of the Evermore Enlightened, its founder, J.C. Hoffman, the Star Center, and especially the part about killing kids.

While I talked, I realized something. Even though I was the youngest one, they thought of me as an equal, maybe even a leader. Nobody had ever turned to me for direction, but the way they were listening and nodding, they wanted me in charge.

Seeing their faces raptly watching me, I felt like I didn't need my leather jacket or my combat boots to be tough. I could reach down deep inside and find the strength I needed already there. And the best part of all was the realization that when I made myself vulnerable and turned to others for help, I was stronger and more powerful than I had ever been on my own.

When I finished talking, Danny sprang up and punched the wall.

"That is some fucked-up, shit. *Vete a su chingada madre*," Danny said. "They come around here again, I'm gonna stuff all of them in this here coffin. In pieces." His eyes glinted with danger. Danny was one of the sweetest and most easygoing guys I knew, but he'd also grown up in a rough part of East L.A. All his cousins were in prison.

John put his arm tighter around Eve, who looked horrified, her eyes bright and her fist held to her mouth. He nuzzled his goatee into her neck, whispering to her in soothing tones for a few seconds. He lifted his head and turned to me.

"I don't know how the hell they got a coffin up four flights of stairs without anyone seeing them," he said. "But I'm going to take a wild guess that they are serious about this warning for you. Which tells me you must be on to something or they wouldn't have gone through this much effort to scare you off."

I nodded. He was right. I was close.

But maybe it was too late.

—CHAPTER—
36

ve had to leave to open up the café and Sadie and I had to work that night, so we agreed to all meet Saturday morning and come up with a plan to find Rain. One by one, everyone filtered out until it was just Taj and me. Alone.

He leaned against one wall staring. I arched an eyebrow at him.

"We need to talk," he said.

The famous words for a break up, but we weren't even together. I shrugged. "Whatever."

Now it was his turn to lift an eyebrow.

I sighed loudly. "So you guys didn't believe me and now you do. I'm over it."

He didn't owe me any special apology. I didn't care. He made it clear he wasn't interested in me the day I took his pictures and he practically ran out of my room.

"I want to explain," he said, standing up and swiping his hand through his hair as he headed toward the window.

"About what?" I tried to sound nonchalant, like I didn't give a shit what he had to say, but a tiny hint of curiosity had edged into my voice.

"My tattoo."

Okay, now I was paying attention. My heart began zinging in my chest. Was this where he told me he couldn't date me because he was hung up on his high school girlfriend or some shit like that?

"It's my sister," he said, and turned back to me.

I must have looked confused because he then said, "My tattoo. It's of my sister. Her name was Angelina."

The relief at hearing the word sister was replaced by horror. My mind got stuck on the word *was*, and it echoed in my brain. *Her name was.*

"She died when she was twelve."

The same age as Rain.

"I'm so sorry," I said, moving toward him instinctively.

"Rain reminds me too much of my sister. That's why I can't deal with her. It's too much. My sister is dead and it's my fault." His voice caught.

"It couldn't have been your fault." I walked over and hugged him. I refused to believe he could have done anything to hurt his own sister.

He buried his face in my shoulder and hair for a second. He seemed to compose himself and drew back talking into my ear. "I wasn't there to protect her."

"What do you mean?"

He pulled away and paced as he told his story, thrust back into the past.

His dad died when he was ten. His mother remarried when he was fifteen and his sister was eleven. One day his sister confessed their stepdad had tried to touch her where he shouldn't. Taj attacked his stepdad, beating him so badly that the stepdad ended up in the hospital. Their mother didn't believe her children. She testified against

Taj. He ended up in juvenile hall for a year. He was frantic, furious that he was locked up and unable to protect his sister. He was a few days from getting out of juvie when his sister killed herself, slitting her wrists as she lay in the upstairs bathtub.

"I wasn't there," he said. I grabbed him and he buried his face in my shoulder, his words fierce. "I was supposed to protect her and I wasn't there."

"Ssshhh," I said, smoothing his hair back. "It wasn't your fault. There was nothing you could have done. It's not your fault."

We lay on my futon and I held him close for a long time, until the shadows grew long and his breathing grew steady as he slept in my arms. I finally understood so many things. We both had dead sisters. Taj had been keeping Rain at arm's length because of his, while I had been drawn to her because of mine.

—CHAPTER—
37

On Saturday morning, my friends and I sat on the floor in my room, poring over *LA Weekly, People* magazine, and several insider trade magazines.

We had a plan—we were going after the three men in the magazine pictures on my wall.

First stop. Rex Walker.

In the magazine picture, Rex Walker, wearing dark sunglasses and a tuxedo, held his hand up to shield himself from the paparazzi as he ducked into a limousine. His black hair was perfectly cut to complement his sculptured cheekbones and Dudley Do-Right chin.

The article, in an industry trade magazine I'd found at the gas station, said Walker had just started shooting an action flick this week at Paramount Studios. With Matt Macklin. My mouth dropped open. The picture showed the strawberry blond Irish actor with his hairless, ripped abdomen on display as he shook droplets of water out of his long hair, walking up from the beach with a surfboard tucked under his muscular arm.

Two of the three actors I suspected in one place. Jackpot.

If we visited the movie lot, we could spy on both actors at once. We could follow them home. Maybe Rain was at one of their houses. It was plausible. I just didn't know if she would be in a guest bedroom or a locked room. I read as I walked to work. I flipped back to the article on Walker to see if I could find out more details and read on. I stopped walking. My hands shook, making the words in the magazine jump around.

Dean Thomas Kozlak was directing the action movie. It was the blockbuster Chad was shooting.

Taj offered to ride his motorcycle to the Paramount lot with Sadie on Monday morning. She had some connection that could gain them access to the studio lot. They would split up so Taj could follow Rex Walker home and Sadie would tail Matt Macklin.

"But if Taj takes his bike, you won't have a car to follow Macklin in…" I said.

John put his arm around Sadie and said, "When you are Sadie O'Brien, you don't need a car. All you need is a face like this."

"Yeah, you're right," I said, and grinned.

That left Andy Martin

According to the *LA Weekly*, the comedian was performing live Monday night. We decided John and Eve would attend the show, tailing Martin back to his place. They would be the perfect ones to attend his steamy, sex-filled comedy act.

"What are we gonna do, home girl?" Danny said, turning to me.

"We're going to Dean Thomas Kozlak's house in Malibu."

Even saying the words made my stomach twist.

I filled them in, starting with that night at Kozlak's house and ending with the surfers' bodies being found. I didn't say their deaths were my fault. It was obvious.

Eve's mouth dropped in horror. "You poor baby." She came over and began rubbing my shoulders. "I'm so sorry you had to go through that."

"So that's how you two met?" Danny said.

"That creep," Sadie said.

"Let Nikki continue," Taj said, and everyone waited.

"Now that we know there's a connection between Rain's guy and Kozlak with that movie being made, I can't rule out that the director's not involved in some way," I said. "Rain got angry when I asked if the mystery guy was really the director so I don't think it was Kozlak in that car. And I truly believe if the man in the car had been working with Kozlak, Rain and I would be dead by now. But think about it: even if Rain went willingly with the guy in the car, which I don't believe, even if she did, what if Kozlak found out about it? The director works with two of the men who might be Rain's mystery guy, so it could happen. We have to go to the Malibu house and make sure Rain's not being held there again."

Also we still had to figure out how to get into the Star Center, I told my friends.

"Somebody didn't like me snooping around there. Enough to kill that homeless man." Something told me the answer to many of my questions lay behind those gleaming walls.

🌴 🌴 🌴

After everyone left, Taj brought his ghetto blaster and about a dozen candles over from his room.

"There's a song I want to play for you."

"I think I've heard this line before," I said, teasing.

But when he hit play, I grabbed his face and kissed him long and hard. It was *One* by U2. He held me close and I listened to the song's words—about dragging the past into the light and carrying each other. I rested my cheek against his chest, listening to the thud of his heartbeat.

Nobody carried me. I took care of myself. I had to. I was so weary of taking care of myself, holding in my emotions. Opening up to these new friends had unleashed something in me I hadn't realized was there. I felt overly sensitive, on the verge of tears all the time. It was a good feeling, but at the same time it scared the shit out of me. I'd never felt more vulnerable in my life.

During the next song, *Until the End of the World*, Taj pulled me up and held my face a few inches away from his with a gaze so intense I didn't think I could look away if I wanted to. He reached for me with a groan and pulled me tighter. But I pulled back and tugged his shirt over his head. I bent down to his tattoo and kissed the wings of the angel ever so gently before I came up and my lips met his urgent mouth.

The next morning, I went into work early to ask for Monday off. I explained what was going on to Amir, telling him one of the church members might have Rain.

His eyes behind his silver-framed glasses made me squirm. If I didn't know him better, it would have frightened me. Even so, the look in his eyes was something I had never seen before and made him seem like a stranger. They held a glint of something dangerous. Maybe he was angry, like I was, at the thought of a powerful, oppressive group hurting an innocent young girl. Maybe to him this *was* a battle worth fighting. Amir had seen some horrific things back in his homeland. Things that might have made him a little bit on the edge of crazy He could be a powerful ally. He dug around in a drawer without meeting my eyes and tossed me a car key on a ring.

"Take the restaurant owner's car. He won't know. He's in Cuba right now. You can keep it until you work again Tuesday."

I scrambled to retrieve it from the floor. "Uh…okay. Thanks."

I didn't know what else to say so I started walking backward toward the door. Amir was already flipping through some papers on his desk. How would I know which car was the owner's? I turned to ask him this, but he'd picked up the phone right before the door slammed shut.

I needn't have worried. There were two cars in the parking lot. I recognized one as Amir's old Volvo. The other was a large—a huge, really—four-door sedan. The little metal plate on the rear end said Lincoln Town Car. I hadn't driven a car since my driver's ed class in Chicago during junior year. I was relieved it was an automatic. Even so, I accidentally peeled out of the parking lot on my way back to the American Hotel.

All night long I had nightmares about returning to Kozlak's beachfront home, chased down maze-like passageways that always ultimately dead-ended in thick brick walls, frantically trying to scale the walls or break through them, clawing at them until my nails were ragged and bloody. And the dreams ended the same way every time: with icy cold fingers digging into my shoulder and jerking me back.

—— CHAPTER ——

38

I let Danny drive us to Malibu, which meant a hair-raising, wild, zipping in-and-out-of-traffic ride on the 101 Freeway. The Lincoln was so big it felt like we were floating down the freeway, bouncing gently at bumps in the road, ready for takeoff. At first I told Danny we shouldn't smoke in the car, but Danny pointed to the ashtray full of cigarette butts, so before long we had both lit up.

"Just don't burn the seat by accident," I cautioned.

The nicotine helped smother the anxiety I felt rising whenever I thought about going back into that Malibu house. Every once in a while, images from my nightmares trickled through my mind, but I blotted them out. I also pushed back images of the surfers' boyish grins.

It was a perfect L.A. day. A breeze brought the salty ocean smell into our car, cooling the heat of the sun on our arms and legs. It felt good to be out of downtown. I smiled at Danny. He returned a blindingly white Cheshire cat grin as a reward. I had missed him. He had such a love of life and childlike wonder in the simplest things that he made something as boring as driving down the freeway fun. It made me feel bitter and jaded in comparison.

"Whoa, man," he said when we turned onto the Pacific Coast Highway, pointing out the window with his lit cigarette. "Look at those surfers ripping those waves."

From our perch high above the water on PCH, we could see giant waves flecked with seemingly tiny bodies on surfboards floating into shore. I didn't want to think about surfers. I cranked up the radio to KROQ and sang loudly until a Concrete Blonde song came on. The lead singer, Johnette Napolitano, introduced the song on the live version, saying it was about AIDS.

"This is for any of you who knows anyone who's lost anyone. This is a song about a woman with AIDS, which someone in this room has, a few of these people in this room have, and you'll go through it, and you'll know it, and you should stop it. This is for Wendy."

I blinked hard to hold back hot tears, sneaking looks over at Danny, who had grown very still and was staring out at the black pavement of the road before us. I unsnapped my seatbelt and scooted right up against him on the bench seat, putting my head on his shoulder. He leaned over and kissed the top of my head. He grabbed my hand with one of his, holding it tight with his other hand loosely on the wheel. We sat there like that until the song ended.

I had told Danny earlier I wasn't sure I'd be able to recognize the front of Kozlak's house. After an hour of cruising up and down PCH listening to the radio at full volume with the windows down, I'd given up. So many houses seemed the same from the road. I decided the next best thing would be to find the parking lot where I had met the surfers. Maybe that would be easier. I tried not to think about those boys. I couldn't. Not today.

Finally, when the sun was directly overhead, the breeze had died, and a sheen of sweat glistened on Danny's upper lip, I spotted the parking lot where the surfers had picked me up. And where their bodies had been found. We parked, rolled up the cuffs of our jeans, and stripped off our shoes, tucking them in the trunk. It would be easier to traverse the long stretch of beach barefoot.

In the heat, I felt a sudden chill as we crossed over the spot where I had first hopped into the surfer's van. This might have been right where those boys died. And now I was going to the house of the man who probably had killed them or had them killed. Although the hot sun was beating down on me so brilliantly I had to squint, a sudden darkness swooped down upon my heart. We hopped the sea wall and headed for the wet sand. I looped my bag with my camera in it over my shoulder, so it hung down my back.

"You sure you can recognize Big Shot's house?"

"Yeah," I said, panting as we walked. I remember looking back at the house and seeing him watching me from the deck.

I wished I'd brought a bottle of water or something. The exertion of trudging through sand knocked back some of the anxious pressure filling my chest. After a few minutes walking, I spotted the deck and the wall of windows behind it.

"Now what?" Danny asked, wiping his brow. He had stripped down to a thin tee and tied his flannel shirt around his head.

As we drew closer, I saw that the wooden plank walkway led from the beach to a side door on the lower part of the house. I tried the handle. It was unlocked. I opened it a few inches. The slivered opening revealed it was a laundry and mudroom. The clanging of a washing machine and dryer filtered out. I swung the door open. The maid was standing there folding laundry. I didn't know which one of us screamed louder.

"*Dios me ayude*," she said, patting her chest.

"It's okay. *Lo siento*." I'm sorry was one of the few new phrases I had learned from the kitchen staff at Little Juan's. Sunshine poured into the cheerful laundry room through the open door, making the house seem harmless and cozy, not the monstrosity from my nightmares.

"Do you remember me?"

Her eyes grew wide.

"*Si*. Yes. You ran away." Then her eyes narrowed. "Why you here?"

"My friend. She's twelve. Her name's Rain. Blond hair. Pink streaks. She was also here that night. Kozlak was keeping her locked up."

The woman's eyes widened. "Locked up?"

"This girl." I held out Rain's photo. It was one I had developed when I took the roll in with the black car's license plate number. She was leaning against my apartment wall, her head tilted back and a small smile on her face.

The woman took the picture and shook her head. "She's little girl?"

I was baffled. She didn't know Rain at all? But Kozlak had kept Rain locked up the whole time.

"Is there a room, maybe a secret room, Mr. Kozlak keeps locked?"

She gave Danny a wary glance. He said something in Spanish that made her seem to relax. She nodded and ushered us in the doorway. We followed her down a set of stairs to a large room set up as a home movie theater, complete with a screen that stretched across the entire twelve-foot wall and plush red velvet seats in rows. There was even an old-fashioned popcorn machine in the back. She pointed toward a door and said, "There. Locked." She sighed. "Is only for garage. And elevator."

Elevator? I was heading toward the door, my heart leapfrogging in my throat. "Elevator to what?"

She shrugged. "I no have key."

She turned to me so suddenly I jumped. "Girl. Yes, girl here. But gone now. With you, right?"

"Yes," I said, my voice rising. "But she might be here again."

"No," the maid said. "Not here now."

A rumbling overhead made her grab my arm, her eyes wide, darting down to a tiny gold watch on her wrist. "Housecleaners."

"You don't clean?"

The woman gave me a look like I was crazy. "I run house. Not clean. Laundry is my own clothes."

I started to head back up the stairs, but she stopped me, pulling me back and toward a small door. "No time. They come down here now. They see you." She fumbled with some keys and unlocked a door that led into a small room. She opened a door and gestured for us to enter. "I come later."

Danny didn't quite trust her. "How do we know you're not gonna keep us locked up until the big guy gets home?"

I also hesitated. Flashes of my nightmare clouded my vision—me running down hallways chased by the icy fingers of death. The noises overhead grew louder, voices and footsteps. The woman scoffed and pushed us into the open door.

"I don't think we have a choice." I pulled Danny in with me and closed the door behind us. The sound of the maid turning the key in the lock sent a chill down my spine.

In the dark, we listened. It wasn't long before we heard the sound of Spanish-speaking voices and a vacuum cleaner. Then the sounds moved overhead, on the floor above. I tried the door. Yep. Locked.

After a few seconds of silence, when we were sure everyone had moved upstairs, Danny flicked open the Zippo I had bought him for Christmas and held it before us. The walls were lined with shelves. Some had books, but most had videos. Well, that made sense.

As Danny moved the lighter across the shelves, I saw something that made my heart leap into my throat. It was that book *Insights*. And not just one copy—more than a dozen. My face grew warm. Was that what the homeless guy was trying to tell me, that Kozlak had Rain? She could be here.

Then the lighter lit up a small section of videos where the spines contained single names where the titles would be. Names of girls. Kelly, Brittany, Jane, Sara, Madison. Christy. Jessica. Kate. Oh my God. They were probably porn. Maybe even child porn. I scanned them all and felt relief when I didn't see Rain's name among them.

"Stop!"

Danny's arm froze. "*Cabron!*" he whispered under his breath. One video didn't have a name, but a gold star on the spine. I grabbed that and two of the other videos, stuffing them into my bag.

"Evidence." I was planning on going to the cops. Now it wouldn't just be my word against Chad's and Kozlak's. Now, I would have proof.

The other shelves contained recognizable movie titles and obscure film equipment. Bored with snooping, we slumped to the ground with our backs against the one wall without shelving. I wasn't sure how long it had been, but it felt like we'd been in the room for an eternity.

"Damn, I'm dying for a cig," Danny said.

"Me, too."

"Should we?"

I shrugged even though he couldn't see me in the dark. God, we were horrible influences on each other. Kozlak smoked himself so he probably wouldn't notice the smell later. I started packing my box of smokes in answer to Danny's question.

He lit it for me and we shared it.

"Probably should only have one." I said.

"Yeah, just this one."

We smoked and waited. Two cigarettes later, footsteps tromped down the stairs leading into the lower level. We stubbed out our smokes on the concrete floor and froze when we heard the steps stop right in front of the door. The crack of light that entered the room momentarily blinded me and I held my hand up to shield my eyes.

"*Vamos.*" The maid batted her hand, trying to wave away the smoke that came out of the room. "They are in the front of the house. You must leave now."

We stumbled into the light, blinking. I ran over to locked door that led to the garage and elevator and yanked the handle. Nothing. I wished I had a screwdriver, but it didn't look like the kind of handle that could be taken off. I pounded on the door with both fists. "Rain?" I whispered as loudly as I dared, putting my mouth to the seal of the door. "Rain?"

"Shhh. No girl there," the maid said. "I hear nothing. To garage. And elevator."

"But where does the elevator go?"

The maid just pressed her lips together and shook her head, lifting her shoulders.

I pounded again, putting my ear to the thick door. Nothing. Danny jutted his chin toward the stairs. The floor above us squeaked as people moved across it.

"Hurry." The maid ushered us to the laundry room. I looked behind me at the heavy door as we left. A glacial wave of fear rippled across my scalp and down my back.

— CHAPTER —
39

We all met back in my room the next morning. Eve brought up a pot of coffee and mugs from the café and we sat cross-legged in a circle on my wooden floor. Danny had borrowed a small TV with a built-in VCR player from a girl on the first floor. After we heard reports back from everyone's day, we were going to see what was on the videotapes from Kozlak's house.

John and Eve told us they had waited around for hours, watching Andy Martin flirt with women in the bar after his comedy show until he left at last call with a young woman on his arm. They followed him back to his Bel Air bungalow.

"From the looks of that place, if Rain was there, she'd have to be in bed with him and that girl," Eve said. "It was like a one-room little cabin."

"Did you see inside?"

Eve giggled. "There was a crack in the curtains. That boy needed to drink some more coffee or something. He fell asleep. His girl was *not* happy."

"There was a big room with a kitchen on one side and a bathroom," John said. "No place to hide someone."

"Okay." That didn't mean he hadn't grabbed her and dumped her somewhere.

"Did you see any drug stuff, like needles or something, on the dresser or whatever?"

"They drank some wine," John said. "That was it."

"Thanks, guys. I bet you're exhausted."

Eve sleepily nodded and gave a slow wink. "Not the first time we've pulled an all-nighter, is it, honey?" She wrapped her arms through John's and closed her eyes.

Taj was next. He followed the bad boy actor from the movie lot. "Get this," he said with a grin that stopped my heart a little. "He went straight to some tiny yoga studio."

Macklin? I'd have thought he'd rushed to meet a high-priced call girl in his hotel room.

"Stayed a few hours. Tailed him to the Chateau Marmont. Put my ear to the door—snoring and Jay Leno. I did ask the receptionist if she'd ever seen the big stud with a young girl. Get this—said the only woman she'd seen him with over the last six months was his wife, who came over to visit from Ireland."

"Wife?" Sadie choked out. "He's supposed to be the biggest player around."

"Not so big, I guess," Taj said.

Then it was Sadie's turn. She'd sweet-talked a crewmember on the film into following Walker home. Unfortunately, the guy drove a beater car that died at a stoplight on Melrose and Western Boulevards. They lost him.

"Oops." Sadie looked sheepish, her long lashes fluttering against her cheekbones. "I'll head back over today. Find a guy with a more reliable car."

Next, Danny filled them in on our visit to the director's Malibu house, saving the videotapes for me. He told them Kozlak was obviously connected to The Church of the Evermore and Everlasting because of all those *Insights* books in the closet.

"There is definitely some connection if we could just figure out what it is. The maid said there was no way Rain was there, but I don't know," he said, telling them about the locked door and elevator. "If these tapes show what we think they will, we've got something to go to the cops with, so maybe they'll believe us and search the Malibu house."

That was our plan. Take the videos to the cops and have them go to the house to rescue Rain.

"Nikki, why don't you tell them what you think the tapes are about."

My mouth felt like I had sucked on a dry sponge. First, I reminded them that Kozlak had wanted me to be in a porn flick starring kids because I looked so young. I swallowed hard and avoided eye contact. I held up a tape.

"This is probably child porn."

"That sick bastard," Sadie said, her eyes narrowing in anger as she took a long puff off her cigarette.

"I know," I said. "I think we should just watch a bit of it to see what is on it, mainly to check whether it is kids, but if it gets graphic, we turn it off. Deal? But if it is a kid, then we need to take it to the cops. Maybe Ernie?" I turned to Sadie.

"That drunk?" she scoffed. "No, if this operation is as big as you think it might be, who knows how far the church's influence reaches. The church obviously has some connection to LAPD or those cops wouldn't have taken away those men in masks. Didn't they tell you not to trust the cops?"

I nodded and she continued. "Something is very fishy with that whole situation. Let's give the tape to Amir and see what he says."

Amir was the most responsible adult we knew. He would know what to do with it. Danny inserted the video with the star on it, pressed play, and we all sat back. I was biting my fingernails. Sadie was tapping her foot. John was tugging on his goatee. Danny perched by the TV, ready to turn it off if it became too much, which we were certain would happen. Sure enough, the first frame showed a naked teenage girl lying spread-eagle on a giant bed. The room was silent.

"Okay, that's enough," Danny said, and punched the pause button with one finger.

But something about it caught my eye. "Wait. Press play again, just for a second."

The picture came into focus. I was right. The girl wasn't there by choice. She was restrained. Tethers strapped to the four corners of the bed bound her wrists and ankles.

"Good God. They are in the movie against their will. It's rape." I put my fist up to my mouth as both fury and horror shot through me.

Danny pressed the pause button. He slammed his fist into the wall. "*Mierda*." He began pacing, jerking his head back and forth and shaking his fist.

At first, the room was dead silent, and then people exploded in sound and movement.

Sadie jumped to her feet, legs planted wide and teeth bared, lips curled back. "That's it. I'm taking my gun and I'm going to that motherfucker's house and shoving it up his ass."

John's eyes were cold and flinty as he comforted Eve, putting his arm around her and hugging her close. Her shoulders drooped and her chin was wobbling. "Oh my God. Those poor girls," she said.

Taj sat there with his head in his hands, running his fingers through his hair. When his eyes met mine, he looked right through me. His intense blue eyes had turned nearly black with fury. He shook his head in disgust, his jaw tensed tightly.

I felt like sparks of anger were shooting out of my eyes. I wanted to take my steel-toed boot and kick out the window overlooking the street. Kozlak gotten away with this and worse. I had seen at least two dozen girls' names on the spines of videotapes.

It was revolting, but we needed to keep playing the tape.

I turned to the others. My voice was calm and precise. "I'm going to fast-forward to the end. I understand if you need to leave the room."

They all stared at me.

"I'm sorry," said Eve, heading toward the door with John. "I can't stay."

"Don't be sorry. I'll talk to you later," I said, giving her a small smile.

The door closed behind them. I looked at my friends' faces.

"Ready?"

They nodded. Danny hit fast-forward so the images were jerky and blurred. I tried not to focus on it, instead vaguely taking in the images of pink and beige flesh moving around on the screen. None of us looked directly at the screen. Taj was back to having his head in his hands, occasionally glancing up at the TV before focusing on the cigarette in the ashtray between his legs. Sadie paced the room, peering out the window in between glances at the screen.

"I just want to see how it ends," I said in a whisper. I didn't tell them why. I didn't tell them that Chad's words that night in Malibu rang in my ears. "*Maybe I'll put you in a different flick, one you'll never have a chance to see.*"

The little strip on the bottom of the screen indicated that the movie was almost over so I turned my attention back to the TV. "Okay, slow this part down to real time."

Then I was on my hands and knees with Taj holding my hair back as I vomited into a plastic bag. Danny was rubbing my back. Sadie had stamped out of the room; slamming the door so hard it knocked my lamp onto the floor.

—CHAPTER—
40

I t was not just child porn. It was a snuff flick. With a teenage girl.

I made myself watch the last part of the movie twice. I never wanted to see something like that again. Ever. But I had to watch it again because something about the man in the video seemed familiar. I never quite saw his face, just his naked body. The person filming was careful about that. I paused the movie. The man had a small tattoo on his wrist. The tattoo had been covered with makeup or something, but some had worn off, revealing a small portion. I grabbed the magazine I had taken from the library and scanned for the picture. Yep, the same small tattoo of a scorpion. In the video, I could only see a tiny piece of the scorpion's tail.

It was Rex Walker.

That son of a bitch was raping kids. And strangling them. That was why people were dying. The church was trying to protect his horrid little secret. And Big Shot Director was in on it.

How could Kozlak and Walker be getting away with this? I'd seen at least two dozen names on the sides of those videotape cases in Kozlak's closet. Then it struck me: they preyed on lost children. Children nobody cared about.

Probably homeless girls, like Rain. And runaways. Like me.

Girls who would never be missed or who were already missing. And that bastard Chad, hungry to curry favor with Kozlak, was one of his recruiting minions. He probably never even liked me, only heard my sob story about wanting to leave Chicago and decided to give me up as an offering to his God—the Big Shot Director.

Maybe Kozlak picked up the other girls at the bus station, just like he had Rain. He lured them with his big limousine and promise of movie stars, fame, drugs. All the glamour and allure of life in Los Angeles bundled up in one outstretched hand. Besides "starring" in Kozlak's sick little side projects, how did Walker fit into all this? Had he lured Rain just so he could turn her over to Kozlak?

Although it was horrible, we fast-forwarded to the end of the other two videotapes. But the other two ended with the girls alive. It was just the one. The one with the small gold star on the case, as if it had won a prize. But both other films looked like the same guy. Walker. The other two tapes were dated last year. The one with the star was dated six months ago. Maybe this meant the killing was something new. Maybe it could be stopped before more girls ended up dead.

When we were done, the room remained silent until Danny stood up. He opened my door, his black eyes bright. "Don't worry, *chica*. They will pay for this."

I nodded, biting my lip, but inside my heart felt like it was shriveling up. Amir was right. Who was I to try to stop something as pervasive and powerful as an organization like The Church of the Evermore Enlightened? Members of the church controlled Hollywood. If it got out that one of their most famous members was a monster, it could ruin them. I knew now, deep inside, that they would stop at nothing to protect one of their own.

My motley crew of friends was tough, but we stood no match for this organization. It went beyond anything I could have imagined in my worst nightmares. And I knew beyond a doubt now.

They'd taken Rain.

A cold wave of terror swept through me, making my face tingle and stomach roil. Her body was probably discarded somewhere, never to be found. The only evidence I had was that tape. What could I do? Who would listen to me? What if I gave it to some detective at the LAPD who had connections to The Church of the Evermore Enlightened? The reach of this organization terrified me.

No, I needed to make sure it ended up in the right hands. Sadie said I would be foolish to turn it over to Ernie. I didn't think he was connected to the church, but he *was* a screw up. I didn't know if I could trust him just because he helped me once or twice. No, she was right, we should turn it over to Amir. He would know what to do.

Meanwhile, we needed to tail Rex Walker.

As soon as I pulled myself together, I asked Sadie to return the Lincoln to Amir and work my shift. I'd take over tailing Rex with Taj. I figured Taj's motorcycle could follow any vehicle. At first Sadie had protested, saying she wanted to be there to kick Rex Walker's ass. But she quickly agreed when she saw how badly I wanted to be there when he led us to Rain.

——CHAPTER——
41

I clung to Taj's back, my face buried into his denim jacket, my thighs tingling from both the vibration of the motorcycle as well as the sensation of my body pressed so tightly against his. We hadn't set out for the movie lot until nearly sunset, knowing that yesterday the actors had knocked off for the night even later than that.

The big studio movie lot, surrounded for blocks by a giant wall, was on a nondescript stretch of road in a less than trendy part of L.A. We parked in front of a Mexican restaurant across the street from an entrance gate to the lot. At first, we sat alert and poised, ready to take off. But as more time passed, I ran into the restaurant and bought old-fashioned bottles of Coke that we sipped sitting on the sidewalk, stretching out our legs with our back to the wall of the building. After about forty-five minutes of waiting, the gates to the lot opened and cars starting streaming out.

Tossing our sodas in the trash, we hopped onto Taj's bike. Sadie had told us Walker drove a yellow Ferrari, not a black chauffeured car. That would make it easy to spot him. After about twenty minutes, a yellow flash emerged from the gate. Walker's car. Taj revved his engine and we pulled into traffic, staying a few lengths behind the Ferrari as it sped along Melrose Avenue, veered onto Van Ness, and made a sharp turn onto Santa Monica Boulevard.

We sped past strip malls and apartment buildings. Walker either suspected he was being followed or else he always drove like he was on a racecourse, weaving in and out of traffic. Taj stayed on his tail, keeping far enough back that we wouldn't be spotted. When we turned onto Sunset Boulevard, I squeezed Taj's waist tighter. I leaned into his ear. "Oh my God, he's headed to the Star Center."

Sure enough, the castle-like fortress soon loomed before us and Walker's Ferrari zipped down the driveway and behind the building, disappearing behind a garage door that slid closed. Taj brought his bike to a skidding halt in the gravel nearby. "Shit."

But I was satisfied. Walker was staying at the Star Center, so maybe Rain was there, too. A camera hidden in the foliage of bushes and palm trees rotated our way. I ducked my head and pulled Taj's face toward me. "Don't look. They're watching us through the cameras. Let's go. We'll come back tomorrow night with the gang. Rescue mission. After dark."

🌴 🌴 🌴

On our way back to the American Hotel, I asked Taj to stop at Little Juan's and wait for me outside. Amir was in his office. I marched in, grabbed the VHS tape out of my bag, and tossed it onto his desk.

"It's a snuff flick. Those bastards who have Rain are making movies where movie stars rape and kill children."

My voice was venomous. I balled my hands into fists, waiting for him to respond. He stared at me. His expression behind the silver-framed glasses was oddly inquisitive as if he were trying to figure me out. Maybe my revelation had shocked him beyond words.

Finally, he spoke. "It's on this tape? You have evidence?"

"Yes."

"Where did you get this?" He stood and was pacing behind his desk.

"That movie director's house—Dean Thomas Kozlak. He's behind it all."

"How did you get it?"

"I can't say," I said. I couldn't admit to breaking and entering. "I need your help. I'm worried if I take this to the cops, I might give it to someone who is part of this group. They didn't believe me before." *He* would understand my distrust of authority. "Is there anyone you trust in the police department you can give this to? We need to do something right away. Rain might still be alive." *She has to be.* "We're heading to the church's Star Center tomorrow night. I think they are holding her there so I need the night off."

His back was to me. I paused, frozen, waiting.

"Okay," Amir finally said, turning, but not meeting my eyes. "I will figure out who we can trust."

My shoulder's sagged with relief knowing Amir was on our side and that it wasn't entirely up to me to try to stop this evil.

—CHAPTER—
42

The next afternoon, I was reading in my room, trying to kill time until it was dark, when there was loud pounding on my door. It seemed urgent so I scrambled to my feet. All my neighbors stood outside in the hall. We weren't supposed to meet until sunset to storm the Star Center and rescue Rain. But the looks on their faces told me something else was going on.

The Rodney King verdict had gone down.

Danny flipped on the borrowed television set, which was still in my room. My hand flew to my mouth in horror. It was on every station—a helicopter hovered over a South Central intersection, filming the beating of a white man who had been yanked out of the cab of his big rig. The man lay on the black pavement beside his semi-truck in the middle of the large intersection at Florence and Normandie.

The footage showed abandoned vehicles stopped helter skelter and crowds of people milling around the sidewalks. When an unsuspecting driver came across the intersection, the rioters swarmed the streets, throwing bottles and bricks, sending drivers peeling out leaving trails of smoke from skidding tires.

Reporters said that earlier more than two dozen LAPD officers had fled the intersection when protesters outnumbered them, looting stores and attacking pedestrians and drivers. Coverage switched to the L.A. County Courthouse where a peaceful protest of some three hundred people had erupted in fighting and gunshots. News helicopters had taken over the skies, being the only reporters who could safely capture the chaos erupting throughout Southern California.

People threw bricks into grocery store windows while others raced down streets with shopping carts loaded with food. Men hauling upholstered love seats on their heads strode down city streets without a care in the world. Other people ran down the street clutching stereo components or TVs, zipping past pedestrians who didn't even look up. Besides the noise from the TV, my tiny room was mostly quiet, broken up by occasional utterances.

"What the hell?"

"No way."

"This is crazy."

"Un-fucking-believable."

Every once in a while we shook our heads. We sat in front of the glowing TV screen, unable to tear ourselves away.

Darkness had fallen when reporters interviewed a man named Bobby Green Jr. The reporters said Green, who was black, had rescued the beaten-up white truck driver, a man named Reginald Denny, by driving him to the hospital.

"Mr. Green, can you hear us?" the male reporter said as the TV showed earlier footage of the intersection.

"Yes"

"Were you one of the people who beat him up?"

"No."

"All right, so that theory is out the window. Tell us what happened..."

Danny sprung to his feet. "*Did he beat him up?*" he said, mocking the announcer's clipped voice. "Dude. What the fuck? They asked him that because he's black. *Pendejo*. Fucking racist pig. He rescued him!"

When the reporter asked how Reginald Denny's condition appeared on the way to the hospital, Green answered, "Really, really, really bad...he had big holes under his eyes...it was like he was ready to go unconscious."

Green said during the drive the truck driver had managed to thank him, but was fading in and out of consciousness.

"Did you ever figure out why he got beat up like that?" the female news reporter asked toward the end of the interview.

Green didn't hesitate in his response. "'Cause he was white."

"That was all, huh?"

"Yep."

We all sat there staring at the TV. Too stunned to move or talk. John had his arm around Eve. Tears streamed down her face.

—CHAPTER—
43

"It's dark now. Let's go." I stood and tugged my leather jacket on. Slowly, heads turned away from the TV coverage of the city erupting in violence.

"What? We can still go, right?" I had my hand on the door. Nobody moved.

A reporter on the TV announced that the mayor had instituted a dusk-to-dawn curfew in the city of Los Angeles.

"I don't know, honey," Eve said, her brow furrowed. "It's kind of crazy out there right now."

That was an understatement. Right when she said that, a cameraman scurried for cover behind an overturned car as a mob shooting guns into the air passed by. At the same time, we heard glass breaking and shouting on the street outside the American Hotel. Sadie sprang to the window and started screaming. A second later, gunfire sent her flopping to the floor. For a second, a cold wave of terror surged through me, thinking she'd been shot. Without lifting her head, Sadie shouted toward the window, "Take your little pissant toy gun and get the hell off our street. I'll show you what a real gun looks like."

Sadie Army crawled across the floor and ran out my door, leaving us all with open mouths and wide eyes.

I guessed we weren't going anywhere tonight.

I kicked the door closed behind Sadie, balled my hands into fists, and began pacing the room. I wanted to punch something. Instead, I kicked the door again. I finally knew where Rain was, but had to sit and wait. And watch my world self-destruct.

We sat in front of the TV, mesmerized by the flickering screen and the seemingly unreal pictures. My anger turned to despair. For the first few hours, I didn't want to eat or even smoke or drink. I didn't want to move from my spot in front of the TV. Everyone brought blankets and pillows into my room and we stayed up all night, unable to take our eyes off the TV. In the morning, we stayed huddled. None of us had slept much, just a few naps here and there.

The sun rose like nothing had happened.

Sadie was acting very mysterious. She had come back to my room with some type of an assault rifle. She sat sentry by my window, pointing the gun out every once in a while. She also had a shoebox-sized phone with a little handle on it like a suitcase. I'd never seen a mobile phone before. Every once in a while, she would disappear into the hall with the phone. Or leave for a few minutes, coming back with boxes of cigarettes, booze, and food.

Once, after she left the room, I waited a few seconds and peeked out the window. A 1950s style sedan with huge tailfins had pulled up by the front door. I saw a blur of blond hair as Sadie ran out to the car barefoot, sticking her head in the window for a few seconds and coming out with a giant box before running back into the building. The car was gone before the front door slammed shut.

By afternoon, the government had ordered the U.S. National

Guard and the U.S. Marines to come settle the city, which was now dotted with blackened, charred buildings.

As if the spell was broken, everyone scattered, leaving only Danny and me shell-shocked in front of the TV, laying on my futon playing Crazy Eights. Danny was flipping through the stations when I yelped for him to stop. They were showing footage of an area I recognized. The coffee shop across the street from the Star Center.

Reporters interviewed the manager who had shut the restaurant after losing power earlier. A burst of noise sent the cameraman swiveling. The rioters—a whirling pack of shouting people bearing sticks and bats—were a block away. The chaotic footage bounced up and down as the cameraman and his reporter ran. The wild-eyed reporter with his hair flopping ducked into a nearby business. The cameraman, who was panting, said in a whisper that he was taking cover behind some bushes but would continue filming. You could hear his heavy breathing and whispering commentary as he filmed the pack of rioters reaching the front of the star center. The rioters began throwing Molotov cocktails at the walls with security guards running around frantically trying to ward off the crowd.

Danny and I looked at each other with wide eyes.

"Now we move," he said, and sprung to his feet.

Within a half hour, everyone had gathered on the roof.

A plan was made. We would wait for dark.

It was going to be dangerous. Kozlak had been willing to kill me. He had killed the surfers. He would kill anyone who got in his way. I turned to Eve and grabbed her by both shoulders.

"I need you to stay here."

"What?"

I had gone over this earlier with Danny and shot him a glance.

"That's right, *querida*," he said. "You need to stay here in case we're wrong and Rain shows up in the chaos trying to find us. You're going to need to be here for her."

Eve looked doubtful for a moment, but then pressed her lips together and nodded. John, who had his arm wrapped around her, gave her shoulder a squeeze.

Now this was going to be the hard part. I turned toward John.

"You need to stay with her. I'm worried about leaving her alone. If someone got into the building, she'd need somebody to protect her. And the building for that matter."

John cast a wild look around before deciding that being Eve's protector suited him. He agreed we could still take his car. The plan was for Taj, Danny, and I to pile in the Caddy as night fell and head for the Star Center.

As the sun set, my stomach knotted with a mixture of fear, excitement, and anxiety. I thought we were all nervous. Sadie paced the roof of the American Hotel with that big gun. I worried her trigger finger was a little too antsy.

"Where'd you get this piece?" Taj asked, taking the gun from her for a moment.

"Didn't you hear?" she said, taking out another gun from her back waistband and checking its ammo with a loud click. "I ditched that married prick, Tony. My new man, Carlos, is leader of the *La Maya Locos* gang in East L.A. He's shown me all sorts of tricks. Taught me to shoot at a range on Rodeo Drive. Did you know the gangbangers and LAPD both practice there? At the same time?" She didn't wait for an answer. "Carlos and his boys are coming along tonight, escorting us. I was going to surprise you all."

I bet Carlos was the attractive, poised gang leader from the restaurant. He was the most charismatic person in any room he was in, a natural born leader. If he hadn't been in a gang, he probably would have been president of a fraternity or something.

"Do you know how to shoot a gun?" Taj asked.

I scoffed.

"I'm going to take that as a no." He turned to Sadie. "Do you my mind if we borrow it for a second?"

She shrugged and walked off.

Taj spent the next half hour showing me how to shoot a gun—without actually shooting it—until he was convinced I could fire it if I needed to. At one point, Danny raced over and grabbed some binoculars from John's hand. He pointed them toward a rooftop a few buildings away in Little Tokyo. I squinted my eyes at two figures on that roof. Sun shimmered on something in their arms. Guns.

I started to move back when Danny chuckled.

"Two Japanese guys. Probably defending their building, too."

Dropping the binoculars, he raised his rifle high in a salute. The two figures raised their guns in acknowledgement back.

Later, as the sun dipped on the horizon, I steeled my gaze in the direction where the gleaming white mansion towered over Sunset Boulevard. Smoke mingled with the setting sun, turning the skies blood red. We would strike when it grew dark. Until then, I had to be patient. I pulled up a ripped lawn chair, took a long drag off my cigarette, and settled back to watch L.A. burn.

— CHAPTER —
44

Finally, darkness fell.

Back in my room, I pulled on my Levis, a long-sleeved tee, leather jacket, and my combat boots. I yanked my hair back in a tight ponytail and smudged dark kohl eyeliner around my eyes. Tossing aside my pink lip gloss, I ran down to Eve's room. With a slash of Eve's blood red lipstick across my lips, I stared at myself in a small mirror and nodded. I was ready. Taj was meeting me downstairs.

I waited near the front door for Danny to pull up in the topless yellow Cadillac. I eyed its open top warily, wishing I still had the restaurant owner's big Lincoln Town Car. A convertible seemed dangerous. Rioters could throw Molotov cocktails at us, pull us out of the vehicle, and shoot us. Any scenario was possible. I didn't like it. But we didn't have a choice. I cringed a little thinking of Amir. When Sadie had called to tell him we wouldn't be into work because of the riots, he'd been furious.

"What? He's keeping the restaurant open?" I couldn't believe it.

"That's a notorious LAPD hangout," John said. "He'll be lucky if that place isn't bombed."

Behind the Caddy, a parade of classic cars pulled up in pastel colors—yellow, pink, and turquoise. Thundering bass poured out of the vehicles, which rose mysteriously up and down like magic. One minute the car was a few inches off the pavement and the next; it had bounced a few feet off the ground. Special hydraulics, Danny said.

A kid hopped out of a pink car and sauntered over to Danny, hitching up his black slacks as he re-tucked a perfectly pressed white t-shirt into them. He stopped in front of Danny, who was in the driver's seat, humming and fiddling with the radio tuner. It was that little punk ass runt-of-the-litter gangbanger from the restaurant. My stomach flip-flopped, but Danny didn't even look up.

The kid ran a diamond-bejeweled hand through his slicked back hair. Without taking his eyes off Danny, he lit a cigarette. Finally, Danny glanced over at him. The kid, who had a giant gold cross hanging down the front of his crisp shirt, poked a finger at Danny's chest.

"Who you with?"

Danny started cackling madly. The kid was taken aback and drew away slightly, his eyes narrowing. "Seriously, *hombre*," Danny said. "Do I look like I run with a crew? Listen, *esse*, not every *Chicano* is a gangster. My only homie is Nikki here, and although she's a badass, I think she has bigger fish to fry than you, my friend."

The kid frowned at me and I glared back, meeting his eyes until a whistle called him back to his car. He left, scowling.

Taj came out the door of the American Hotel, tucking a switchblade into his belt. The three of us had decided to leave the guns behind in case we were pulled over by the cops. Eve and John could use them to defend the building if they needed to.

Danny stood up in the driver's seat and waved his index finger in a big spiral. Engines roared to life behind us with eager feet revving gas pedals. Time to go. Taj and I climbed into the big back seat of the Caddy. Danny drove with one hand, taking swigs off a bottle of tequila and handing it back to me. I tried not to choke as the fiery alcohol hit my throat. My mouth burned with the flavor of tequila mixing with nicotine. Adrenaline surged through me, making every part of me feel alive. As we peeled out and swerved around the corner, Taj looked over at me and even in the dark I could see his grin. He must have felt the same way I did—a mixture of surrealism, excitement, and fear. The energy of the uprising was in the night air. How could anyone *not* feel it?

The feeling that I'd been thrust into an alternate universe made my limbs weak as we passed a parking lot that had been turned into an armed camp by soldiers. Camouflage netting was strung twelve feet in the air as if protecting against an aerial attack. Men in full body armor and masks carrying submachine guns and rifles patrolled the lot. I hoped the soldiers didn't think we were rioters, but they barely looked up as our little convoy passed. To the east, an empty dirt lot behind a strip mall was now lined with trenches. You could see the helmet and guns of the soldiers laying down in them.

Danny made me nervous by howling like a wolf every time we skidded around a corner, but his war cries were absorbed into all the other chaos—tires squealing, fires crackling, glass breaking, and people shouting.

The night air was thick with the smell of smoke and gasoline. Everywhere, bands of people were running and yelling. We flipped U-turns when we spotted overturned cars on fire. We passed people with sweaty and dirty and angry faces pulling down store awnings and ripping them to shreds. The dark was punctuated by blue and red squad car lights that briefly sent groups scattering into the shadows. But tonight something different was happening—police were the ones retreating, reversing vehicles out of blocks teeming with too many people.

For some reason, I'd never felt so alive. Energy surged through me, prompting me to hop up onto the top of the Cadillac's backseat with my legs dangling down by Taj. He grabbed my shins every time we swerved around corners so I wouldn't tumble out of the car. Just like the rioters, I wanted to attack something, too. I gave my own whooping war cry as we sped toward the Star Center, pumping my fists in the air and feeling like Sadie, I shouted, "Watch out, motherfuckers. Here we come!"

— CHAPTER —
45

The streetlights on Sunset Boulevard were dark, casting everything in shadows. The Star Center appeared in the darkness as we grew closer—a hulking, looming silhouette with jagged turrets jutting into the night sky. The Cadillac glided into a spot near the entrance to the driveway, my pulse thumping almost painfully in my throat as I slid down into the backseat from my perch.

This was it.

I leaned forward and mimed to Danny, showing him the security cameras bolted onto palm trees. Every once in a while, little red lights on them blinked. Danny nodded solemnly before hopping out of the car and running back to the caravan of classic cars behind us.

Danny returned with two guys from Carlos's crew. With barely audible pops they extinguished the two blinking red lights with their long guns.

"Check it out," Taj whispered into my ear. "These must not be small time gangbangers. Those rifles have night scopes and silencers. Cool."

With their backs to the ivy-covered walls, the two boys crept up the driveway, faces pressed to their rifles. They made their way up and around a corner until their dark figures disappeared. Carlos and Sadie appeared at my side.

"Recon, baby," Sadie said in a low whisper. "They're scoping out what's up." She turned to Danny. "Can you stay here, ready to go? We're going to need a getaway if the shit hits the fan."

Danny turned around. Every one of the gangster's cars behind him had a driver waiting at the ready. "Sure thing, sister," he said. "I'm your getaway man." He settled back into his seat and took a long swig of tequila before handing the bottle to me.

A low whistle sent the rest of Carlos's gang scrambling up the driveway. Sadie grabbed my arm and pulled. "Let's go."

I tossed the bottle to Danny. Our footsteps seemed too loud on the cobblestone driveway. At the entrance to the lobby, two of the center's security goons lay on either side of the door, motionless. I raced up the stairs and caught up to Sadie, who was inside the lobby behind the receptionist desk tearing through a stack of papers, a small flashlight in her mouth.

I felt sick. "Are they dead?" I asked, gesturing to the two men on the sidewalk outside.

She didn't bother taking the flashlight out of her mouth to answer, making her sound like she was underwater. "Nope. Just pistol-whipped into a brief pavement nap. They'll be fine."

She kept flipping through the papers, throwing them on the floor. "Here we go." She had her finger on one page. "Top floor, baby."

Not surprisingly, Rex Walker lived in the penthouse suite. Sadie rummaged around in a drawer, tossed me an elevator access key, and jerked her head toward the elevator as a few streetlights flickered back to life.

Taj was at the elevator door, waiting, holding it open. I ran inside with him as Sadie leaped over the receptionist desk, her long blond hair flying behind her. At that moment, power was restored to the building and the lobby's chandeliers turned on, illuminating the scene before me. Before, in the dark, I hadn't noticed Sadie was dressed in fatigues and boots. Like a guerilla warrior. She turned and winked at me just as a volley of gunfire erupted, shattering the glass front doors of the center and sending me cringing into the corner.

Sadie crumpled. She'd been hit.

"Sadie!" I shouted, horrified.

I scrambled on all fours toward her, but at the last second, Taj yanked me back into the elevator. Sadie crawled behind the desk. When she sat up, blood was seeping through her pant leg near the knee. She scooted most of her body behind the receptionist desk and pulled a gun out of her waistband, checking the ammo. She met my eyes, pointed up, and mouthed, "Go. Now!"

"They shot Sadie!" I screamed to Taj as the elevator doors slid shut.

"She'll be okay," Taj said. "She's one tough chick. And besides, Carlos's gang is not going to let anything happen to her."

"Okay. Okay. Okay. You're probably right." I was repeating myself and distraught. I caught a glance of myself in the elevator mirror. My eyes were wide. I had a smudge of something on my cheek. My hair, half out of its ponytail, swung madly around my face as I paced. I looked like a crazy lady.

As we grew closer to the penthouse, Taj and I each took a spot pressed against opposite walls. When the elevator came to a halt, I braced myself. It seemed like an eternity before the doors slid open. The smell of a cigar reached me right before I saw the giant white mane of hair.

Dean Thomas Kozlak.

Smiling around the cigar in his mouth. I frantically punched the door close button, but it was too late. Two men who had been standing behind Kozlak had already grabbed Taj despite his cursing and punching. In the chaos, an arm wrapped like a steel band around my chest. A cloth pressed to my mouth and my vision began to fade.

—CHAPTER—
46

The view before me was spectacular. A wall of windows revealed a distant fairy village sprinkled with colored lights. The City of Angels was below me in all its glory. But I didn't want to keep my eyes open long enough to take it all in. My entire body was warm and cozy like I was wrapped in a fur blanket and plopped in front of a roaring fire on a cold day. My limbs tingled pleasantly and a wave of pleasure lolled through me as I licked my dry lips. In the back of my mind a nagging thought told me that I shouldn't be feeling this way. Something was wrong, but I didn't know what it was.

With blurry eyes I scanned the massive room lit softly by ornate chandeliers and filled with art and massive floral arrangements. My memory was hazy. Where was I again? Why did my arms hurt? My wrists were bound to the thick wooden arms of the chair I was in.

Fragments of what happened started floating back. "Taj!" I jerked but couldn't move. My ankles must be bound as well. I swiveled my head. The movement made me nauseous.

Taj was tied to a chair beside mine. His head slumped onto his chest. Strangely, I didn't care. It was fine. Taj was supposed to be tied up in this dream, too. Something fluttered across my memory. *No, that's not right. This isn't a dream. But what is it? We're not supposed to be tied up.* Then, movement across the vast expanse of the room shifted my gaze.

In the corner, a man sitting in a large armchair crossed his legs. He shook his head and light from the chandeliers glanced off his silver-framed glasses. For some reason it seemed perfectly natural for him to be sitting in the penthouse of the Star Center.

"Hey, Amir." My voice echoed as if it were going down a long tunnel. Cool. I closed my eyes and repeated it, "Amir, Amir, Amir," liking the sound it made.

Something flickered across my brain. He hadn't moved or said anything. I couldn't see his eyes from across the room, only the glint of light reflecting off his glasses.

"Amir?"

He remained silent, sitting casually with one pressed gray trouser leg crossed over the other. He started swinging his foot, making a tsking noise.

Finally, he spoke. "I told you to leave it well enough alone."

"What?" No, I wasn't dreaming. We were at The Church of the Evermore Enlightened Star Center. In the penthouse. Had I been drugged? What was Amir doing here?

"Nikki...you spoiled Americans think life is all a big game," he said in a scolding manner, and gave a big sigh, unfolding his legs and pushing up from the chair. "I warned you."

As his words sunk in, I felt a sudden icy chill in my core. It was all coming back. What was he doing here? And why was I tied up? The skin on my face and arms began to tingle and my heart raced. Was I hallucinating? I must have been given something. Again. Oh God, after all this did somebody shoot me up with heroin? I glanced down at my bare arms. No needle marks. Looking back at Amir, I felt a wave of sadness.

"I thought we were friends." My voice sounded funny to me. "Don't you like me?" I sounded whiny and childish, but I felt like a child right then. Was there any adult on this planet I could trust?

"Sometimes you have to sacrifice for the greater good. These people," he gestured around the room, "they are extremely valuable to our cause."

"Your cause?" I could feel my forehead scrunching.

"Haven't you been listening? You Americans are so sheltered, so egocentric, so greedy, and so blind to the fate of others in this world. You are the most selfish country on this planet." He stood and even in my foggy state I could tell his growing anger was dangerous. "You think life is all about fun. You think that you matter? You don't matter."

He began pacing and rambling as if I weren't even there. I kept trying to listen and plan a way to escape but I was so very tired. It took all my effort not to close my eyes.

"It is true that these people, this group that calls itself a church," he said with a sneer, "are worse than nothing. But they are useful. I give them what they want. They give me what I want. They wanted the tape. I gave them the tape. They wanted you. I gave them you.

"They provide money to help my people who are oppressed. You gave me the idea to introduce myself to them. When they learned you had the tape and that I knew where you were, they were more than happy to help with my cause. You didn't heed their warnings. It is your own fault, not mine. You will die because of that."

Inside, I knew he was right. I'd known since the day they lowered my mother's casket into the ground that my stay on this earth was limited. I was destined to die young like she did. Like my sister did. I deserved to die. I had blood on my hands.

But I remembered why I was there. Rain. I struggled against the restraints.

"Where is she? Where is Rain?" A little bit of spit flew out of my mouth as I said it.

"She is not here," Amir said. "Anymore."

I was right. Rain *had* been here.

"Where is she now?" I glared at him.

He paused, hands behind his back, looking out the floor-to-ceiling windows at the lights of the city spread out before him. "You will be there soon." Amir moved on, pacing the polished marble floor. "You are so very, very naïve. You do not realize that your life, one single life, is inconsequential in the greater scheme. My life, too, is worth nothing. That is why I will gladly give it to improve the lot of my people. What is one life compared to hundreds, thousands if you count the generations of children and grandchildren who will have a better life because of our sacrifices?"

My vision cleared a bit. Maybe I hadn't been given heroin like I feared. It was something else. I tried to move my legs but it was as if the signal just wasn't reaching them. They remained still. I tried to talk logic to a crazy man, hoping he would respond. "What happens now?"

"In a few minutes, I take you to the beach house. You will die there, but not before Mr. Kozlak sees you again. He has big plans for you."

I knew all about Kozlak's plans. Bastard.

I nodded toward Taj.

"He will die," Amir said. "He is no use to them."

I heard a moan. Taj was waking up. "Let him go," I said, jutting my chin at Taj. "He knows nothing. If you let him go, I won't fight. I'll come along willingly. Just let him go."

Amir gave me an odd look, his eyebrows scrunched together, and shook his head. I needed to up the ante. What did I have that he would want? The tape.

"If you let him go, I'll tell you where the copy of that videotape is."

He made another tsking noise. "No, but you forget. You gave me the only copy."

In the Rodney King videotape, the man had taken it to the TV reporters. "I wasn't sure I could trust you so I made a copy. It's hidden in a safe place, but if I disappear, it will be mailed to the TV station. I left those directions. If I don't come home tonight, it goes to the anchor at the news station."

He paused, tilting his head and squinting at me.

I wasn't sure he believed me, but I figured he was afraid to take the chance that I was telling the truth. "If you don't hurt him, I will walk out of here without fighting." I paused for a second. "But if he gets hurt, I promise you, I will fight you to the death. I will *never* tell you where the other copy is and you will show up with my dead body at the beach house. I don't think that is what you want, is it? I don't think your new friends would be very happy if that happened."

Amir's expression didn't change as he walked over to me. He stood right above me holding a big knife. Distantly, I noted that the blade matched his silver hair color. My blood was pounding in my ears and I was hyperventilating, but he merely slid the knife between my wrist and chair and cut me free. He kneeled down and did the same to my ankles. With his bare neck bent over at a vulnerable angle, I knew somewhere inside that this was my chance to strike. I could hit him and maybe hurt him enough to escape. Maybe I could bite his neck? As my mind mulled over this option in slow motion, I also knew I could barely lift my arm. There was no way I could strike him. My entire body felt mushy and weak.

Amir tied my hands behind my back and pulled me to my feet. He led me over to the elevator, around the corner from Taj, and shoved me into a velvet chair. My legs were wobbly and not following directions well.

Around the corner, Taj came to, shouting in a hoarse voice, "Nikki?"

I jumped at hearing his voice. Amir picked up a phone from an end table and spoke into it. "We're ready."

— CHAPTER —
47

I kicked the lid of the trunk with my boots, but the sound of shouting, gunshots, and breaking glass outside drowned the noise out. As soon as the trunk lid had slammed down, engulfing us in darkness, I'd felt a surge of energy brought on by pure fear and adrenaline. The wooly feeling in my head was gone.

The car bumped and lurched, sending me flying up to smack the lid. We must have just left the parking garage and were on the street outside the star mansion. I was flung sideways as the car squealed around a corner. I was lying on something slippery that stuck to my bare legs. Plastic? I bumped into Taj's body as the car swung around a corner.

He rolled up against me, his face pressed against mine. He kept moving his Duct-taped mouth against mine, mumbling. In a flash of understanding, I felt around with my mouth and grabbed a corner of the tape with my teeth and yanked on it. Nothing. I tried again. No luck. I worked down to the other corner and it was a bit looser. I used my teeth to gnaw at the edge of the tape until I got a grip and was able to yank the whole thing back with a loud rip. "Thank God," Taj said. I collapsed from the effort. He pressed his mouth against mine. This time in a long kiss before drawing away.

"Let's hold that thought," he said. "We've got to figure out how to get out of here. Scoot over and bring your hands up to my mouth. I'm going to try to work on the knot."

The calm in his voice quelled the terror and panic surging through me. The trunk was dark and cramped and I scraped my cheek on a piece of something sharp as we both tried to maneuver in a position where Taj's head was down by my hands behind my back. I felt the rope around my wrists tightening and could feel Taj's warm breath on my hands as his teeth worked on the knot. The ride was making me nauseous. I gulped and concentrated on not throwing up since rolling around in a big pile of puke would not help us. A bump and sudden screeching stop sent us tumbling toward the front of the car. I accidentally bit my lip and tasted blood.

"You okay?" Taj asked. He was still tugging on the rope around my wrists. Within seconds, I had my right hand free and a loose wad of rope around my left hand. I felt around for a latch to undo the trunk lid but only managed to slice my finger on a sharp piece of metal.

"Give me your hands!" But Taj had already scrunched around so I could get at him and I managed to untie his knots.

With our hands free, we both started kicking at the taillights, loosening one panel and putting out one light. Maybe Amir would get pulled over by a police car and we'd make such a racket the cop would hear us. Then, I remembered that with the rioters taking over the city, a burnt out taillight would be the last thing the cops were worried about.

At least we weren't tied up. That meant when the trunk opened we would come up fighting. But whatever they had drugged me with, combined with the exertion of the last few minutes, had zapped all of my energy.

"We need to make a plan," I said, resting my head on Taj's shoulder. "But I'm so sleepy."

"It's the drugs they gave us." Taj ran his fingers down my arm and it took all my concentration not to drift off. The darkness, combined with the lethargy that swept over me, lulled me into complacency and apathy. All I wanted to do was close my eyes. That short burst of energy when we pulled out of the Star Center had wiped me out. I felt exhausted. And defeated. I still hadn't found Rain. I'd failed.

"It's going to be okay."

"No. It's not. If she's dead, it's my fault."

"What are you talking about?"

He sounded baffled.

"If Rain's dead, it's my fault," I said it more slowly this time. "Just like my mother." I said the second part so quietly I didn't think he'd heard me.

But he had.

The thudding of my heart seemed suddenly very loud.

"Nikki, as soon as all this is over, we need to talk about your mother."

I didn't answer.

"Okay?"

"Okay."

Right now we needed to focus on getting out of here alive. We needed a plan.

Amir didn't know we had untied ourselves, so the only thing we really had going for us was the element of surprise. In the darkness of the trunk, we decided that because Kozlak apparently had "plans" for me before I died, Amir would be less likely to kill me. But as soon as they found out there really wasn't another copy of the tape, Taj would be dead. I wouldn't be able to bluff about the copy much longer.

We decided that when the trunk opened, I needed to distract or delay Amir long enough for Taj to escape and get help from a neighbor or passerby. Our plan was pretty rudimentary and involved me tackling Amir long enough for Taj to run away.

The car slowed to a stop. Go time.

—CHAPTER—
48

I jumped at the squawk of the trunk lid opening. I blinked in the dim light. Instead of Amir, a man with a Dudley Do-Right chin looked down on us. Rex Walker. Up close. Pockmarked skin the camera hid. Surprised to see him instead of Amir, I momentarily froze.

"You're right. She is perfect," he said to someone over his shoulder. "I don't need him, though. Thought you were going to get rid of him."

When Walker turned his head for a second, Taj came up swinging, clocking Walker enough to send him off balance. Meanwhile, I scrambled out of the trunk on cramped and weak legs and jumped on Walker, clawing and scratching. Out of the corner of my eye I saw Taj as a blurry figure disappearing into the darkness. A gun went off, echoing in the garage, and several people swore loudly. Walker tossed me off of him and I turned, heart leaping into my throat, in time to see Taj slipping through a hedge. I closed my eyes, hoping he hadn't been hit.

Walker and Amir loped after Taj's figure shouting and swearing. I started to follow when something cold pressed into the small of my back and Kozlak drawled, "I don't think you want to do that."

My eyes darted around frantically for an escape route. We were in a spotless three-car garage with polished black painted concrete floors. Besides Amir's car it contained a big black Jeep with fog lights on its roll bar, the same car that had followed me down the beach. And through the open garage door I could see it in the driveway—another car I knew well. The big black one.

This was not the driveway Chad and I had pulled up to when we visited. But this must be Kozlak's house. That was his Jeep. This garage must be on the lower level, by the room Danny and I'd hid in. A secret entrance.

"All this nonsense could've been avoided if you'd have agreed to star in our little film a few months ago," Kozlak said, chomping on his cigar. He was dressed in a white suit with a white silk scarf looped around his neck like he'd just come from a formal dinner. "Damn good thing your Iranian buddy gave us back that tape. Not sure how you managed to get ahold of that." He leaned over and trailed a chubby finger down my cheek. My palm connected with his grizzly cheek with a slap. My fingers tingled and vibrated from the impact. Kozlak immediately gripped my hand in his, his fingernails digging into my palm.

"Not very ladylike." His eyes bored into mine for a few seconds. My heart was racing and I was panting. Then, just as abruptly, he shoved me away. My back smacked into the trunk and I winced. He held up the gun and casually shoved it into my mouth, so far that I gagged. A dirty, metallic taste filled my mouth. Sweat dripped from my temple.

"Don't. Ever. Do. That. Again." His eyes bore into mine.

Walker returned, panting. "Lost him, chief."

Kozlak pulled the gun out of my mouth and shoved me toward Walker. "She gives you any trouble, tell her I'm going to shoot her little friend, Rain. That should keep her in line."

"Where is she?" I asked as I careened into Walker's chest and jerked back, repulsed. Walker said something I couldn't hear.

"Don't worry," Kozlak said to Walker. "You get Rain first. I keep my promises."

"Don't hurt her," I said. My throat hurt from where the gun had scraped my tonsils.

"Nobody will touch my angel," Walker said.

My face scrunched up. What the hell was he talking about?

Kozlak turned to me. "When your little Iranian buddy forked over the tape, he also told me where Rain was. Of course, as soon as I confronted him, old Rex here had no problem giving up the ghost, fessed up to finding Rain and keeping her at his penthouse. And I have to give him credit for finding her. He knew she'd end up back downtown near Union Station where I found her. I didn't think she'd be so stupid. But Rex did. He knew. But he wants to help now. Don't you? Otherwise, Rex, I'm afraid I can't use you in my little side project films anymore."

Walker fidgeted. Kozlak slapped him on the back.

"No worries. All is forgiven," Kozlak said. "Rex is being a good boy so he gets his reward—making a little movie he can have as a keepsake."

I was filled with fury. My jaw clenched and I balled my hands into fists. It took all my self-control not to plant my steel-toed boot in Kozlak's crotch.

Walker and Kozlak were oblivious to my rage.

I sighed with relief when Amir emerged from the bushes. Alone. Taj must have escaped. For once, the Iranian man's silver hair was mussy and his tie was off center.

"He headed for the beach," Amir said.

"Go find him." Kozlak tossed a set of keys.

Amir leaped into the Jeep but then leaned out to speak to Kozlak—white head close to the silver one. I couldn't hear what they were saying over the sound of the Jeep's engine.

Amir peeled out of the garage. A finger on my chin lifted my face to meet Kozlak's dangerously glittering eyes. He said through gritted teeth, "Where's the copy of the tape?"

I shrugged. His palm raised and came at me in slow motion. The sting of the slap seemed to echo in my mind as my cheek tingled and vibrated. I laughed incoherently. Right back where I started—getting slapped at Kozlak's house.

Pull yourself together. I reminded myself that my goal was to stay alive until I found Rain. This time I wouldn't run away. This time I would stand my ground and fight. There was another big difference this time. This time I wasn't alone in the world. I had something, actually someone, worth fighting for beside myself.

While Walker held my arms behind me, Kozlak took out a knife and ran his finger along the blade. "Tell me where the tape is. I'm going to wait here while I send someone to retrieve it. If they can't find it. You die. Right here. Right now."

He pressed the blade against my neck. I swallowed hard. I felt a tiny prick.

"Amir has the only copy. I lied." The pressure on my neck eased. He brought the knife to his face and licked a small drop of blood from the blade. He stared as if daring me to crack and confess something more.

I met his gaze without blinking. "I swear. You have to believe me. It was a bluff. I wouldn't even know where or how to go to make a copy of it anyway. How would I know how to do that stuff?" It was the truth and Kozlak knew it.

Kozlak looked at me for a long moment and then laughed.

"Walker, take her to the set. I'll meet you there. I need to clean up and change." The director disappeared through a door in the garage, toward the back.

"Come on, sugar," Walker said, and jutted his cartoonish chin toward the door where Kozlak had disappeared. Up close I could see the deadness of Walker's eyes. Instead of reflecting the fluorescent lights in the garage, his eyes were dark pits that seemed to suck in all the light like black holes. His gravelly voice was sexy to ninety percent of the female population in the world, but I flinched at the sound and shrunk away from his extended hand. He was a pervert and a murderer.

When I jerked away from him, he said calmly, "Suit yourself, darling."

I stood stock-still. "Where's Rain?"

"She's safe." He gestured toward the door. "Ladies first."

Walker turned to me and raised his hand. I braced myself, anticipating the sting of another slap, but instead, I felt the back of his hand caressing my cheek.

"I'll take you to her, sugar. She's in a…well, let's just call it…a holding pen."

"Holding pen for what?" I spat out.

"You're both going to star in my new movie."

"What?" I asked, my eyes darting around ready to run.

"The church has put the smack down on some of my…more controversial desires. See, I didn't mean to kill that girl. That one in the tape you had. I was planning on letting go of her neck—eventually. But in my excitement, I got a little carried away. But then…oh my God. The rush. It is even better than sex, little princess. The power to take someone's life. To watch their essence extinguished in their eyes. There is no other high like it. Now I know. Now I know why people kill. And then do it again."

His eyes had grown glassy and it was almost as if he forgot I was there. Then he came back to me, gently placing his hand on my shoulder and bending down so I could feel his warm breath.

"But that was a mistake. An accident. It has to have been done on purpose. To achieve the power, you must sacrifice the child in a meaningful way. And the child must be pure."

The brochure the masked men gave me said that some church members believed this was the way to unlimited power.

"My plan was to wait until the summer solstice. That seemed the most auspicious day, but then when the riots started, I realized it was a sign. It must be done on the third day of the riots. The number three is very important in our world, did you know that, my sweet? Well, the third day is today. We only have a few hours left."

He looped his arm through mine, like he was escorting me to my seat at an awards show. I walked, dragging my feet, but just a little. I needed Walker to take me to Rain. The sooner I found Rain, the sooner we could get out of here.

We stepped through the door into a small hallway that contained an elevator and another door at the far end. Walker stopped in front of the elevator and punched the button. I didn't know if we were going up or down.

The other door opened and Kozlak peeked his white mane in. Beyond the door I could see that it was the room near the closet the maid had hidden us in. Not far away was another door to the beach.

"We'll get started as soon as the camera guy gets here," Kozlak said gruffly to Walker around the cigar he was chomping on. Camera guy. Chad. He turned to me. "He'll be happy to see you. You've been a loose end for much too long."

"Why Rain?"

"I saw her one day here, at Dean's house," Walker said. "She looked so innocent and helpless. I knew she was the one."

We were standing in the narrow hallway in front of the elevator doors. He had yet to push the button, caught up in talking about Rain. Darting a glance at the direction Kozlak had gone, I tried to keep Rex Walker talking.

"Kozlak said you knew she'd go back to Union Station, so why didn't you just grab her that first time you saw her downtown?"

"That's not how it works." He ran his fingers through his hair and gave me an exasperated look as if I was supposed to know all of this. "For the ultimate power, she has to willingly sacrifice herself. She had to want to go with me. I courted her until she felt the same way as me."

"She didn't want to go with you." Again, I glanced at the door. That was my escape path. The door to the beach. But first to get Rain.

"You know who I am?" he asked, squinting, and gave a small laugh. "Well, of course you do. So you know that I can pretty much have any woman I want, right?"

I refused to answer.

"Well, let me tell you, that gets old fast. When you can sleep with the most dazzling women in the world you can't help but start to get bored a little. They've seen and done it all. They all start to blend into one. But young women on the verge of adulthood? It's different every time. It's fresh."

"It's rape," I spit out, glaring at him.

He shrugged. "I am, above all else, a gentleman. I don't need to force them. I don't need to even ask. They want my love."

I glared, thinking of the girl tied up in the video.

"Then why do you need to tie them up?"

He swiveled his head toward me.

"It enhances our pleasure. The game we are playing. In essence, it is all acting, a role. They are the headlining act. For once in their life, they are the stars of the show. The girls I meet are the ones nobody loves. Nobody cares if they live or die until I come into their lives. I am doing them the greatest favor anyone has ever done. I give them more than they ever dreamed." He paused. "I give them me—a fantasy, a dream come true. I dress them in designer clothes, put them in my penthouse bedrooms fit for princesses, feed them gourmet meals delivered from Spago.

"And the price? Not much. Just to satisfy my desires, which they long for as well. Most of them end up begging me. They get down on their hands and knees and beg me to let them stay. But I can't keep all of them. I mean, my God, where would I put them? But Rain, now she is different. You see, sugar, unlike the other girls, Rain has never been with a man. I found her first. And she loves me. Really, truly loves me. Her love is just like her—pure and innocent and genuine. That's why her sacrifice will bring me the ultimate power I seek."

"But she didn't go willingly," I said. "You had to force her. That's not love."

"No," Walker said, his eyebrows drawing together in the first sign of emotion I'd seen. "No, no, that's not right at all. I didn't force her. I'm afraid you are mistaken. She wanted to be with me." He pressed the button, summoning the elevator.

"That's bullshit," I said. "You forced her into the car. I know. I saw."

A thin vein popped on his forehead and his jaw clenched. For a second, I thought he was losing his temper, but then he took a deep breath and looked at me with a gleam of triumph in his eyes. "She loves me. That's the truth. She wanted to come with me. She was just trying to play hard to get, but she loves me."

I felt sick because it was true. Even if she didn't go with him willingly, I thought she'd been protecting Walker all this time because she thought she loved him. But at least he hadn't raped her. Yet. My hands clenched into fists and my eyes narrowed.

"You bastard." It took all my self-control not to throw myself at him and claw his eyes out. There would be time for that later, once Rain was here before me, safe. I needed to see Rain first.

—CHAPTER—
50

The elevator doors slid open. The room beyond was dark. As soon as we stepped into the room, a flood of automatic lights switched on. It was the room used in the movie with the dead girl. The room was dominated by a giant bed placed center stage, resting several feet off the ground on a circle platform. Cameras on wires hung from the ceilings. Leather straps were attached to each corner of the bed and a leather contraption hung above it. On a nearby brick wall, several chains were bolted to the wall at head level. On the other side of the short, thick chains were restraints—thick metal bands that went around someone's neck, some medieval torture device.

As I took it all in, my hand flew to my mouth. Before I had time to react, Walker turned and, with a force that surprised me after his previous gentleness, pulled me over to one of the neckbands. When I fought, he slammed the back of my head into the brick wall, stunning me long enough to fasten the cold metal around my neck, sticking the key to it in his pocket. The click of it closing sounded like a death knell.

"Sorry, darling, I know that wasn't gentlemanly, but I can't afford to have you escape. Not now. This will keep you out of my hair, little princess, until we're ready for your debut. You'll have to excuse me. I'm anxious to see Rain."

He was off his rocker. I'd read that The Church of the Evermore Enlightened didn't believe in psychiatric treatment or drugs. And this guy needed both. How long had this been going on? I suspected the church had been protecting him for a long time. Walker stepped over to the only other door in the room and slid back a large metal bolt. I arched my neck and pulled the chain connecting my torture device to the wall. But I couldn't see inside the door.

"Rain," I shouted as the door slowly swung shut. The muffled sound of voices filtered through the thick door. I strained to hear if it was Rain but there was only the sound of a thump. Then silence.

After a few seconds, the motion-activated lights went out, leaving me shivering in the dark. I kicked out my feet and arms to trigger the lights, but I must not have been standing in the right place. It stayed dark. I pried at the metal band around my neck until my fingernails broke and bled, plunging me back into the memory of my nightmare where I tore my nails to the quick trying to climb a brick wall. Just like in that dream, I wasn't going anywhere. I knew then I was going to die.

A clicking sound made me freeze. It was the elevator. The door whooshed open with a quiet hiss. Then nothing. No sound. It was still dark.

I felt a chill run through my body as I strained to see in the darkness. The automatic lights flickered on, momentarily blinding me. I blinked and focused.

It was Ernie. Holding a gun pointed right at me. His eyes met mine and his hand with the gun dropped to his side. He ran over. I blinked, my face scrunched in a frown. I shrank away from him. I started to scream, but he clamped his hand over my mouth. What was the drunken cop doing here? Was he in on it with Amir? No scenario I could imagine made sense.

The fingers on his other hand felt around the edge of the medieval style restraint around my neck. He drew back. His eyes were not blood shot but clear and alert and intense.

"I'm going to take my hand away now. Please don't scream. I'm on your side. You have to trust me. Okay?"

I paused for a second, then slowly shook my head back and forth, staring right into his eyes. No. Why should I believe him? Every other adult in my life had let me down. Why would he be any different? His eyes looked sad and he pressed his lips tightly together, nodding. "You're right. I'm a fuck up. I know it. Everyone knows it. But I'm trying to make things right. I swear it. Let me help you."

For a few seconds we stared at one another. Against all odds the drunken cop, with his thinning hair and bushy moustache and red nose, wanted to help me.

"Okay?"

I nodded warily. He removed his hand.

"Walker. In there." I nodded toward the door. "He's got the keys."

Ernie crept over to the door, gun drawn. Slowly, he turned the knob. With a loud crack, he burst into the room. Straining my neck against the metal, I tried to see into the room but the door swung shut.

Within seconds, Ernie raced back into the room with a jingling sound and unlocked the band around my neck. The elevator door made a small noise. His eyes darted around the room and he pushed me, sending me sprawling toward the door he had just come from. "Go now."

"No way." I had seen Walker go in there. I don't know how Ernie got the keys from him. I hadn't heard sounds of a struggle. Maybe it was a trick. It was irrational but in my mind that door opened up onto the world of my nightmares—endless passageways leading to dead-ends where a faceless evil waited to wrap its dead fingers around me. I couldn't shake the belief that death waited for me in that room. I'd rather die here in the light.

"I'm not going in there. I'm not." My voice was trembling and my words barely coherent.

I started scrambling backward on my hands and knees toward the elevator. Ernie crouched down and looked in my eyes.

"Trust me."

That word again. I closed my eyes. I wanted to trust him. I wanted to believe that an adult would help me, not hurt me. I wanted to trust someone enough to walk into a room where I was certain death waited for me. My mind was screaming to run away. *Danger. Don't believe him. Danger! Go in that room and you will die. Don't trust him. Don't trust anybody.*

But maybe it was time to listen to my heart instead of my head. And he did unchain me from this torture device. I decided.

I would do it. I would trust him.

Springing to my feet, I raced for the door, ducking inside and slamming it shut right before the elevator doors slid open. There was no lock on the inside of the door. I was afraid to look around me. Where was Walker?

Slowly, I turned, my eyes widening in surprise. Before me, in a room done up all in pastels with a giant canopy bed filled with stuffed animals, sat Rain. Huddled in a corner. Even paler than I remembered. Dirty blond hair stringy and longer. Pink streaks gone. Holding a bloody piece of wood in her hands. Staring at Rex Walker.

He was face down on the ground. Blood billowed out around his body. Then, I noticed that the path of blood led to Rain. I took it all in within seconds. Behind me, in the room I had just left, a series of gunshots made my blood run cold. I had to block this doorway, keep us safe. I leaned over and pushed and pulled, shoving a big bureau in front of the door before I leaned against the dresser, breathing heavily. I wanted to run to Rain, but she wasn't there. Not in any way besides physically. Her eyes never flickered my way. But she was alive. There were more shouts and gunshots on the other side of the door. Then nothing.

The sound of the doorknob turning made me gasp and I leaped across the room and pressed my body as hard as I could against the dresser blocking the door. I dug in my boots and put my weight into it until I heard the footsteps retreating.

—CHAPTER—
51

It was unearthly quiet outside the door. I waited. I counted to fifty. Then to one hundred before I turned to Rain. She hadn't moved. I crawled over to her. She was covered in blood. One hand clutched her ripped blouse to her chest.

"Rain? It's me. Are you hurt?"

She swiveled her head toward me. "Nikki?"

I felt relief flood through me. "Yes. Can you stand up? We need to get you out of here."

"He said he loved me. He told me if I didn't go with him that you would get hurt. But then he brought me back here… to this house." She choked on a sob. "He…he tried to…he was going to…" She closed her eyes.

I gently took the jagged piece of wood out of her hands. Its painted pink edge was dark with blood. She must have broken it off of a piece of the furniture. I pulled her to her feet. She only moved when I directed her. I had her sit on the chair near the door, facing away from Walker's body while I pushed the dresser out of the way. Without the big rush of adrenaline I had when I came into the room, it took longer to shove it aside.

I pressed my ear to the door. Nothing. Slowly, I cracked it open and the lights flickered on. The movie set room with the giant bed seemed empty. I led Rain, holding her hand and keeping her body behind mine. I headed toward the elevator but stopped when I saw a pair of legs sticking out from the other side of the big bed. Instinctively, I shielded Rain's eyes and put my finger to my lips.

Creeping around the edge of the giant bed, I saw that it was Ernie. Face down. A puddle of blood surrounded his head. My hand flew to my mouth. I ran over to Ernie to see if I could feel a pulse. There was nothing. I sank to the ground, holding Rain behind me.

Then I noticed him. It was Amir. Standing in an alcove I hadn't seen. Holding a gun by his side. Fear trickled down my scalp. There was no place to go.

I shoved Rain further behind me.

"You killed him. You bastard." My eyes never left his.

Amir's face darkened with anger. "He was trying to destroy me and everything I'd worked toward. The director will be here any minute. He will know why I had to kill him. And why when we find your boyfriend, we will kill him, too."

I closed my eyes for a second with relief. Taj had escaped.

Amir, lost in his anger at Ernie still, seemed to be talking to himself, reassuring himself that he wouldn't be in trouble for killing Ernie. He was pretty much ignoring me, the gun hanging in his hand at his side. As if I were no threat whatsoever. That was when it struck me. He didn't consider me a threat. At all. This was my only advantage.

I could use Amir's own philosophy against him. He had told me that Ernie's mistake with the gang members was thinking he was invincible. That Ernie's sense of power was his Achilles heel. And Amir warned me to never "underestimate the little guy."

Now I was the little guy. I'd always had been, of course, but now Amir was the big guy, and he had underestimated me.

As Amir paced, talking about what a terrible man Ernie was trying to ruin his "cause," I scooted closer to Ernie's pant leg. I had seen something black near his ankle. A gun? Rain was nearly comatose, huddled with her arms wrapped around her knees. Her head down in her lap, staring at nothing.

Thinking of Ernie brought a thick sob to my throat. I tried not to look at his face, but scooted closer to his body. It *was* a gun strapped to his ankle.

I couldn't grab it without Amir seeing. I had to distract him.

"Amir?"

He stopped pacing and stared at me, as if just realizing I was in the room with him.

"I think Rex Walker is hurt. He's in that room over there. He was bleeding and moaning. He said something about transferring funds to some account or something…"

Amir cocked his head for a minute, stomped over to the door, and flung it open. In an instant I had grabbed Ernie's gun out of the ankle strap and yanked Rain to her feet. We were at the elevator and I had jabbed the call button when Amir reappeared. His hand holding the gun was shaking. Pointed right at me.

"You cannot leave," he said, eyes narrowed when he noticed the gun in my hand.

When the elevator door slid open behind me, I pushed Rain behind me, letting the doors close with Rain inside.

In one smooth movement I clicked the safety off the gun like Taj had showed me on the rooftop. I stretched out my arms, now both hands clutching the gun in front of me. Seeing this, Amir startled me by laughing.

"You? You shoot me? You are a child. A naïve, silly child. I told you already." He raised his gun up higher, toward my face instead of my chest. "You are the innocent sacrifice made to achieve our goals. Today you will die for the greater good. Today you will die for my people. Today—"

The retort of the gun sent me tumbling back off balance against the elevator doors. My mouth involuntarily dropped open as a wide crimson stain spread across Amir's chest and a small bubble of blood formed at his mouth as he tried to finish his sentence. He made a motion moving toward me and I reached behind me, frantically punching the elevator call button until it opened behind me. I stepped backward into the elevator, not taking my eyes off Amir, who had crumpled to his knees, his mouth wide open, looking at me in astonishment.

"Today...is not my day to die," I said as the elevator doors slid shut.

I hit the down button and slumped to the floor.

My heart seemed to stop and I burst into what was a combination of laughing and crying. *I must be in shock.* I stared glassily in front of me, seeing nothing, feeling nothing except an icy pit in my stomach and hearing my heartbeat pounding in my ears.

The scene before me came into focus. Rain stared at me as if only now realizing I was there. "Nikki?" She crawled into my lap and I held her close, stroking her hair. Staring at nothing. The elevator door slid open and lights and sound greeted us. People running and yelling and the sound of sirens and static from radios. But I couldn't even force my head to look up. Someone was shaking my shoulder, kneeling down and peering into my face. Somewhere inside, I registered that the person was wearing a police officer's uniform. A radio clipped to his shoulder emitted some static.

"He's dead..." I grabbed his collar and spoke so quietly he had to lean in to hear me. "They both are. Dead."

He leaned into his shoulder and said, "Code four here. We've got two DOAs. Send in EMT ASAP."

"Are you hurt?"

I stared straight ahead.

— CHAPTER —
52

Blindingly bright red and blue lights flashed and a cacophony of screeching sirens greeted us in the driveway. A tall female officer led Rain and me past an army of rushing police officers with guns drawn and white-shirted ambulance drivers hauling what looked like small suitcases and stretchers.

In a flurry of motion, Rain was swooped away by a medic. When I realized what was happening, I made a lunge for her, but the lady police officer grabbed me. "She'll be fine. You'll see her in a sec."

The officer led me to the back of an ambulance. I looked wildly over my shoulder, trying to see where Rain went.

"Where's my friend?"

"It's okay," the police officer said, gently taking my elbow. "Let's have the EMT guys look at you first. They're checking out your friend, too." I relaxed a little. Rain wasn't really hurt. It was Walker's blood. The medics began asking me questions. After a few moments, one of them said, "Well, physically she's fine."

My eyes widened at the sight of a familiar figure emerging from the mass of people. It was Taj. I ran to meet him, ignoring the medic's protests. When I reached Taj, I choked back a sob that sprung from a mixture of relief and sorrow. Within seconds, I was wrapped tightly in his arms. "They just took Rain away in an ambulance," he said into my ear.

I struggled to free myself but he held me back.

"It's too late," he said. "The ambulance is gone. I think she's fine, just doped up on something and they want to keep her overnight for observation."

"We should've gone with her."

But it was too late.

After the paramedics gave me the all clear, a police officer came up to me and gently touched my arm.

"Can I give you two a ride home?"

I eyed him suspiciously. His eyes were red like he'd been crying. He had curly brown hair and that same cop moustache that Ernie had. He leaned down. "I'm Officer Craig Nelson, Ernie's partner. I'd like to talk to you."

Taj nodded his okay saying, "He helped me earlier."

The story unfolded as we made our way back to the American Hotel through streets still filled with smoke and rioters. Vaguely, in the back of my mind, I realized a squad car might not be the safest place to be during the riots. But the story Craig told us distracted me from anything outside.

Apparently, Ernie had been on to Amir for months, suspecting him of arms dealing to the Iranians. All those drunken nights at Little Juan's were staged. Part of the LAPD's undercover operation. That wasn't to say that Ernie wasn't a drunk who really did lose his entire family to his drinking and had been put on probation with the department for his drunken screw-ups. But this undercover operation was his fresh start. It was going to be his way to redeem himself, not only with his superiors, but also with his family. He told Craig that once he put Amir behind bars, he would have earned the right to contact his two little girls again and be part of their lives. But until he atoned for his previous sins, he didn't feel worthy of their love. Hearing this as I sat in the back of the squad car, I vowed right then and there to make sure Ernie's children knew he died a hero. When I told Craig this, he became very quiet. He swiped a hand across his face and inhaled loudly.

"Thanks." It sounded choked. "He was a good man. And a great partner."

Craig went on to tell us how he and Ernie had tailed Amir from the restaurant to the Star Center earlier in the day. They were on stakeout when we arrived, and later, when they saw Amir's car zoom out of the underground parking lot. Craig hopped out of the car to go investigate inside the center while Ernie followed Amir's car to the beach house.

Meanwhile, backup officers arrived at the Star Center and burst in searching for Taj and me, not realizing we'd been in Amir's trunk. It took a while for everyone to sort out what had happened.

After backup arrived at the Star Center, Craig raced over to the beach house to help Ernie, unsure what he would find. On the way, he'd received a garbled radio message for help from Ernie. Worried, Craig called for backup. A few houses away from Kozlak's place, Taj stepped into the middle of Highway 1 to flag him down. They sped to the beach house together with an army of police cars and ambulances only moments behind them.

"Did you see Rain?" I asked them. I couldn't forget her dazed look and demeanor. I was still worried that they had taken her away in an ambulance.

"They just want to check her out. She probably was drugged for the last few months," Taj said.

"She was pretty out of it," Craig agreed. "But she looks like a fighter. They'll make sure she's okay at the hospital."

"Let's go there. Right now." I leaned forward toward Craig.

"I already asked about that," Craig said. "They won't let you see her right now. Only family. But they said you could go by during visiting hours tomorrow morning."

I sat up. "But we are her family. We're all she has."

"Let me try one more thing." Craig got on the radio and made some calls. The dispatchers told him that the supervisor on duty at the children's hospital was a no-nonsense, everything-by-the-book nurse, and that we had no chance of seeing Rain tonight.

"Head there first thing in the morning," Craig said. "You don't have to talk to detectives until tomorrow afternoon. I told them I knew you—I figure I sort of do after everything Ernie told me—so they released you into my custody."

"And they agreed?"

"Not really," he said, chuckling. "But I'm the only one who knows your names or where you live. When they figure out you're gone, it will be too late. I sent a message to the detective bureau saying you'd be there tomorrow at three. I figure you could use a good night's sleep first."

When he pulled up in front of the American Hotel, Craig said he'd pick us up tomorrow at a quarter to three and take us downtown for our interviews. Upstairs, Taj led me to his room and tucked me into his bed like I was a child, pulling the covers tight up to my chin, kissing me on the forehead. I didn't protest.

But I sat up in bed when the realization struck me. Rain was now in the system. That meant they would put her into the foster care system. The last place she wanted to be.

"She has nobody," I told Taj, who was sitting at his desk writing.

"They're going to make her some anonymous face in the system and stick her in some home with other kids and nobody to love her. We can't let them do that. She belongs here with us. We're her family."

Taj turned with a serious look.

"I know. I've been sitting here racking my brain over it. Trying to figure out a way to stop that from happening. I just don't know."

I sat up, pulling the covers around me.

"Taj, I have to tell you something. Something I did tonight. It's about Amir."

He was at my side in a second, holding me, his lips pressing down on my head, kissing me and stroking my back. "I know."

"See, the thing is, it's not just him. It's also the surfer boys..." I paused and swallowed hard, my mouth dry, "...and my mother. I've got a lot of blood on my hands." The words came out wobbly. "The last time I saw my mom she told me I had killed her and she wished I was never born."

——CHAPTER——
53

When my sister, Adele, was stillborn, my mother sunk into a deep depression. She didn't come out of her room for two months. At the time, I didn't know it was another chapter in my mother's lifelong struggle with depression and addiction.

When she finally got out of bed, we were so relieved we didn't notice that she'd become addicted to the painkillers prescribed to her. When these ran out, she went looking for something stronger. My dad and I didn't know. She hid it well. That is, until she got hooked on crank.

After she ran out of pills, my mother, desperate, contacted a distant druggie cousin for help. The bastard hooked her up with a local drug dealer who introduced her to crystal meth. Within a year, she had left us and fled the suburbs to inner city Chicago with her new drug dealer "boyfriend."

I was fifteen.

My dad fell apart. He began traveling for work, leaving me home alone for weeks on end. When he was home, he was drunk. He hired a housekeeper to cook and clean. I rarely saw him.

Once when he was gone, I watched a TV show about a girl who found her mom after filing a missing person's report. I went to the police station. The cop told me it was hopeless. "Sorry, kid. I'm sorry to be the one to break the bad news, but you better just accept it now. You ain't ever gonna see her again."

But he was wrong.

One day, my friend Rob told me my mom was back in town. He'd seen her walk into that old abandoned house on Johnson Street on the edge of town—the place where homeless people squatted. He took me aside and whispered it to me in the hall at school, and although I was grateful for that, it really didn't matter if anyone else heard. At that point, nothing could humiliate me anymore. The entire school knew my mother had become a drug addict and left her mansion in the suburbs, her new Mercedes, and her family.

After school, instead of going home, I took a city bus over to Johnson Street. The wind had picked up and blown in dark gray clouds that swirled above me, making me pull my hands up into the sleeves of my jacket. Fast food wrappers and cigarette butts littered the curb. The houses had peeling paint and lawns were bare or brown, piled with cars. Besides the wail of a baby and the angry screaming of a woman in response, the only other sound was the howling of the wind and the creak of an unlocked screen door rattling back and forth.

I paused outside the house Rob had told me about. It was a two-story Tudor that had fallen to ruin. Tiles were missing from the roof and cardboard was taped over all the downstairs windows. I made my way up onto the porch, which was littered with trash—an old black shoe, soda cans, a stack of cigarette butts. The doorknob felt cold under my fingers, but turned easily. The interior of the house was darker than the gray outside. I closed the door behind me and paused, waiting for my eyes to adjust, hoping I wouldn't find a bunch of people staring at me when they did. But the first floor was empty, just strewn with trash like the porch. A big staircase lay before me.

Slowly, I made my way up the stairs, apprehension flooding over me. At the top, more light seeped in from an upper window. Three open doors lay before me. The first one contained some blankets and trash. The room smelled so badly of piss and sweat and filth that I gagged. A homeless man wrapped in tattered rags sat in the corner raving to himself about something. I tried the next door.

That was where I found my mother.

At first I didn't notice her. She looked like a wadded up blanket on the floor in a dark corner. I was about to close the door when she moved. I crept closer and saw a pale face that didn't look like my mother anymore. The woman before me was so emaciated that her face looked like a skull. Her skin was drawn back tightly on her cheeks and her eyes sunk into dark hollows.

"Is that you, Veronica?"

Her voice was raspy, weak. Her blond hair dark with grease.

"Yes, Mama. It's me." I knelt beside her. She grabbed my hand. It felt like I was holding a claw.

"Oh, my baby is here. Please help me. You've got to help me."

"I will, Mama. That's why I'm here. I came to get you and help you."

"Thank you. That's my girl."

"Mama, can you walk?" She seemed so weak. "Will you be okay for a minute? I'll go call Daddy."

"*No!*" The screech sent a chill through my body. Her eyes were wild as she struggled to sit up, managing to pull herself up onto her elbows. "Is he here with you?"

"No, Mama."

She sunk back onto the blanket. "Good. I need you to go find

Darwen. I need you to help get me some stuff, some important stuff I need to make me feel better."

She acted like I was still a child who believed her when she told me her drugs were her special "adult candy."

"Mama, I can't. I'll do anything but that. Mama, please let me take you home. Let me take you home where we can help you. Daddy will know what to do. Please."

"He won't help me." Her voice grew louder. She was growing increasingly angry and was clutching my hand so tightly her claws were digging into my palm.

"Mama, you're hurting me."

The door below slammed and footsteps pounded up the stairs.

"Hey, kitty cat, who you got here?" The man's eyes were bloodshot and bulging. His beard was tangled and his clothes rags. I could smell his sour, unwashed stench from across the room. Another man stayed behind him in the shadows.

My mom's eyes lit up with excitement. "Is that you, Darwen? You got something for me? Did you bring something for me?

"Oh, I got something, but what you gonna give me?"

"You know I'm good for it, Darwen. I just need some time."

"I gave you time. You said your old man would give you some money if we came back here."

I looked at my mother in surprise. She came back to town to get money from my dad?

My mom slumped back in defeat. "That didn't work."

"You saw Daddy?" *And he didn't tell me.*

She leaned toward me and in a hoarse stage whisper asked, "Listen, baby. Do you have any money?"

I shook my head sadly. She grabbed my arm, twisting it. "How about jewelry? You got any jewelry you can give him, honey? How 'bout a necklace?" She clawed at my neck, her fingers trolling around, feeling around for my necklace, which she then yanked off, ripping the worn fabric of my shirt as she did so.

"Mama, please don't. Please, please come with me."

She eyed the necklace, saw it was cheap costume jewelry, and tossed it onto the ground.

Her eyes raked over me, taking in my torn blouse. She turned to face the guy across the room. "Darwen, this is my girl. My baby. Isn't she pretty? She's twelve."

"I'm almost sixteen, Mama," I said, trying to ignore the men across the room.

My mom ran her jagged fingernails down my cheek and she smoothed down my hair. "Veronica, why don't you go over and introduce yourself proper like to Darwen. He's my new old man."

"No, Mama. We're leaving. You're coming with me." I could feel the men staring at me and dread coursed through me, making the back of my neck tingle. Turning, watching the two men with my peripheral vision, I grabbed my mother under the arms and lifted her. It felt like I was grasping a small load of dirty laundry, she barely weighed anything. I had my arms around her back and her head on my shoulder but she was not even attempting to support her own weight, just lay in my arms like a floppy doll. I tried not to hold my breath, but her stench made me gag. I almost had her to her feet when she whispered in my ear.

"There's one thing you have that I know they want."

I paused, trying to think of what I had that they wanted. I didn't even have a purse with me.

"You know what it is. I saw the way they looked at you when your shirt ripped. You got one thing they want. Can you please give it to them for your mama? Pretty please, baby. Be a good girl and give them what they want. Otherwise, your mama is gonna die. If I don't get what they have, I'm gonna die."

My vision started to close in. I let go of her and she slid back to the floor. I stood frozen, staring at the skeletal body at my feet, paralyzed as bony arms reached toward me and long, thin fingers wrapped around my ankles.

"You give them what they want." My mother's voice was an unrecognizable wheezing shout.

Blinded by the tears in my eyes, I jerked my foot away from her and started running for the stairs. As I pounded down them, I kept expecting to feel a man's strong grip on my shoulder, jerking me back. There were no footsteps following me. Only the echo of my mother's wails as I left the room.

"You leave me here, I'm gonna die. You just killed your mama. Please come back. Don't leave me here."

I paused at the bottom of the stairs, frozen, sobbing with guilt at the terror and pleading I heard in my mother's voice.

"Veronica? Veronica? You little bitch. I wish you were never born. I wish you were dead."

I lifted my head and walked out that door. I never looked back.

That night at dinner, I didn't speak. My dad asked me what was wrong, but I just glared at him. I left my food on my plate and locked myself in my bedroom.

Two days later, a police officer knocked on our front door. He held his hat in his hands. I already knew what he was going to tell me.

My mother was dead. It was my sixteenth birthday.

— CHAPTER —
54

By the time I was done telling Taj this story, my face was sopping wet from my tears and snot dripping down my face and into my hair.

"You're the first person I ever told this story to," I said with half a laugh, half sob. "So, it's not just Amir. It's my mom, it's that homeless guy, it's those to surfer boys, and then it's Amir. That's five! I've got five dead bodies on my conscience."

Taj was silent. That was when I knew. Of course he hated me. What kind of monster would let her own mother die? He must really be disgusted to not say anything. But then I felt him scoot up against me. He wrapped his arms around me and kissed my eyes. Very gently.

He exhaled loudly. "Is this what you've been living with?"

I sobbed, uncertain how to answer that question. I had nothing left to hide.

"You can't blame yourself. She was the mother. She was the one who was supposed to take care of you. Your job was to be the kid. Your job wasn't taking care of her. I don't care if that's how your dad made it seem. You were the kid. Hell, you still technically are a kid. You couldn't save your mother. I don't care what you think you could have done to save her, I'm telling you this and it is the utter truth—there is nothing, nothing in the world you could have done to save your mother. Got it?"

"But I didn't tell my dad. If I had, she'd still be alive."

"That's not true. Your dad knew she was there, remember? He didn't go get her. He could've gone and gotten her, but he didn't because he knew he couldn't save her either."

I didn't answer. The echo of Taj's words in my mind made me cry even harder. *"She was the one who was supposed to take care of you."*

He was right. She was supposed to take care of me. And she didn't. And I thought, deep down inside, that was what hurt the most. That was why I had made sure that I always took care of myself without anyone else's help. And I tried to be the adult with Rain. But I wasn't an adult. Not yet.

Taj continued holding me close, breathing warmly into my hair, occasionally kissing it. I turned and buried my face in his chest, feeling weak and emotionally exhausted from the relief of telling someone else my deep dark secret.

"Listen, your dad probably knew that there was nothing he could do to help your mom. Giving her money for drugs was only going to prolong the inevitable. If she didn't want to be in treatment, there was not a damn thing you or your dad could do about it. That's the truth. When you are a drug addict, nothing is more important than your drugs. Nothing was more important than drugs to your mom. No her own life. Not your dad. Not you. Nobody. Nothing.

"And those other people—none of them were your fault. Even Amir. You would be dead right now if you hadn't done that. You told me it wasn't my fault Angelina died. How do you expect me to believe that when you won't believe your mother's death wasn't your fault? You're the one who is supposed to help me believe that."

We both had been carrying around entire truckloads of guilt for a very, very long time.

"Yeah," I said with a rueful laugh. "I guess we're both pretty messed up."

But maybe, just maybe, Taj was right. Just like I knew in my heart he couldn't have saved his sister, maybe I couldn't have saved my mother. Amir had said almost the same thing—"You can't save someone from themselves."

We lay still and he stroked my hair. "Shhh. Just close your eyes now."

Finally, the exhaustion I'd been fighting overcame me. And despite everything I fell asleep. I slept ten hours and woke to bright sunshine and Taj's arms around me.

——CHAPTER——
55

John and Eve came creeping in after I yawned loudly the next morning. Eve crouched down and hugged me tightly. "Oh thank God you're okay."

Taj sat up, running his fingers through his hair, making it stick straight up, just the way I liked it. "Can't a guy have his girl over without it becoming a slumber party for crying out loud?"

His girl? I didn't have time to think about that because John thrust the *LA Times* in front of us. Although the newspaper was almost entirely filled with stories about the riots, Rex Walker's death also made the front page. I had to flip to the inside section to see a mention of Ernie's death. All it said was an unidentified police officer had been killed in a shootout with a suspect. The story basically said that Walker had been found dead at Kozlak's house under suspicious circumstances and that Big Shot Director had been arrested for conspiracy to murder and child pornography. Apparently, they nabbed Kozlak and Chad hiding in a safe room at his Malibu house. Had the maid given him up?

They also found that girl from the video's body. Stuffed in a barrel of acid in Kozlak's basement.

I knew Chad and Kozlak would never see the blue sky above them again. But I hoped they would suffer much more than that. I wanted them to rot in prison and have unspeakably horrific things done to them while they were locked up.

Then I read something that made me whoop and jump to my feet with joy. The police said they were going to ask the Department of Justice to open an investigation into The Church of the Evermore Enlightened practices and how they covered up illegal activities of their members.

And Amir had said it would be foolish for me to go up against The Church of the Evermore Enlightened. He scoffed at me, saying there was nothing one person could do. He was wrong. I had proven that. The man who filmed King's beating had proven that. The man who pulled Reginald Denny to safety had proven that. One person could change history. One person could change the world.

Speaking of Amir, there was only a very small mention of him—a tiny, vague paragraph saying that police were investigating a second homicide victim found in the house and weren't sure how the death was connected to the other crimes.

Homicide victim.

I leaned over and vomited.

"It's okay." Taj held back my hair. "You only did what you had to do to survive."

The next minute, Danny and Sadie came racing in the room, swooping me up in a giant hug. Well, Danny ran. Sadie limped. She had on cut-off shorts and a giant bandage across the outer edge of her thigh.

"Just grazed me, kiddo."

The six of us piled into John's convertible and headed for the L.A.

Children's Hospital. Taj and I had to go talk to detectives at the police station at three, but we had a few hours until then.

Inside the hospital, we hurried under the enormous colored balls and model airplanes suspended from the vast ceiling to the receptionist desk, which was just as cheery and brightly colored. The woman behind the desk had a warm smile, curly brown hair, and funky eyeglasses.

"We're here to see our friend. Her name is Rain."

"Sure. I can help you. What's her last name?" She said it cheerfully as if she were certain we would be able to produce the last name. I had no idea. I looked around at my friends. They didn't know either.

"I don't know. Oh God." I closed my eyes for a second.

The woman winked. "Don't worry. I'll find her by her first name. It is so original there can't be more than one Rain here, right?"

The woman tapped her long pink painted fingernails on her computer keyboard. A frown appeared between her brows.

"I don't show any patients by that name."

"What?" My eyes widened. "What does that mean?"

"It could mean she checked out…" Her words trailed off.

Taj put his arm around me and turned to the lady. "Is there anything you can do to find out what happened to her? Please."

The woman looked at us for a moment and her face softened. "Okay. It could get me in trouble…" She turned away and spoke quietly into a phone. After a few seconds she hung the phone up and turned back, speaking in a low voice. "She's fine. She was released."

But it was still bad news. The woman said they had released Rain into state child protective services' custody. She would be in a foster home within two days. Privacy laws prevented her from disclosing any more information, or so she explained when I begged her, saying she had already said way too much.

My insides felt hollow, empty. A heavy weight seemed to press down on me, making my movements sluggish as I walked out of the cheery hospital. I would probably never see Rain again. I knew she was safe now, which was some small consolation, but I kept imagining her alone in some sterile room waiting to be placed in foster care with some uncaring money-hungry, system-milking parents. It made me sick.

But it made Danny furious.

He kept punching the back seat the entire drive back to the American Hotel. When we pulled up, he leaped out of the backseat and ran into the building, leaving us behind. He acted mysterious about it the rest of the day. He and Sadie kept whispering in the corners. At one point, they disappeared, supposedly to go smoke on the roof. When I next saw Danny, he had a firm set to his mouth.

"We're gonna find Rain for you. Don't you worry."

And that comforted me. Sadie could talk anybody into anything and Danny had a loyal streak a mile long. The two of them together were like a heat-seeking missile.

CHAPTER
56

On the drive to the detective bureau, Officer Craig told us the same thing. He'd also dug around trying to find where Rain was, but had struck out.

"They gotta keep all that stuff locked up tighter than a nun's…" He paused. "Uh, you know what…to protect the kids. Say some jackass abusive dad tries to track his kid down or something."

"But you're a cop," I said. "Can't you find out anything? You should be able to if anyone can."

"I'm sorry. Even if I knew, I wouldn't be allowed to tell you. I'm very sorry."

The streets were quieter now, almost eerily deserted. Instead of rioters, soldiers in full body gear roamed the streets.

At the police station, Craig talked to the receptionist. "Debra here will call me when you're done and I'll give you a ride back home."

We sat on a love seat in the lobby and I clung to Taj's hand.

"I don't know why, but I'm kind of scared," I said.

"Yeah, I'm not really looking forward to talking to the cops either.

I know we didn't do anything wrong, but you just get the feeling they'll look at us—you with your combat boots and me with my tattoos—and just assume we're fuck ups, you know."

I cringed, remembering the feel of the gun going off in my hand. "Maybe *you* didn't do anything."

Instead of answering, Taj rubbed his jaw and looked away.

A door to the back offices opened and a gray-haired, pudgy-bellied cop called my name. "Veronica Black?"

Taj seemed surprised when I stood. To him I was Nikki. But he was no more surprised than me. How did they know my real name? Taj tugged on my hand with a question in his eyes. I pulled my hand out of his and said, "I'll explain later."

Taj stood up with me, but the cop barked, "Just her. Someone will come get you."

I followed the man with his creaky gun belt down the hall. He flung open a door and I shrunk back, eyes wide.

My dad was sitting in a chair, his head in his hands. I stood in the doorway, my lips pressed together. I wanted to throw myself in his arms but was waiting for some sign from him. The door swung shut with a loud click and my dad raised his eyes. He stood, his chair toppling behind him, and started to take a step my way, but then turned around to right his chair and sat back down. He looked like shit. I was used to seeing him clean cut in a three-piece suit, but he had on khakis and a wrinkled shirt. He needed a haircut and a shave.

I stood still, not moving into the room. I just wanted him to hug me. I wanted him to run across the room and scoop me up in his arms like he did when I was a little girl. But that was too much to ask. It was too late and that filled me with a deep sorrow.

"Hi, Daddy."

"Hi, Veronica. How are you?"

The cop who had brought me into the room was sitting in the corner and seemed to be doing a good job cleaning his fingernails. Or pretending not to listen.

I blinked. "I'm okay."

Before we could say anything more, two other men came in, another officer, and a man in a suit who said he was an assistant district attorney. They told me they were going to question me about what had happened the night before. Why was my dad there?

By the end of my story, the district attorney guy said it was clearly a case of self-defense, but that I still would probably have to testify during a coroner's inquest and also at Kozlak's trial. I'd told them about the homeless guy and the surfers, as well. One guy raised his eyebrows while the other rapidly took notes.

My dad wouldn't meet my eyes the entire time. When we were done, the detective and DA guy left, both thanking my dad for being there, but the first officer remained in the corner as if he were security.

"How did you get here? How did you know what happened?" I asked my dad, eyeing the officer on the chair who was now reading the newspaper.

"They called me this morning. They needed to have your legal guardian to question you anyway. I took the next flight out."

"You didn't have to do that."

"You're my kid and you were in trouble. Plus, I think I told you I'm working the program, you know AA and NA and part of it is that I had some amends to make and I wanted to tell you in person I didn't handle your mother's death very well and I'm sorry. I know it wasn't your fault." He had the decency to swallow hard and look down.

It was what I had wanted to hear for so very long. But it was too late.

"You blamed me." I was shaking, my hands clenched to my side, my face warm and my vision blurry. "You called me...horrible...names and you blamed me...for Mama's death."

He swallowed hard and without meeting my eyes said, "I'm not saying it was right. I'm working on all that right now."

We sat there for a few seconds in silence. I figured he wanted me to forgive him, but I wasn't sure I was ready. He cleared his throat.

"And you know I've been with Julie, well, the thing is, she's pregnant and so we're getting married." He paused, waiting for my reaction.

"A baby? You're having a baby?" My voice choked on a sob. It was like a punch in the gut. For a moment I couldn't breathe. I didn't know what I felt. Sadness, fear, and then, there it was, a glimmer of joy.

"It'd be nice if you came out to visit and went to the wedding," he said.

My heart ached at the thought of having a little brother or sister. And then my dad's words sank in—come to *visit* for the wedding. Visit him, not come home.

I would skip the wedding and save my money so I could fly out when the baby was born. How could I not? I would make sure that no matter where I lived I would be a part of that baby's life. But meanwhile I had to start my own life here in L.A.

—CHAPTER—
57

I had two whole weeks to myself.

When Taj and I got home, Sadie told me that Little Juan's was closed temporarily while the owner found new management. The owner was so ashamed at Amir's behavior that he gave all us employees a paid vacation.

I didn't know what I was going to do.

But Eve did. She told me that rather than moping around about Rain, I needed to help her with a project. The owner of the café had just promoted her to manager and told her he wanted to bring in more events, such as art openings and live acoustic music once a month. The "opening night" would be in one week.

"I've got John and Taj lined up to play some music, but I need some art. That's where you come in," she said.

Eve's idea involved blowing up poster-size pictures of my portraits. Somehow she had talked an artist friend of hers who lived in the lofts across the street to be the benefactor for my new exhibit. I needed to give him my film by Friday.

"I can't possibly get done by then," I protested.

"Sorry," she said breezily, continuing to wipe up a nonexistent spill on the counter. "You're going to have to."

The artist had his own production studio and darkroom so all I had to do was hand over the film with the shots I wanted blown up. It would have been nice to have this connection the day I was so frantic about developing the film with the license plate number.

I started to get excited about the idea, which momentarily helped me forget about Rain. I was looking forward to going through those shots I had taken of Taj and finding the perfect one to enlarge. He was so beautiful with the light on him that day, I knew it would be a stunning picture—the one where he was looking at me, exhaling right when I snapped the shutter so his intense blue eyes pierced through the cloud of smoke.

And I had a few of Rain already. I just had to decide which one to use. Thinking of her little face made my stomach hurt, but not like before. At least she was alive.

I'd decided to include the snapshots of the surfers in my exhibition. It was my own small way of paying tribute.

🌴 🌴 🌴

Right at nine on Friday night, I flung open the door of the café. My friends were all waiting on the sidewalk. We had told them to dress in their finest and they had outdone themselves. I handed each of them a flier that said, "The faces in my heart and mind, an exhibition by Veronica 'Nikki' Black."

A few people looked confused and turned to me.

"That's my real name," I said sheepishly, ducking my head and hiding behind my hair. I searched for Taj's face in the crowd. He gave me a long, slow smile that sent a ripple down my arms as my friends laughed and joked, filing into the café.

John walked up, wearing a pink ruffled tuxedo shirt and shorts with a top hat. When Taj got closer, he took my breath away with his black blazer over a tight white tee.

Sadie, Eve, and I had spent yesterday afternoon at the thrift store trying to find the perfect dresses. Eve had dug up an old cornflower blue prom dress and looked like a princess, and Sadie had unearthed some sleek silver sheath that made her look like a movie star.

I'd picked out a butterscotch yellow sundress with tiny white flowers. I liked the way the skirt swung around me as I moved. It had taken me nearly as long to find sandals to match—strappy beige ones that made my legs seem about two feet longer. They were about half a size too big, but for two bucks, they did the trick.

Danny had slipped away earlier, telling me he was going to be a bit late but had a surprise for me. I hoped it was some more of those yummy tamales from East L.A. No brownies, though.

I smiled at the picture I had taken of Danny. He was sitting on the ledge of the roof of the American Hotel, strumming his guitar with the downtown skyline behind him.

The portrait of Sadie was one of my favorites. It was inspired by the night she saved me from the mugger and showed her as the avenging angel she really was. In the picture, she stood spread eagle in the middle of the street in Little Tokyo at night with all the neon lit up around her. The portrait was of her sexy silhouette holding two giant guns at her side like a James Bond girl. The only part of her that was more than a dark figure was her blond hair streaming out behind her, backlit from some lights Eve and I had strategically erected.

Danny had helped me find Frank so I could ask him to pose for me. I spent an entire morning trying to adequately capture the wondrous map of wrinkles on his face—those lines that told a thousand stories and held just as many secrets. He had promised to stop by the opening, saying he had an announcement to make that would concern all of us. I was baffled but excited to hear what it was.

My favorite portrait was the one of Rain. It was taken after she had first kicked heroin and we had taken a walk over to Olvera Street to buy some churros. One of the vendors, a man selling ponchos from Mexico, had a big shaggy dog. Rain spent nearly a half hour petting the dog until the man unwound the dog's leash and told Rain to take the dog over to play in the grassy park nearby. Her eyes grew wide with excitement. Over on the grass, Rain and the dog wrestled and chased each other up and down the narrow strip as I took pictures. The one I blew up for the art show showed Rain flat on her back on the grass, laughing hysterically as the dog licked her face. In it, she looked like the little girl she still was deep down inside. A little girl who didn't have a care in the world.

Taj noticed my sudden sadness and put his arm around me, hugging me close as the rest of our friends walked around oohing and ahhing at the pictures. Taj leaned down and whispered in my ear, "Veronica 'Nikki' Black, you look amazing. I don't think I've ever seen you wearing something other than black."

I couldn't help it. I blushed. The sound of my name coming across his lips put a smile on my face I couldn't hide. He knew me. All of me. And it was okay. I felt him press something into my hands. It was a small stuffed seal.

"I know it's not your mom's, but maybe it could remind you of her and keep you safe."

I grabbed his face and kissed him for so long that people started cheering.

Frank came in wearing pressed slacks and a crisp button-up

shirt. He leaned over and gave me a kiss on the cheek. I fought my inclination to shy away and instead smiled up at him. "So what's the announcement?"

He cleared his throat. Eve hushed everybody.

"You are looking at the new janitor for the American Hotel. I'll be busy keeping that place spic and span. Have any questions, you can come find me in my room—number one oh one."

I started clapping and everyone else joined in. I hugged him. "That is great news. Congratulations. I'm so happy for you."

"Don't get too used to seeing me around, though. I'm only doing janitorial stuff part time for free rent so I can get some money saved. Most of the time I'll be busy teaching kids at L.A. City College."

"Oh, Frank! That is fantastic news! Those students are so lucky." I gave him a kiss on the cheek.

After a while, Taj and John got busy setting up their guitars in a corner. They were going to debut Taj's new song, *City of Angels*—the one he said was inspired by our conversation that first night on the roof.

After a while, a horn honked outside. The windows were black with night, reflecting the party inside the café and hiding anything outside. With a whoosh, the café door slammed open, startling us all into silence. When I turned, I caught my breath.

It was Rain.

Danny was escorting her into the room. She had on silver sandals and a pink sparkly dress. A tiny tiara rested on her golden head. She smiled shyly at us.

"Hi, everybody."

The first person to greet her was Taj. I hung back as he walked over and ruffled her hair.

"Hey, little one."

She beamed up at him and wrapped her arms around his chest, hugging him and smiling. I ran over and grabbed her in a hug. A sob caught in my throat. I hugged her tightly and said, "Welcome home."

EPILOGUE

We threw another party on the roof last weekend. We had good reason to celebrate. Eve was knocked up and couldn't be more thrilled. John had proposed to her immediately and they tied the knot at L.A. City Hall on Saturday afternoon. We all cried, but I thought John might have cried the most. The couple was saving their money to rent a little bungalow in Echo Park, but until then, Taj and Eve had traded apartments so the newlyweds could be together in the bigger room.

It was also a going away party for Sadie. She'd decided being a gangster's girl wasn't for her. She and Carlos had parted ways amicably and she was dating one of the security guards she had manhandled at the Star Center. He'd quit his job and was working as a bodyguard for Matt Macklin. They'd rented an apartment together on the West Side.

Danny couldn't make the party.

He was in jail.

Apparently, he had staged a virtual jailbreak to bring Rain to our party. He showed up at the foster home while the adults were at work and grabbed Rain. Probably not the smartest move ever. Cops got him the next day. He was sitting in L.A. jail right now. They had arrested him on suspicion of kidnapping.

But Ernie's partner, Officer Craig, said that because the details of what happened when Danny arrived at the house were murky and nobody could prove Danny did anything other than give Rain a ride back to the American Hotel, the DA was considering dropping the case altogether.

I went to visit Danny. The jail was only a few blocks away from the American Hotel. He had somehow talked a guard into letting him have his electric guitar in his cell so he sat there all day, playing it, unplugged.

I felt so bad thinking of him being HIV positive, wasting what little life he had left sitting in a cold, crappy jail cell. But he was his usual goofy, nonchalant self—as if he couldn't have cared less.

"This ain't my first go round in the pokey and…" He made the sign of the cross, "…if I'm really lucky with this HIV positive thing, it probably won't be my last."

Then he cackled madly—the Danny I knew and loved.

Last week, Taj asked me out on a date for this Saturday, which I thought was cute since we'd never had a real date. He was borrowing John's car and said I needed to wear a dress. I'd surprise him and even wear my sandals, too. I asked if we could make a special trip to the cemetery so I could put flowers on Ernie's grave.

I had written Ernie's daughters a long letter about how their dad had died a hero, saving my life. Craig said he'd make sure they got it. I told them when they were older I would give them all the details, but for now they should be very, very proud to have had such a brave, heroic dad who loved them so very, very much. I even lied a little and said that right before he died he told me to tell his girls how much he loved them and that he would be watching them from up in heaven.

It was what I had always hoped my mom had said about me before she died. And honestly, I bet if Ernie had had the chance, he would have said that exact same thing.

Rain was living with Officer Craig and his wife. They'd been trying to have kids for years and had finally given up and become foster parents. He was able to pull some strings and take Rain into his home while they made arrangements to adopt her. He promised all of us we could visit her any time we wanted. We had an open invitation each week for Sunday dinner, which at least Taj and I planned on keeping. The first thing Craig and his wife did was enroll Rain in a middle school near his house in Burbank. Rain loved school, especially her photography class. I gave her my camera and now she had plans to attend Central L.A. High School as a freshman next year. The downtown arts school specialized in dance, music, theater, and photography.

Rain and I were both in therapy. It was Craig's idea. He was right. I went once a week. I was trying to figure so much out. I needed to learn to live with so many things. My mother's death. The surfers' murders. Killing a man. Even being able to say that showed how far I'd come.

I had thought Rain was my second chance, my opportunity to do things differently with her than I had with my mom. I had lived for so long thinking that walking away from my mom was the wrong thing to do. When Rain came along, helping her seemed to me the only way to right that wrong. But my therapist explained that walking away from my mother had actually been the right thing to do.

My dad knew my mother was there. But even he couldn't save her, so I had been wrong to think saving her was within my power, a teenage girl. It never had been. Even though the therapist kept telling me this, it would take a while for me to believe it. I also hoped that with therapy I'd be able to create a better relationship with my dad. And as the weeks passed, I was even more determined to be a part of his baby's life—my little brother or sister—even if it was a long-distance part and only on the holidays.

I'd also gotten a gig volunteering at the homeless shelter that helped Frank. Once a week, I went and served meals. It was funny because even though I was supposed to be helping them, those Tuesday nights had become the most fulfilling, gratifying thing I'd ever done.

Every once in a while I found myself sitting down, sharing a meal, and listening as someone told me their story. What went wrong, and how they ended up on the streets. In my head, I was taking notes. Everyone had a story. And everyone had a story worth telling. I wanted to be the one to tell some of these stories. This was partly why I gave Rain my camera. Not only had therapy made me see I was using it to hide, to stay detached from life instead of truly living it, I'd also discovered a different way to make art.

Writing.

I enrolled in L.A. Community College. I was going to study creative writing. If the scholarships I applied for came through, I'd transfer to USC in two years. I'd also borrowed Danny's typewriter while he was in jail and began writing a memoir. It was going to be a bit about my mother and hopefully by writing about her I would be able to forgive her, and fully forgive myself. But more than that, it was the story about how a motley crew of misfits came together to form a family. That first night I slipped the crisp white paper into the typewriter and pounded out my title:

The American Hotel.

—— CITY OF ANGELS ——

City of Angels
She's calling out to me
Saying, find yourself some shelter
Here beneath my wings

She is so forgiving
To my restless heart that sings
Out my songs of indignation
Her redemption brings me peace.

Salvation is somewhere on her streets
And I know a neon halo
Is waiting there for me.

I want it. She's got it.
She's offering everything up for free
The keys to the kingdom
Are within my reach.

City of Angels
Caress my soul
Free me from the bondage
That's kept me low.

I don't want forgiveness
For all the things I've done
I just need your arms around me

For I got nowhere else to run.

I want it. She's got it.
She's offering everything up for free
The keys to the kingdom
Are within my reach.

All the angels say Hallelujah. Hallelujah.

She sets them up
I knock them back
The rounds are never ending.
I'm blinded, by the lights that shine
Like stars a burning in my eyes

I want it. She's got it.
She's offering everything up for free
The keys to the kingdom
Are within my reach.

Come on now. Give it up now.
Give it up, give it up, give it up to me.
Angel of mercy
Gonna spread her wings.
I'm talking about Los Angeles.

–Michael Miller, @2008

ACKNOWLEDGMENTS

My deepest gratitude to my amazingly talented writer's group— Sean Beggs, Kaethe Schwehn, Kate Schultz, Coralee Grebe, Sarah Hanley and Jana Hiller. I am so thankful for early reads of my crappy first draft from stupendously talented writers: Owen Laukkanen*, Samantha Bohrman, Trisha Leigh, Phyllis Bourne, Claire Booth, Bethany Neal, Kat Asharya and Sarah Henning. *Special thanks to Laukkanen for reading it a second time and giving me a quote!

In addition, I'd like to thank Devin Abraham, Meg King-Abraham, Matt Keliher, Erica Ruth Neubauer, Gretchen Beetner, Emmy McCabe, Taloo Carrillo, Sharon Long, Erin Alford, Douglas Cronk, Mimi Ryan, Mikki Clark-Pennington Ashe, John Bychowski, Steve Avery and Bill Wehrmacher.

Also thanks to David Pennington, a talented writer and high school friend, who was a good sport when I told him I was using his "other" name: Taj. Huge thanks to my best friend, Manisha Dhanak, for letting me use the poem she scribbled in my journal a few decades ago!

ABOUT THE AUTHOR

Kristi Belcamino is a Macavity, Barry, and Anthony Award-nominated author of four crime fiction books, a newspaper cops reporter, and an Italian mama who makes a tasty biscotti. Her first novel, *Blessed Are the Dead*, was inspired by her dealings with a serial killer during her life as a Bay Area crime reporter. As an award-winning crime reporter at newspapers in California, she flew over Big Sur in an FA-18 jet with the Blue Angels, raced a Dodge Viper at Laguna Seca and watched autopsies.

Belcamino has written and reported about many high-profile cases including the Laci Peterson murder and Chandra Levy's disappearance. She has appeared on Inside Edition and her work has appeared in the *Miami Herald*, *San Jose Mercury News*, and *Chicago Tribune*. Kristi now works part-time as a police reporter at the *St. Paul Pioneer Press*. She lives in Minneapolis with her husband and her two fierce daughters.

Visit her online at www.KristiBelcamino.com and follow her on Twitter at @KristiBelcamino.